The Bride's Room

THE ADVENTURES OF MILDRED BUDGE
(BOOK 3)

Daphne Simpkins

Quotidian Books

Montgomery, AL

Daphne Simpkins/Quotidian Books

Montgomery, AL

The Bride's Room/ Daphne Simpkins. —1st ed.

ISBN 978-1-7320158-6-9

Contents

For the Millbrook Girls
Lori, Jennie, Sue, Guin, and Shelby

"Every day is a good day."

—MILDRED BUDGE

Part 1
Something Old, Something New

1
The Don't Sell *IT* at Estate Sales

It happened suddenly but had been a long time coming.

Retired school teacher Mildred Budge realized that she had left her springtime self behind while walking through a crowded room of shoppers at an early morning estate sale.

The Southern church lady was accustomed to being invisible here and there.

But this time it wasn't only that others didn't see her. Something vital and alive that once had been was now gone.

With each step the church lady took crossing the room, Mildred tested this new knowledge. Yes, yes, *it* was gone. The youthful self-awareness associated with vigor and progress was missing. The inherent rhythm that sometimes in some people becomes a swagger or a prance had laid itself down and gone to sleep.

It was gone, and Mildred Budge knew the truth soberly the way from time to time she had known that a friend who had been convalescing had died in his sleep. When the news came later in the day to Mildred Budge, like church ladies everywhere who are too polite to prove that they know more than they are expected to, she feigned surprise.

Church ladies are always sobered and saddened by the news of someone's passing, but they are not often surprised.

People die, and a church lady sometimes knows that before she is told.

And now a part of her had died, and Mildred Budge, church lady of the South, knew that too.

Each step Mildred Budge took confirmed this surprising new truth.

No heads of other shoppers at the estate sale turned to watch the church lady pass through the big living room of a recently deceased person where furniture and knickknacks had price tags hanging on them. Those little price tags with dollar values suggested vaporous facts to prospective buyers.

Competitive vendors of used household goods like herself were hunting and gathering from the remains of someone's estate, which was being cleared out by relatives who wanted the cash and had no attachments to any potential sentimental value of desks, brass hat stands, floor lamps, paintings (landscapes, cloudscapes, flowers), silver-plated pitchers, or even a hand-crocheted cross bookmark the like of which once upon a time Mildred's Aunt Betty had sent to everyone on her Christmas card list so they would have something to remember her by. Mildred kept her lavender crocheted cross in her Bible next to Psalm 103, and she remembered her Aunt Betty every day.

There was a bowl of similar crocheted bookmark crosses on the end of the long display table next to two mystery boxes. Mildred touched the delicate pastel crosses, running her fingers across the intricate stitches, comforted by the idea that a woman like her Aunt Betty had lived here with her spools of crochet thread and her needle working, working, while her thoughts kept her company. And now the lady of the house's turn was over.

"I'm not dead yet, but my turn is apparently over too." Mildred Budge whispered the words to herself, feeling the undertow of knowledge that some of her best friends had probably already experienced this--had most likely known for some time what she was just now facing.

And not one woman in her Berean Sunday School class had told her to expect this. According to the world, an older church lady becomes not only invisible but irrelevant.

The experience of that knowledge produced a soft, self-effacing smile of surrender to appear on her older though incongruously innocent face.

The church lady said the words softly to Jesus, "My turn is over. I knew it could happen, but I didn't see this coming."

Spying a chair, Mildred Budge sank down onto it soberly with this new knowledge. In the good chair that had a price tag on it of $175, she sat there watching others go by with a foolish smile of realization on her face that didn't worry anyone. Women old enough to have retired from their plain-Jane occupations—and Mildred Budge had been a plain-Jane fifth grade school teacher--were expected to wear a slightly foolish expression from time to time.

Her bemused reverie was broken suddenly by an older man whose voice was a soft entreaty, warm, intimate and clear, "Love, would you mind terribly if I took your picture?"

Mildred Budge heard the question from far, far away, inside the private space called thinking. Her heart beat twice, and she looked up.

Before she could think of a polite reply, the smiling gentleman in front of her held out his cell phone and began to move his index finger across the screen, taking one picture and then another of Mildred Budge.

Mildred blinked rapidly, her private personhood invaded, and she would have said something like "Go away, please" except the gentleman taking her picture lowered his iPhone, tilted his nicely shaped head sideways, and smiled disarmingly at her.

His was a beautiful smile.

Just that quick, the part of her she thought that had died came right back to life.

It returned.

Mildred's left hand automatically moved to the back of her head, where she fluffed out her two-day old brown curls and wondered hopefully, but without any confidence, if she had remembered to apply lipstick that morning before leaving the house.

2
Hello, Beautiful

"Why did you take my picture?" Mildred asked, tasting her lips for any left-over gloss.

He studied her carefully before answering, his eyes smiling. "Sitting there like that, your thoughts somewhere else, the expression in your eyes reminded me of someone. A woman I knew once." He stifled an apologetic laugh. "A very beautiful woman," he added quickly. "And later, you know how it is. Later, I will try to figure out who it was you reminded me of and what about you reminded me of her." The gentleman shook his head slightly as if to clear his thoughts.

It was only a reflex, a habit. This man knew what he was thinking.

Mildred Budge had a knack for recognizing men who had all their faculties, and his brief head shake was only a self-effacing movement, not really some sign of dementia or forgetfulness of the inconvenient or even tragic kind.

He straightened up, standing taller, having finished with his picture taking. And when he stood, the light passing through the living room window landed on him kindly. He was a handsome self-assured man who had once been something to behold.

That's what Mildred thought. And a new thought tumbled upon that one: 'You are still something to behold.'

"I knew if I had a picture of you, what I am trying to remember now could come back to me later. My memory isn't what it used to be," he confessed, allowing a rueful smile to show up in his sparkling eyes and nudge playfully the corners of his generous mouth.

He shared a slightly roguish grin, lips curling up at the sides whether he was smiling or not. And his eyes? The color almost didn't matter at first. The light in his eyes mattered more. His eyes gleamed with a warm and friendly curiosity. They were dark. But were they brown? Were they grey? Mildred couldn't tell, and she didn't dare stare long enough into his eyes to find out. Instead, her hand reached toward the floor and her purse while catching a glimpse of his teeth. People her age often took one another's measure by assessing their teeth. This smiling man had strong teeth, and he smelled good, like an old-fashioned bar of thick green soap with an Irish name that she could almost remember. The fragrance was like treetops on a brisk day—refreshing, and then, vaguely—Mildred inhaled deeply—it was also like pine straw.

He wore a classic dark wool-blend blazer that had aged with him. While the tweed blend of grey and blue looked good with his thick greying hair and, oh, yes, she saw them now, they were forest green-brown eyes, the cut of his jacket was old-fashioned, the length a couple of inches too long to be a new purchase, the sleeves frayed by wear at the cuff from the passing of time and use. The pattern of the tweed was too wide to be this year's style or last year's or even the year before that. He had gotten and was getting his money's worth out of what had once been an expensive, high quality jacket, and Mildred Budge heartily approved of that thrift in someone else. However the styles might change, she liked to wear out her clothes, too.

"It is probably your mother's smile. I remind most men of their mothers," Mildred Budge said without bitterness. It was simply the story of her life—the truth. "Or, I remind them of an aunt. Or an older sister. Or a Sunday School teacher," she said with resignation. When her obituary was written the words "Sunday School teacher" would be in it. She taught the Berean

Sunday School class in a church in Cloverdale, the garden district of Montgomery.

"I do hear school teacher in your voice," he said, stopping himself from offering her a hand up.

Ah.

He had been raised to offer small gallantries of help and courtesy to women; but in the current times refashioned by discussions of gender equality and social distancing, now he was cautious, careful not to overstep or offer his hand where it might not be wanted.

"I taught school once upon a time," she confirmed simply, rising. "Today, I am supposed to be looking for houseware bargains. My best friend and I have two booths over at a local antique emporium, and I was looking for objets d'art to be replacement inventory. The Emporium is hosting an event in three weeks, and we need more inventory for the annual Super Saturday Sidewalk Sale."

When he didn't say anything in response, Mildred attempted to fill the awkward silence. "My friend and I are always selling out. A booth's floorspace can't remain empty for long, or we would be out of business."

Mildred Budge heard herself use the words objets d'art cavalierly, as if she casually spoke French all the time, but she had never said that expression out loud before. Never.

Later, she would tell Jesus in prayer that she should have gone on high alert right away when she saw that this man who took her picture had triggered some inner urge to speak French.

"The items on sale here are not exactly right for us, my friend Fran and I," she explained, with a small flicker of apology, too. For Mildred meant no disrespect of the newly deceased's taste in home decor. Mildred simply meant that shoppers who browsed for home goods at the antique Emporium didn't want the kind of jewelry holders and bathroom tissue disguises that she had found and rejected on the display tables in the other rooms.

The jewelry holders on the accessory table were ceramic stylized heads of women with mostly blond bouffant hairdos, and the bathroom tissue covers were hand-crocheted (thick course thread in too bright colors used!) antebellum dresses into which an undressed Barbie doll had been stuck, her torso playing a meaningful part in hiding a roll of tissue paper. But a nude Barbie was under that crocheted skirt, and the flouncy skirt could cover a mega-sized roll of Charmin. Once upon a time, a gentle woman had thought that a crocheted full-skirted, plantation era dress with a toilet paper roll disguised under a Barbie doll's dress was a good decorating idea. Few shoppers who visited her booths at the Emporium thought so now.

Mildred would tell Fran exactly what she had seen, but her recounting of the inventory would not satisfy her best friend and business partner. The explanation of the paucity of resalable goods at the estate sale wouldn't be an acceptable explanation for Fran Applewhite, the business brain behind their enterprise and the one who was always able to find something to buy and resell in their booths no matter how many naked Barbies were stuck inside rolls of toilet paper.

"You're feeling all right, aren't you?" he asked suddenly, concern growing in his voice. "You did sit down rather suddenly. Do you need some water?"

"I sat down because I needed to think," Mildred explained truthfully to the man with the iPhone, surprising herself.

"Time out to think," he repeated, amused. "Most people don't admit to needing time to think." He turned his body slightly, pivoting to look around the room and take the measure of others who were milling and shopping and talking. None of them was taking the time to think.

Mildred's hand hurriedly fluffed the hair at the back of her neck while she tasted her lips to see if there was any lipstick there at all. Not a bit. Her left bra strap was slipping off her shoulder, and Mildred wondered now as she had off and on throughout her life how she could tug the wayward strap back up without this courtly gentleman who had taken her picture seeing her do it.

Buying time, Mildred rose, purse hoisted automatically, and tried to saunter back toward the display table with the crocheted crosses and the two brown cartons labelled mystery boxes. As soon as her back was turned, she adjusted that straying strap; and then to disguise the motion, Mildred let her hand fall upon a large brown cardboard box with a question written in black Sharpie ink: *Feeling Lucky? $10.00.*

The mystery box was heavily sealed in tan masking tape that had been stretched and pressed down by someone who had wrestled with it. The wide sealing tape was wrinkled and bunched in places. The cardboard box had been previously used for mailing and was now repurposed at the estate sale to hold items that would most likely not fit any kind of category and so had been crammed together in a mystery box which was positioned near the bowl of hand-crocheted crosses. A scrawled sign said the crosses were twenty-five cents each.

Someone with a black marker had scratched out the recipient's address on the brown box. Instinctively, Mildred craned her neck to read the name on the box the same way that you occasionally overhear a bit of conversation at the next restaurant table and in spite of your upbringing and respect for others' privacy try to piece together the story being told by leaning in to hear, albeit discreetly, another fact or two.

"I see that we are both treasure hunters," he said, falling easily into step with Mildred while she surveyed the table of wares. "Are you going to buy that mystery box?" he asked.

The question felt like a dare.

"Why wouldn't I?" she replied smoothly, letting her hand rest upon the top of the box as if she already owned it. Mildred had decided in the other room to leave empty-handed and go to Jack's for a breakfast biscuit and a cup of coffee and sit by their sweet fireplace and wonder if she would ever rent a cabin in Gatlinburg and spend a snowy week or two by herself becoming the woman she was meant to be. It was a desire of her heart that she had experienced off and on for most of her adult life. Presently, Mildred qualified for most senior discounts everywhere. She did not feel fully grown, however, and there was a part of her that still expected an adventure of change that wasn't about illness and death but the romance of becoming a woman she did not yet know but would welcome.

To welcome the many versions of yourself as the days and seasons passed was a virtue among church ladies that was not often discussed, but it existed. It did.

He laughed softly, the kind of laugh she had not heard in a very, very long time. His laugh was free of derision, free of polite reflex, free of any undertone of mockery at her for any reason. His was an honest easy-to-be-with affable, welcoming companionable laugh.

And though she did not know it, his good-natured laugh made Mildred's brown eyes shine.

3
FEELING LUCKY?

"If you are feeling lucky today, I don't know why you wouldn't buy that box," he said. The smile in his eyes teased her gently.

Mildred turned and faced him directly, her hand remaining on the *Feeling Lucky?* box though she had already spied its sister box just a little further down. That box had its own message, different than this one. Mildred registered the other words, breathing them in and storing the dare: *No Peeking!* It, too, cost $10.

Less than five minutes ago Mildred had not felt lucky at all. A good-natured smile and a teasing laugh from a good-looking stranger had brought it right back.

A clerk appeared beside them, and still holding the gaze of the man in front of her, Mildred Budge said without equivocation, the tone of her voice higher than usual, "I'll take both mystery boxes. This one--the *Feeling Lucky?* and at the end of the table, the one that says, *No Peeking!*"

The young man's eyes widened. One light brown eyebrow rose higher than the other, more a salute than a show of surprise.

"You're not going to lift the box? To consider the weight and how much might be inside? You're just going to buy them both? Just like that?" her gentleman companion asked.

"I am," she declared stoutly, waiting for him to laugh at her.

He did not laugh. Instead, he eyed her with a growing regard.

"Just like that," she said firmly, handing over the twenty-dollar bill for the two boxes. "And those crocheted crosses in the bowl. How much for all of them?"

The clerk eyed them skeptically. They were just a wad of colorful thread to him.

"Twenty-five cents each. Five dollars for the lot?" he asked. "I haven't counted them."

"I'll take all of them," she replied instantly, adding a five-dollar bill that was in her other pocket, next to some singles. Mildred Budge shopped estate sales with cash in both side pockets so that she didn't have to sift through her wallet in front of strangers.

The man with the friendly forest-green eyes and generous laugh stepped back while the clerk grabbed the crosses and stuffed them unceremoniously into a cellophane bag.

"A woman who knows her own mind is a rare find these days. I'm Mark the Gardener. Happy to know you."

"And I am Mildred the...B." She stopped herself and started over. "I am Mildred Budge."

"Of course, you are," Mark affirmed, as if she were famous.

The clerk scrawled a quick receipt. Mildred automatically tucked the receipt into the side pocket of her big church lady purse. "And what are you doing here other than taking pictures of women who remind you of your mother?"

"You said that. I didn't. I told you the truth. I came to look at the garden." He turned to face the back of the house.

The back yard was big, shaped like a lengthy rectangle and stretched toward the golf course that was part of the country club's grounds. It was flat and mostly green—a kind of green that Mildred Budge had caught a glimpse of and wondered what kind of chemicals did they spray on their grass to make it that artificial color. Almost immediately after wondering that, she wanted to see the grass covered in snow. Snow would blanket and erase that unholy shade of golf-club green.

"These stately neighborhood houses sometimes have the kind of merchandise I am looking for, which is old plants. I am in the heirloom plant business. I was just coming back from their rear garden to get to the front street where my station wagon is parked out front when I saw you. You changed right in front of my eyes," he marveled. "I haven't seen a woman do that in a long time. You sat down with such conviction and purpose as if to make sure you would remember what you seemed to suddenly know, and I was impressed with the resolute expression on your face."

He studied her with a friendly interest. "I'm curious, though. What changed? What changed inside of you while walking across the room?"

Mildred Budge fluffed the curls at the back of her neck again. The smile she offered was unlike her regular self. It was coy. She took a breath and avoided telling the truth by changing the subject. "What kind of plants do they have outside?"

"Nothing I need or want," he replied easily. "It was all so very tidy out there," he explained in a confiding whisper. "I have never been a great fan of tidy yards. It bothers me to pass a house where the inhabitants have pruned azalea bushes into perfect squares. They cut off flowers to achieve a box shape, and there's something troubling about that. You don't do that, do you?"

"I knew a man once who would stop to comb the fringe on the rugs in the church hallway. He used his own moustache comb to do it."

"Do you still belong to that church?" he asked, his dark gaze instantly concerned.

"Yes," she said. "If you left a church every time an elder combed the fringe on a rug or attempted to tidy someone else's theology out of a similar impulse, you would be moving around quite a lot. I would miss my sweet friends. That man is a sweet friend, too."

Mark nodded. It was an almost imperceptible nod. If she hadn't been watching for his reaction, she might have missed that nod. But when she saw the gentle acquiescence of understanding, Mildred Budge relaxed. A tautness in her shoulders that stayed with her slightly eased. A catch in her chest, which is where tension settled after routinely biting her tongue, loosened.

A man who seemed to listen to you was one kind of event. But a man who could understand you was another.

Mildred gave Mark her undivided attention, as the back of her neck began to perspire. The moisture collecting at the nape of her neck made the short brown hair curl back there. Riotously. She felt warm and hoped it was only the temperature of the house. Hot flashes, though infrequent now, were very inconvenient when they did occur.

"Everything in that backyard garden was new," Mark reported, with regret. "All of it planted in the last ten or twenty-years range. I look for vintage plants and flowers, something with a history and a lineage. I'm kind of a broker for southeast nurseries that specialize in heirloom plants. You could call me a matchmaker," he added mischievously. "I work for myself, and I work for them. I hunt and gather, and then I deliver the right plants to elite nurseries whose customers prefer some heritage— some history-- in their blooms and foliage."

Sensitive to the nature of their instantly friendly conversation, the hospitable clerk pointed and whispered, "Here's your loot, ma'am," he said, handing her the cellophane sack with all the crocheted crosses stuffed inside. "Your two boxes are by the front door. We have someone who can help you tote them to your car."

"That won't be necessary," Mark replied, dismissing the clerk easily. "Are we leaving now?"

Mildred's mouth went dry. She nodded.

The Kelly-green scarf in his jacket pocket brought out the color of his friendly eyes.

Mildred wondered for the second time, *Am I wearing any lipstick at all? Do I have on my eyebrows?* She didn't remember holding the eyebrow pencil or even if she had brushed her teeth that morning. *Surely, I brushed my teeth.* She tugged self consciously at the hem of her grey blouse with the cute

Siamese kittens on it. Simultaneously, she wished she were wearing the green blouse with the red robins. She felt more like wearing red in that moment than she had earlier when she had decided the grey Siamese kittens was a better fashion choice for an estate sale.

"Do they call you anything other than plant broker or Mark the Gardener?" Mildred asked, tracing her right eyebrow with her forefinger. Maybe some of the lightly sketched feathery lines from yesterday's eyebrows were still there.

"I answer to both. My last name is a happy coincidence. My name is Mark Gardiner. It made sense to call my business Mark the Gardener," he said, extending his hand, "although I've been called a few other names in my life."

"Haven't we all?" Mildred said, for she was aware of the number of nicknames people had used over the years about her: FussBudget, Mildew Budge, Midriff Bulge, and Miz Budge—she who rarely budges. Mildred Budge was a slow driver and a slow mover.

Slowly, Mildred reached out and took his hand, preparing herself for a handshake that would tell a significant portion of the life story of the man in front of her.

If his grip was cool and limp, then he was mostly talk and lacking ambition.

If his handclasp were too strong a grip, he was an aging bully who had played football one season too long and had never gotten over needing to conquer or tackle everyone he met.

Just as she was about to forecast what it meant if he took only three fingers of her hand and squeezed—three-finger handshakes made her flesh crawl—Mark Gardiner warmly grasped her whole hand. He had the sensibility not to reach out with the other hand and seize her wrist and hold her captive. No, this matchmaker of beautiful vintage plants, this Mark the Gardener lightly met her hand with his own that felt like he had done some real work in the world, and from the pace, grip, and tenderness of that greeting she knew he was a hard worker and would be a good dancer. *Maybe even a good kisser.* That last idea came so suddenly out of nowhere—faster than the pace of moseying which Mildred had decided was her forever pace—that Mildred began to blink in wonder, this time at herself. Then she spoke, saying words she had never planned to utter, "I own a rental house in Cloverdale, the Garden District, with a grand old backyard that might have some vintage plants in it. I'm getting the house ready to rent. Would you care to take a look sometime?" Her right shoulder twitched upward in an automatic imitation of serial widow Liz Luckie when she was feeling coquettish.

Gone was the idea of a warm biscuit at Jack's eaten by their sweet fireplace.

Mark's reached into his pocket from which he extracted a card, and he held it out to her. "With pleasure. This is my business card, just in case you begin to wonder later if what I said this morning is some kind of pick-up line."

Mildred took the card and looked down, studying it. It would never occur to her to wonder if Mark had used a pick-up line because no one ever tried to pick up invisible women who fluctuated between having *it* on some days and not having *it* on other days—well, moments, apart on the same day really.

She looked up, repeated her name, and said, "Merci'. I'm glad to know you, Mark. I am a retired public-school teacher. They used to call me Miz Budge," she reminisced, and then she gave him the address of the house across the street from her own and which she had bought to preserve the property values in her neighborhood. "You could come take a look. It's over grown right now. Perhaps you could find something you could salvage."

She looked up at him to see if *salvage* was a word that offended him. Perhaps she should have said saved or rescued.

Mark nodded, yes, *salvage* was a good word for him.

"I live across the street in the small brick bungalow with the cherry wood front door. We could work something out," she said, smiling mysteriously. That particular smile hadn't been on her face in years. Tiny muscles near her ears and eyes stretched in a way that they had not moved in eons.

Mark grinned and held up his cell phone and clicked her picture.

"Why did you do that?" the church lady asked.

"You changed again, and I saw it. I saw you change, and I wanted a record of it while the smile was on your face and in your eyes. You have a trustworthy gaze. Has anyone ever told you that?"

"Once or twice," she replied with an airy wave of her hand. *Reliable. Dependable. Steady.* Those were the words that had been most often written on her teacher evaluations annually by school principals who were relieved that she possessed those qualities, but the virtue of dependability routinely year after year usually only earned her the standard median raise.

At the front door, Mark lifted the two boxes without asking Mildred, squinting momentarily as he registered the weight of the second box. "One box is heavier than it looks," he said, bracing his hands underneath.

He wasn't complaining—just observing, preparing Mildred for when she got home and tried to lift the boxes out of the car by herself.

"I'm parked over there," Mildred said, as if he were the bag boy from Publix who was pushing a cart behind her. She marched ahead, leading the way, until she realized that she should have been keeping pace with him and making the kind of conversation women make with men who are helping them.

Mark the Gardener didn't seem to mind, and there was a quality of getting along with women that she saw came easily to him: no struggle to gain control, no suspicion that she needed or wanted anything more from him than the time of day and some help to the car. Mildred was just registering this understanding when she heard herself say, "I've got someone looking at my house to rent tomorrow afternoon, so if you came by tomorrow morning…" her voice trailed off. She didn't sound like herself. "That is, if you want to come tomorrow."

"I wouldn't be in anyone's way if I came in the morning tomorrow," he acknowledged amiably, eyes twinkling, as she opened the passenger side of her black and red Mini-Cooper for him. He settled both boxes on the seat. He patted the second one, testing the balance to determine whether they would skid to the floor when she braked. He was a careful man.

Mildred adored careful people. She told him the street address and then repeated it.

"I'm an early riser," he said. "I'll check out that backyard early tomorrow. If I see something promising, I'll walk across the street and knock on your door," he promised, offering a slight tilt of his head and a sudden turning of good-bye. "Until tomorrow!" he called lightly over his shoulder.

"Au revoir," she said. Hearing herself speak French again, Mildred muttered, her left eye flickering in an inconvenient twitch, "Jesus, have mercy," as they finally parted, with more brief waves of farewell and the acknowledgement that a salvage operation might begin between them.

Looking carefully before pulling out in the street, she said to Jesus, "What is happening to me? I'm not myself today."

4
YOU CAN BE A WINNER, TOO

"Your new best friend's picture is on a billboard out on the interstate," Fran announced the next morning instead of saying good-morning. She came through Mildred's front door with a rush, but Fran often arrived as if she thought she were running late. After slamming the door hard, Fran gripped and twisted the doorknob to make sure it was locked. That was usually the signal that Fran had something she wanted to talk about, and she didn't want anyone else coming inside to interrupt them.

"I've seen that billboard. Liz Luckie is very photogenic," Mildred replied neutrally.

Dropping her bulging handbag on the floor, Fran kicked off her canvas slip-on shoes and walked flat-footed across Mildred's living room floor wearing her red and blue plaid pants ensemble that looked like it was getting bigger. It wasn't. Unlike Mildred, Fran lost weight easily. Planning her wedding to Winston Holmes was burning off the calories fast. Fran settled down on the floor beside Mildred, where she was trying to open one of the mystery boxes.

"What have we got?" Fran asked, growing concentrated.

Mildred didn't answer the question. She was attacking the *Feeling Lucky?* box with a pair of scissors from the kitchen drawer.

"Give me those scissors and let me try this corner," Fran said.

"Have at it," Mildred replied, shifting her weight. She was stiff and needed to move. She really needed to stand up, but she didn't want to have to get all the way back down on the floor again.

"Our Liz does take a mighty good picture," Fran said, as she flexed the scissors open and used one extended blade to slice expertly through the stubborn sealing tape. "The billboard claims that Liz Luckie won $10,000 at our hometown casino. She is inviting the rest of us to try our luck gambling, too. On the billboard, Liz says, and her teeth have been brightly whitened, 'You can be a winner, too.'"

The sealing tape gave way, and Fran pushed back the flaps of the *Feeling Lucky?* box. "Let's see if we are winners."

"Christians don't believe in luck," Mildred mumbled automatically. It was the kind of rejoinder her closest friend expected her to say.

"Lucky at cards. Unlucky in love, and that's putting it mildly for Liz who has buried four husbands." Fran reached out and flipped open the other half of the cardboard box top. The new diamond engagement ring on Fran's left hand caught the light. It was big and sparkly.

"It appears that we have won a box of used Legos," Fran announced as her right hand dug deeply inside and extracted hands full of Lego pieces. She laid them on the floor, making a significant pile. "And here's a longish Christmas garland with little white lights. Every family needs one of these," she said. "Although we could use it for decoration on one of our display tables."

Fran the business woman eyed the string of lights thoughtfully. "But that would involve an extension cord, and who wants to risk using one of those where people are walking and might get a foot caught and trip?"

Mildred's heart sank. So far, there was nothing to sell. Ten bucks down the drain.

"What's this?" Fran asked, lifting out a small wooden box. She sniffed it. Fran often sniffed items they were considering buying for their booths, which Mildred considered very brave.

She didn't hold foreign objects up to her face and inhale them for fear of the microbes that might be attached and drawn into her body. No, sniffing foreign objects did not feel lucky to Mildred Budge.

"Eau de sandalwood," Fran said. "Very old. The box is not very pretty," Fran lamented, as she opened it carefully. "But there's treasure inside," she said, lifting out a few pennies, a couple of worn, thin dimes, and one old grimy silver dollar.

Fran held the silver dollar up to the light to find the date of the coin. "My grandfather used to give me a silver dollar every Christmas Eve. I spent them the day after Christmas on comic books at the drug store. If I'd kept them, they might be very valuable now."

"The silver dollars or the comic books?" Mildred asked.

"Both, probably," Fran replied, scrutinizing the coin and shaking her head. "I can't make out the year, but it looks pretty old."

"Doesn't Winston collect old coins?" Mildred asked.

Whether Winston was or was not a collector of old coins, the tall string bean of a man who had fallen in love with Fran seemed like the kind of guy who might collect old coins.

Fran asked, as if talking to herself, "Does he?"

"Why don't you take that old silver dollar to Winston? He'll like it. And it's something old for your wedding. Something old, something new, something...." Mildred said.

"Borrowed. Something blue. He might like this old coin," Fran said, finishing Mildred's thought. She knew immediately what Mildred was doing. Her best friend was sending a let's-get-along gift to the man who had won Fran's heart. It would be one of many little intentional niceties that would occur which would nurture the friendship between Winston and Mildred in order to help Fran be comfortable in her new upcoming role as Mrs. Winston Holmes.

"The coin might be worth something," Fran said. "Is it fair to our business to give it to Winston just because we like him?"

"Business is one thing. Winston's another. Whatever the coin's dollar value, if he likes it, then that silver dollar will be worth far more to him than to us," Mildred said, sealing the arrangement.

Pleased, Fran slipped the silver dollar into her pocket, nodding. "Liz Luckie won ten thousand dollars. That's what the billboard said. Why is it people who don't need money win ten thousand dollars and the rest of us end up with Legos, a Christmas garland, and a tawdry box that once upon a time held a bar of cheap sandalwood soap?" Fran's nose wrinkled disapprovingly.

"And Winston Holmes," Mildred added hurriedly.

Like the offer of the coin, the suggestion that Winston was a prize was another pledge of support. It meant: I plan to love him, too, as your best friend, and together we will both always see Winston Holmes as your very good fortune to love.

"My Winston is a prize," Fran agreed happily. "But what I wouldn't do with ten thousand dollars. What would you do with ten thousand dollars?" Fran asked, standing up more easily than her age suggested she could. A couple of years older than Mildred, Fran was amazingly agile and energetic.

They had another box to open, but Fran wanted something first. Mildred waited to see what it was.

Fran headed to the kitchen. Though limber, there was a momentary slight hitch in her gait that was new, caused in that very moment by rising suddenly from the floor. Both Mildred and Fran routinely challenged themselves to positions of flexibility like sitting cross-legged on the floor. But when they got up, sometimes—sometimes—that rising caused a little hitch. They did not acknowledge any sudden hitch that might occur, believing that paying attention to any kind of hitch only made it grow, like a weed. Attention to pain was like sunshine and rain to a bothersome weed.

"You got coffee?"

"I did, but Sam came by and drank it. I made him a peanut butter sandwich and off he went." Mildred said, following Fran to the kitchen.

Fran would make her own coffee, but Mildred would keep her company, standing like a visitor in her own kitchen watching her friend.

"I'd give some of that ten thousand dollars to the women's shelter. They are always running out of toilet paper over there. I'd keep some for something I haven't thought of yet. Probably put some in my envelope in the junk drawer for whatever."

Fran rinsed out the coffee pot, added water, and then counted scoops under her breath while answering her own question. "You could make a down payment on a new car. Yours isn't getting any younger," she suggested. "Winston and I would go to Paris for our honeymoon on ten thousand dollars. I saw a movie once where a woman went to Paris for her birthday and ate a roasted chicken at a café in Paris. She was all lit up over that chicken. She said that it was the best roasted chicken she had ever eaten. The woman who played that part is our age. Maybe older. If I suddenly had ten thousand dollars, I would watch that movie again, find out the name of that café in Paris, and Winston and I would go over there and eat that roasted chicken."

Fran leaned back against the counter while the coffeepot made its first gurgling sounds. Something was on her mind besides Liz Luckie winning money. But you could never rush Fran to talk about what was bothering her until she was ready. "Can you imagine what it would be like to discover a new kind of roasted chicken that is better than any other roasted chicken you have ever tasted? It would give you a fresh hope that a long life was worth living after all!"

"I imagine that just about any place you go on your honeymoon will have a roasted chicken. Besides, if you were in Paris wouldn't anything you eat there taste better than it would anywhere else?" Mildred replied, sensibly.

"What are you going to do while I am out of town with Winston?" Fran asked abruptly, her face still bearing the trace of a smile that was as much inside of her as it was on her face. It was a recently released smile—one that had grown out of her love for Winston Holmes, who could reach any light bulb in the house and change it without needing to stand on a chair. He had no major health problems, he was good-natured and quiet, and occasionally, he kissed the fool out of Fran, causing her to arrive in more than one place--and that included church-- with her lipstick smudged.

Her sudden jarring question was similar to the offer by Mildred of the coin. This gentle inquiry was a form of assurance: *I am in love, but you and I are till-death-we-do-part friends. Sisters, really. Nothing that happens will change our commitment to one another's welfare. I will always want to know what you are doing; and if you need me, nothing I'm doing and no matter where I am will stop me from coming to be with you.*

That commitment was a great puzzlement to people outside the Christian faith. Inside the Christian community, it was as common as the dust they acknowledged they were made of.

"I'll be doing what I always do," Mildred promised, releasing her friend to get married, go on her honeymoon, be in love and eat a roasted chicken if that's what she wanted. "I'll hold down the fort. Keep the world running. Bring in your mail. Finish fixing up that house over there so I can rent it. Mark the days off on my calendar...."

"Until I come home?"

"Yes. But stay gone as long as you like. Little Mister won't be due until two weeks after your wedding," Mildred took a deep breath. She was going to foster a newborn baby until his mother got released from prison.

"Your house is kind of small. You've got room for a baby, but if the Baby Mama lives with you, she will fill up your house. Promise me you won't give up your writing room. It was your daddy's study. It's your writing room now. Don't give that up," Fran asked, just as a loud rap on the front door interrupted them.

"Does Sam knock now?" Fran asked, turning with irritation toward the sound. Fran had something she wanted to talk about and everything that she had already said was simply a preamble to the news she wanted to share.

Mildred shook her head. "Sam never knocks."

Fran reached the front door first and opened it. Mildred arrived just as Mark the Gardener filled the doorway.

Mark was standing there bigger than Mildred remembered him and dressed to work outdoors. The thick durable denim overalls he was wearing as a plant salvager suited him better than his vintage Brooks Brothers jacket.

He spoke first, nodding to Fran. "Hello, I'm Mark the Gardener."

Before Fran could reply, Mark spoke over her shoulder to Mildred, "You've got some gold back there, love," he said, taking a step inside.

Mark Gardiner looked around the foyer approvingly before he said with satisfaction, "Girls, I found treasure."

5
HIDDEN TREASURE
IN THE BACKYARD

"Treasure?" Fran asked, confused.

Simultaneously, she followed Mark's gaze and saw with chagrin what Mildred spied at the same moment: an elaborate spider's web stretching across the corner of the foyer ceiling! Short as she was, Fran wanted to jump up and slap down the artifact of poor housekeeping to preserve Mildred's reputation with this handsome stranger who was smiling at both of them.

"I told you about meeting a plant man. Mark carried our mystery boxes to the car for me yesterday," Mildred explained quickly.

"You told me about the boxes but not about treasure," Fran said, taking a step back from both of them. Her body stiffened as she processed that more than she knew had occurred between Mildred and the plant man.

Suddenly, Fran was the outsider in her best friend's house. The experience, familiar to Mildred because of Winston, jolted Fran.

Mark waited while Mildred explained. "Mark harvests heirloom plants for nurseries, and I told him if he wanted to take a look at my rental house, he could come and see what was there. I didn't know what he would find," Mildred said, raising both hands in wonder. *I'm not keeping secrets. He really is a plant man, and I really didn't know what he would find.*

Mark grinned, patient with how women talked among themselves. "You've got a good back yard over there. Someone used to grow herbs. I found some old sage, old thyme, and some dried-up mint. You've also got some wild onions growing." Frowning, he added, "I have tried to talk myself into liking wild onions. But I don't like the taste of wild onions in a stew."

"Me neither," Fran chirped up. "And the texture is stringy. We don't ever have to eat wild onions. They sell plenty of the good kind in the grocery store."

Mildred cast her friend a surprising glance. *What did Fran know about eating a wild onion?*

"I did not know that old herbs and the onions were there. The grass is so high that I haven't done much exploring in the backyard. I've been working inside the house."

"Want to see? I'll show you now," Mark offered, with a quick grin. "If you've got a minute."

"We've got all the minutes you need," Fran promised, moving to put on her shoes. "I'm coming too. If you've got gold in your backyard, I want to see it," Fran said, falling in behind. The hot coffee would wait. "Oh, and I'm Fran, Mildred's very best friend," she said, catching up with Mark and doubling her stride to match his long-legged gait.

"The first sweep is always the most exciting," Mark explained, energetically leading the way as they crossed the street. "We're going through here," Mark said, pointing toward the large swinging wooden gate that marked the entrance to the backyard of the old Garvin house. The gate had a fussy metal latch coated in rust.

"Careful here," he advised, pointing to a small patch of earth. "The ground is damp and mushy."

They stepped over the boggy patch of ground.

"At first, I thought you had an underground water leak, because that's an unusual spot for water to collect. But then I found that water hose. Its nose was buried in the grass.

Somebody didn't turn it off completely. How has the water bill been?"

Mildred shrugged. "Not bad. No one's been living here. Modest," she replied.

He nodded. "All's well that ends well."

"I'm glad you found that hose," she said, casting a concerned glance at the dark green tubing. There was mold growing on it in places. Mark had rewound the hose and placed it under the wall spigot. She tried to check on the inside of the house every day, but she had not wanted to tramp around the overgrown backyard.

Fran passed through first, and Mark stepped back, holding the gate for Mildred.

"It really is a mess back here," Fran said, hands on hips as she planted both feet wide apart as if she were about to do something about it.

The size of the overgrown backyard did not bother Mildred, who had become over time someone who was attracted to a big mess. It was an expansive capacity in her nature that had been developed while she had served on various outreach ministries at church. The messier the ministry in the church the more potent it was in the fulfillment of missions. Mildred had tasted that potency of various ministries increasingly as she aged, and now her appetite for life-spreading ministries was focused on the really hard messy jobs at church or hard messy jobs outside of church. The labor was more satisfying. You can't confront the work of missions—of spreading the gospel far and wide— without developing a great capacity to tackle a big messy job with hope and vigor.

As a result of this training in her nature, Fran's business partner was not afraid of the mysteries hidden in the overgrowth of her rental house or the decisions to be made about clearing it out. And now this! There was an adventure unfolding right in front of her: a plant matchmaker who had lived long enough to know what he was talking about had told Mildred in front of her business partner that there was buried treasure literally at her feet.

"It's a mess all right," Mildred said with a broad, pleased grin.

Mark motioned for them to stay put. "It gets thorny over here," he said. "You don't want these little daggers stuck in your shoes or in your legs. Let me clear you a small walking path."

Reaching down into the grass, Mark picked up a short scythe. Using some quick motions, he began to swing the blade, lopping off thorny vines and the too-tall grass so that the women could see where to walk.

Fran and Mildred hung back as Mark forged through the overgrown yard, briars reaching out and snagging his thick working man's pants. In some places, he lifted his legs higher as he worked, and that was a sight to see—tall legs rising that high in the air.

"You found him at the estate sale?" Fran confirmed. "I'm going with you next time."

"Him and those two mystery boxes and a bowl of crocheted crosses I haven't shown you yet," Mildred replied with a hint of self-satisfaction. It wasn't often that Fran spoke with that kind of awed regard in her voice.

"We may have to use the scythe for most of the yard. Grass this high and what's growing along with it could choke out a regular lawn mower," Mark called out. "I've got a young man I'm going to send over right away to take care of this for you."

There was no opportunity for Mildred to ask, 'How much will that cost me?' Mark had decided. Though she was a church lady who was not afraid of a messy job, Mildred quickly accepted that this particular backyard cleanup job was too big for her.

Mark slowed his pace, giving the women a chance to catch up as he continued his assessment of the perimeter of the yard, peering, bending, and occasionally leaning close enough to inhale the fragrance of a late-blooming flower or something green that Mildred did not know the name of. Neither did Fran. Mark took leaves between his fingertips and rubbed softly at the green, smiling to himself. Once he tasted his fingertips, and then closed his eyes thoughtfully, as if he liked the taste and was trying to remember when he had experienced it before.

Mark suddenly leaned over and plucked a small stem of a flowering plant and brought it to Mildred.

When she didn't reach for it automatically, Mark the Gardener picked up Mildred's hand and laid the delicate orange blossom in the center of her open palm, his dark eyes rich with admiration.

"What am I holding?" Mildred asked.

"If I'm not wrong, and I could be wrong, you may be holding about two hundred dollars, depending on how many nurseries want a piece of it," he said. "That little darling has a formal name, but I will need to research it. Don't let me say something now that I'll regret later."

"Oh, no. Don't say anything you will regret," Fran said, and a small giggle escaped her.

"This is the first time in a long while when I've been in a yard that didn't have poison oak. But that green plant back there against the fence post, you could make some tea out of that and put someone out of commission for a while if you were inclined. And that tree in the corner back there. I don't know what that tree is called. It's been ages since I met a tree I didn't recognize, but I don't know her. I don't see trees I don't know very often...." Mark's voice trailed off as he stared with wonder at the mysterious tree.

Fran and Mildred politely stared at the mysterious tree in the back corner, and swapped glances. It was green. It was a tree.

"Isn't she a beauty?" he asked, gazing warmly at the tree.

Southern women, they nodded agreeably.

Mark pivoted slowly, absorbing the view. "There's an old-fashion barbecue pit over there hiding under what looks like a bush. It's not a bush though. It's a bunch of vines that have grown over it. They need to be cleaned out and burned. I'll get the lad to do that, too. What I ought to do next is take a few pictures. And I want to take those plants back there home with me for safekeeping, if that's okay with you. And I'll take the one I just showed you. They are sweet babies. I'll take good care of them. I have a safe place for finer plants like those in my home at Red Bluff in Cottage Hill. I want to do some research before I start making any pitches to nurseries down in Florida and over in Georgia. I don't know about Mississippi." Mark shook his head regretfully, remembering some incident he didn't share.

"They're peculiar. And so is Louisiana. You kind of need to know what your baseline value is before you entertain bids. Then, I'll come back tomorrow to make a second turn and harvest the others. I need to do a little sleuthing tonight. The other babies might just need to stay here," Mark added, talking more to himself. "I need time to think," he said, flashing Mildred another smile.

"I like to know what we really have before someone makes us an offer; and if we could get multiple offers, we would have a better sense of their market value. We won't know whether a number is too low if we don't know what other people are willing to pay for it. Sometimes a nursery wants exclusivity. I always think that's rather small-minded. Petty, really," Mark said, shaking his head. "Who cares what other people have in their backyard if you like what you have in yours?"

"I agree completely," Fran said as she elbowed Mildred. "You may come out all right," she said, eyeing her friend with fresh regard. "I should have gone halves with you on this house," she said with a tinge of excited envy in her voice.

There had never been any discussion of going halves on buying the Garvin house. Mildred had made the decision to buy the property on a kind of inspired impulse. The decision had intermittently scared her and excited her. In that moment of the backyard jungle, the feeling of excitement was winning.

"Are we good to go?" Mark asked suddenly, his demeanor changing. He was formulating a work plan, and his body was raring to be in motion.

Mildred nodded yes. "I'll need to pay the young man you send over to clean it up."

"If you trust me, I can work that out once we get some offers on the plants and subtract his fee from what we get on the first sales. We go fifty-fifty after expenses. I provide labor and contacts. You provide the plants. The young man is reasonable. And so am I," Mark assured her.

Fran jumped in. "Mildred is the most reasonable person on the planet. No doubt about it," she promised him.

"I have my unreasonable moments," Mildred said, casting a strange glance at Fran. "But go ahead. I need the help with the yard, and I'm curious about the plants you've found."

"Don't you love it?" he asked, pivoting slowly. "This is the best part of my job. You have got yourself a big fine mess here, girl. A big, sweet, dirty mess."

"I like dirt," Mildred said, swallowing hard.

"She really does," Fran asserted quickly. "Mildred never minds getting dirty at all."

Mark smiled. "We share that love of dirt, darlin'. But this is a big messy job, and you need to save your pretty hands for other kinds of activities." His voice was teasing.

Mildred couldn't quite place it. And then she recalled the word for what this man was doing. Mark the Gardener was flirting with her. It had been a long time since an eligible man had flirted with Mildred Budge. Sometimes, married men flirted with Mildred in the presence of their wives, but there are all kinds of reasons married men flirt with an older single woman. Most often, it is because they don't know how to make conversation with a woman, and flirting with her is their idea of small talk. Sometimes, they are showing off for their wives when they flirt with you: *See there? I've still got it. I'm letting your friend see that I've still got IT so that you can appreciate me more when you start to take me for granted. And you've been taking me for granted for a long, long time, by the way.*

Mildred moved awkwardly to the side as Mark left them to retrieve his gear.

"Well, you are full of surprises, Millie Budge," Fran said. "I was wondering why you were wearing lipstick this morning, and you have on a pair of eyebrows that the woman at the Clinique counter taught you to draw on with one of those little pencils that cost eighteen dollars. I was surprised you spent eighteen dollars on an eyebrow pencil; but when all is said and done, that eighteen dollars was money well spent. We women need all our tools."

Focused on his work, Mark walked purposefully to a plant in the far-right corner of the backyard, carrying four blue empty buckets and a shovel. Jabbing the shovel hard into the earth, Mark stamped on it authoritatively with his left foot. In a few efficiently placed moves, he hefted a three-foot tall plant up and gracefully shifted the foliage and root system to one of his buckets.

It was a beautiful sight to see: a man who could use his hands and body with such fluid movements.

Mildred and Fran watched him in admiring silence as he brought up another plant nearby. The earth didn't fight him. He wore the sunlight well. Standing in silence together, both women took long appreciative breaths of the refreshing breeze that suddenly blew across the backyard. Somewhere nearby a wind chime tinkled.

Oh.

There was a wind chime hanging from the tree that had no name.

"A man like that can open any jar that he brings home from the grocery store," Fran mused dreamily.

"He does seem strong," Mildred agreed. "Men our age...." She began another sentence and didn't finish it.

"Don't let Liz Luckie see him," Fran advised sharply.

And then the woman who was going to get married to the love of her life in six weeks said the most amazing words: "Let's keep Mark the Gardener for ourselves."

6
COME. GO. EAT
WEDDING CAKE!

Back at the house, flushed with the idea of profits for her friend, Fran sipped a now celebratory cup of coffee while she made grilled cheese sandwiches and heated some tomato bisque for their lunch because Mildred wanted to stand in her living room and watch for Mark to leave or come back over—whichever happened. She had combed her hair again and put on some fresh red lipstick. Fran hid a smile. That's when she had started making a platter of sandwiches in case they had company for lunch.

"Do you want to eat a sandwich and the soup while they're hot?" Fran called out.

"In a little bit," Mildred replied, pulling in her stomach. She needed to lose a little weight—buy a new lipstick. Maybe a different shade.

Fran joined her at the front window. "The soup is on low. The sandwiches are on the table. They're going to get cold."

"Cold," Mildred repeated, not moving. Mark was lowering the tailgate of his station wagon and rearranging the contents in the back. "We can eat whenever you're ready," Mildred said, but she didn't move. "Did you make sandwiches?"

"I see," Fran said, amused. "I'm going to open this other mystery box while you are not of a mind to help me. It'll be easier that way," she explained.

Mildred didn't take offense. Occasionally, both women got in each other's way, and the simplest strategy to avoid conflict was to do just what Fran was doing: work alone while she could.

Using the scissors, Fran expertly snapped back the flaps of the second box and peered inside while Mildred continued to watch for Mark.

Oblivious to the trail of germs she would leave behind on the tablecloth, Fran placed the contents of the second box on the dining room table.

"We've got ourselves an ancient cast iron Dutch oven. The kind cowboys use. I haven't seen one of these since the last time I watched a Western, and the cowboys cooked pinto beans over an open fire. This pot has a metal handle across the top so that it can be hung over an open fire."

"Did cowboys really cook?" Mildred asked, turning as Mark finally slammed the tailgate. Pots and pans were iffy in terms of resale value. Pyrex sold pretty well, but nowadays, homemakers liked easy-to-clean pots and pans that were not so very heavy. Dishes needed to be microwave safe or have a picture of Lucy and Ethyl making candy or that woman from the show "Bewitched" on them.

Reading her mind, Fran said, "Somebody did some cooking on campfires once upon a time, and this is the kind of pot they could have used. It would make a good door stop. It could hold open a big heavy door."

"Would anyone use it for cooking today?" Mildred asked, distracted.

"Truly doubtful. It's heavy. Do you know that they have some kind of new cooker that fries with air?" Fran eyed the campfire pot thoughtfully. "This is one of those things we aren't going to know the truth about until we sell it. Let's put a big price on it and see what happens."

Mildred eyed it dubiously. "How much is a big price?"

Fran hesitated, and then said, "I'm thinking forty dollars. Maybe thirty-five because it's not pretty. But there's a real cowboy craze in popular fiction if you pay attention. Amish and cowboy stories rule. Somebody who likes to fantasize about cowboys might buy this campfire pot for reasons of her own. I've heard of a recipe for cowboy beans. A woman in love with a cowboy might buy this pot to cook those beans for him. But that's all I can see for this item."

"Still—cast iron is so heavy," Mildred said, shaking her head ruefully.

"I know," Fran said, shaking her head skeptically. "I'll set it out on your sunporch until we make up our minds. Let's think about it later and eat now."

Before they could sit down at the kitchen table, Sam appeared in the back-porch doorway, and without waiting to be asked, came inside. He eyed them in that strange one-eyed glare that had become his means of focus when he was trying to decide the names of the people in front of him. He gave up on saying their names.

"Girls, trouble's coming," he warned. "I can feel it."

"I know you can, Sam," Fran replied kindly. "But come over here and have a sandwich. Whatever happens, everything will be all right."

Fran tugged another chair over, and Sam sat down unceremoniously, unshaved, hair uncombed, his T-shirt too thin from washing, and his legs bony inside loose-fitting grey stretch pants. Strangely his posture was still good. Erect. Military. Sam Deerborn would be a retired colonel until the day he died.

He grabbed a sandwich and began to eat. No blessing. No waiting. No sense of eating with others. He just ate a sandwich. Fast. He chewed hard, for his life, watching them intermittently as if he just hadn't figured them out yet. Then, their friend Sam looked at the other sandwich and before either of his old friends could say, *yes*, he grabbed it too. "Got things to do. People to see," he said, backing out of the kitchen, his eyes alert. He sniffed the air. "Mark my words."

"Trouble's coming," his two old friends replied in sync.

It was Sam's mantra. His new hello and good-bye. And then Sam was gone just that quick.

"Do you want me to make another sandwich?" Fran asked. "You've got just enough bread."

Mildred shook her head. "Crackers are enough. Let's eat the soup before it gets colder."

"Does Sam come by for food all the time?" Fran asked.

"All the time," Mildred said, but she wasn't complaining.

"Belle?"

"Belle is Belle," Mildred replied cryptically.

They spooned their soup, moving into the easy shorthand way of talking that old, old friends have learned.

When Fran was almost finished, she sat up taller in her chair and announced the newest decision in her wedding plans. "I've decided not to have a wedding cake. They are too expensive, and cupcakes are easier to serve. I can order cupcakes from the grocery store and place them out on the table and that will be that."

Fran made the statement flatly, expecting no argument from her best friend, who had, with resignation and dread, agreed to be her maid of honor. *Me? I'm too old to be called a Maid of Anything.*

"Cupcakes?" Mildred blanched, sitting back hard against her chair.

Currently, the world was smitten with cupcakes, and she didn't see the attraction. Cupcakes were often badly constructed. There was too much icing on too small a piece of cake, and that icing was often gluey and bedecked with toppings that were hard to chew, like little hard jelly critters and small shiny silver beads which were supposed to dissolve like sugar in your mouth but usually didn't. Decorations on cupcakes often got stuck between your teeth and stayed there, shredding any piece of dental floss that you used to go after it!

Cakes were different. The very size of them made you happy to see them, and when a grown-up cake was decorated with flowers—why, you could find a pastel icing rosette on your slice of cake and feel, well, lucky. Mildred didn't believe in luck, but she liked to feel lucky. Yes, Mildred Budge had a great fondness for tall wide cakes, or at weddings, gleaming satiny cakes that looked like they were made of snow and were sometimes blessedly bedecked with edible white roses.

"I've lost my appetite for bakery-made cakes since I watched that TV show about that man who bakes specialty cakes. Manhandled the cakes is what it looked like. That baker should have been a brick layer instead," Fran said, staring off into space, her attention wandering. "What he did to cakes, he should have been doing to bricks."

And that's when Mildred knew that this discussion of wedding cakes was a blind, a subterfuge. Fran was using the wedding cake discussion to avoid talking about what was really bothering her and had been since she had first come in the house and closed the front door behind her hard and locked it.

Mildred tried to read her best friend's mind and failed.

"I don't want to eat that frosting that they dig out of a big plastic container and slam down in mounds and roll out so they can drape it over the cake layers. I can't remember its name."

"Fondant," Mildred said with a wince because her appetite, which had always been healthy for cakes, had been severely dampened for a brief spell by watching that bakery show, too.

"I am not going to have a wedding cake made with that fondant," Fran repeated emphatically. "I can hear the arteries of my friends clogging up from eating all that lard." She shivered, gripping her opposing elbows with both hands.

Fran was repressing anxiety, and that wasn't like her friend. Ordinarily, Fran Applewhite wasn't a nervous sort. Not at all. Mildred wondered if she was having second thoughts about getting married. *Oh, my. That would be a hard conversation to have. Very hard. You could be terribly in love and not want to marry. Yes, yes, you could.*

"We don't know that fondant is made of lard. It just looks like it could be. I read somewhere that the base of fondant is something like melted marshmallows," Mildred recalled.

That gluey fondant stuff had looked awfully like lard to her, too. The idea of eating lard lingered in her awareness no matter what else anyone said fondant was.

"I heard another person on one of those cooking shows say that fondant was too sweet for some people. Well, Mildred, you know as well as I do that when something is too sweet, it isn't naturally sweetened. What do you suppose makes fondant too sweet for some people, Mildred? Whatever happened to jelly cakes?" she asked suddenly. "You haven't made one of your jelly cakes in a long time."

"Would you like for me to bake a wedding cake for you?" Mildred offered suddenly.

Mildred Budge did not know she was going to say those words. They tumbled right out of her mouth without forethought. Mildred tasted the idea of her offer after she had said the words and discovered that she didn't mind. Actually, the idea of finding a white cake recipe, practicing that recipe, and offering other people slices of celebratory cake filled her with a feeling similar to the way Fran described wanting that roasted chicken in Paris.

"Why would you want to take on the job of baking a wedding cake when there's so much you need to be doing, like getting that house across the street ready to rent and this house ready for the baby?"

"Because people love cake, especially wedding cakes," Mildred replied quietly. "Although the slices they give out are usually very small. I always think that's sad. Small pieces of cake served at a wedding celebration just isn't right."

Mildred had lost count of the number of weddings she had attended in her life, but it was mostly the cake that made going to a wedding bearable for her. She was a great optimist about life itself, but there had been many times when she had seen a man and woman join hands during the ceremony leading to holy matrimony, and right before the vows were taken and the congregation was asked, 'Does anyone here object to this union?'

she had repressed the urge to call out, "It's not going to work out for you. I can see it as clear as day from here."

But like everyone else at weddings, Mildred remained as a silent witness, smiling faintly through the vows, brushing away an occasional tear of sorrow for the grief and regret she foresaw in their soon-to-be permanently pledged, self-deceived futures.

"If you want to bake a wedding cake just to see if you can, go ahead," Fran said in an uncanny understanding of her best friend's motives.

It was hardly a gracious response and so very close to the truth that the reply irritated Mildred. Fran's best friend almost snapped and said, *'Fine, serve itty-bitty cupcakes to people who want to scream at weddings and will have a hard time thinking a lone grocery store cupcake is a reason not to do it. And by the way, we don't exactly know what kind of icing that they squirt out of the big tubes onto those store-made cupcakes which may have just been thawed out—not baked on the premises. Much of what was sold as freshly baked at her local grocery store was often very cold in the middle and underneath where you placed your hand on the box. Whatever the color the frosting happens to be, it always looks like Halloween no matter what the season or occasion. Have you looked at those grocery store cupcakes?*

But Mildred, the designated maid of honor and skilled multitasker of mixed motives and tumbling emotions, believed in that moment that Fran Applewhite would regret not serving a proper wedding cake at her wedding to Winston Holmes. Fran Applewhite was throwing wedding jobs to do off the ship of her life like ballast that she couldn't handle the weight of anymore. Later, Fran would certainly be glad to have had a wedding cake. Friends had to look out for each other during their seasons of stress-induced blind spots, and as far as a wedding cake was concerned, Fran had a blind spot.

"You just leave it to me," Mildred urged in a strange show of bright confidence that was not her usual way of talking. Sometimes, the important nature of a problem caused one to speak with more confidence than was ordinarily felt about any given task.

"Okay. But don't buy one of those crazy cake toppers of a bride dragging a groom down the aisle by his hair. Or he's wearing a tuxedo, and she's wearing that long white night gown they call a dress. Don't put some stupid little statue like that on my wedding cake. Winston and I are both grown up. And no dogs either. Or cats. Or birds. Not even white doves. I don't want a bird sitting on my cake."

Mildred didn't know about cake toppers--had not imagined buying one. But apparently, a wedding cake required one. Mildred inhaled deeply, wondering if it were too late to back out. Baking a cake was one thing; decorating it was another. She forced herself to sound more confident than she was. "Do not fret. It only causes harm. I believe I know you and Winston well enough to choose an appropriate cake topper."

"Well, just make sure it's pretty. And if you decide to add some fruit, don't choose anything with seeds in it because most of the people who will be at the wedding can't take seeds in their teeth or in their bridges. And some of them have diverticulitis. No seeds. Stay away from kiwi or grapes with seeds. People usually decorate the groom's cake with red seedless grapes, and it is always chocolate. Chocolate on chocolate. Are you going to make a groom's cake too?"

"Too?" Mildred waved aside the reckless question. She hadn't said a word about a groom's cake. "I know who the guests will be, and I know about seeds. Do you want me to run the cake recipe by you when I have figured it out or do you trust me?"

And that's when the confession came. The question 'do you trust me?' unlocked the secret that Fran had been keeping to herself by fretting over the wedding cake. Fran did trust Mildred. Her pent-up secret came out in a great gush, her voice growing louder in the room. And it wasn't concern about the lack of inventory for the Emporium's annual Sidewalk Sale.

"They have kicked me out of the Lunch Bunch, Mildred," Fran announced suddenly, her bright blue eyes wide open in reverberating shock and a kind of fading innocence, haunted in a way that happens when one is truly surprised. Mildred understood Fran's shock and a kind of embarrassment that accompanies rejection of any kind.

Esteemed church lady of the South in her own right and the go-to person for advice about church doings and etiquette, Fran Applewhite had been kicked out of the Lunch Bunch after over twenty years of eating Sunday lunch once a month with other church ladies. Expelled. Dismissed. Rejected.

Mildred should have seen it coming.

Shoot, Fran should have seen it coming.

But eviction from the Lunch Bunch had come, and best friends Fran and Mildred—veteran church ladies of the South who knew the written and unwritten rules of social engagement-- were now both blindsided by Fran's expulsion from the Sunday lunch gang just because she had fallen in love with a good man and was going to get married.

Her best friend's feelings were hurt by the rejection of long-time friends even though she knew the unwritten rules: single women belonged in the Lunch Bunch; married women did not.

"They sent me a letter with a gift certificate to The Vintage Year and said, 'Good luck. We'll miss you in the Lunch Bunch.' That's how they kicked me out. No one person signed it. She just wrote 'Lunch Bunch.'"

Mildred Budge did not know which one of the members of the Lunch Bunch had bought the restaurant gift certificate or written the dismissal note. The other church ladies had had enough sense not to ask Fran's best friend for a financial contribution for the gift certificate that ousted her best friend from their circle of abiding, you-can-always-count-on-me friendship.

"Why do you suppose that once you marry you get kicked out of the Lunch Bunch? It's not like we have a set of rules written down, and that's one of them. There are no rules; but if you get married, you have to leave the Bunch. Is it because they don't want a man at the lunch? I thought we were all so old now that we didn't even think like that anymore."

Every now and again even Sunday School classes that were all female occasionally had a man hang out with them for a while. There were some rules written down somewhere in a book about church order that forbade that. Still, when a man hung out in a woman's Sunday School class for a while it was mostly ignored and, once his curiosity was satisfied, he eventually went away. Too, there were church-sponsored, women-only night-time events that often caused a devoted protective husband to chauffeur his wife because she no longer drove at night but wanted to go. A sweet husband, rather than go home, eat alone, and come back an hour later, came on inside and ate supper with the girls. No one cared. That good man wasn't treated like an outcast. His wife wasn't treated like an outcast who had betrayed them all by letting her man come along.

But there were no formal rules that governed who ate with the Lunch Bunch. And there had been times when a woman had brought a man along if he were visiting in town and needed to eat. Those occasions had been overlooked, too. In short, there was a great history of exceptions to the rules except this one about getting married.

Other women had married and left before they had been kicked out, and Mildred hadn't given it a second thought. But now, as her wedding approached and she hadn't formally resigned, Fran had been formally ejected, and during this wedding season of disorientation and big emotions on high alert her feelings were deeply hurt.

"Are you going to keep eating with a bunch of girls who have kicked me out just because I have chosen to marry the man I love?" Fran demanded suddenly.

Mildred was caught off guard by that question. It had not occurred to her that she was being forced to make a choice between the Lunch Bunch and Fran, but obviously, Fran felt that a question of loyalty and friendship was at stake.

Did she want to stay in the Lunch Bunch without Fran? The answer surprised Mildred Budge for whom eating lunch was always a small but delightful adventure.

Mildred didn't have to think for long. She registered the stricken look on Fran's face that was the result of being rejected by long-time friends, and she said without hesitation, "If the Bunchers don't want you, the Bunchers don't want me."

Fran was satisfied by that, and her mood lifted. "I think a wedding cake would be kind of nice. Make it a big one, Millie. I think there's going to be a good turnout."

7
YOU NEED A
WEDDING DRESS, TOO

"What do you want me to do with these crocheted Bible bookmarks?" Fran asked, pouring the crosses out on the table and beginning to smooth them, instinctively using her hands to press them down, the way you use a cold iron. "These bookmarks are lovely! We've got yellow, pink, lavender and mint green."

"I thought so, too. I haven't counted them. I don't know how many we have," Mildred explained, feeling a twinge of self-consciousness. She should have counted them, at least.

"I think I used to have a handmade cross like these, though not as pretty. I don't know what happened to it," Fran said, holding one and then another. "Why did you buy them?"

"Impulse," Mildred admitted with a shrug. "They reminded me of the bookmarks my Aunt Betty used to crochet. When I saw the basket of them, I thought of her and all the church ladies who sit around crocheting baby blankets, booties, afghans, and crosses like those and how after she's gone, her handiwork ends up in a pile with the price tag of twenty-five cents," Mildred explained. "And I didn't pay twenty-five cents apiece for them. Bought them all for five dollars."

"I'm glad you bought them," Fran said, her eyes growing steely with a protective resolve. "We'll figure out something good to do with them." Her voice dropping, she added reflectively, "You know, they'll be going through our stuff one day and selling it off, and no one will care what it was worth to us or how much time and energy it cost us."

"And it won't be worth much to anyone else," Mildred said, picking up a small lavender cross made of delicate thread. "This woman made up her own pattern. Look at this. Her work is exquisite."

Fran peered closely and nodded approvingly. "And she probably had arthritis, too. Who doesn't? These crosses need to be soaked in Woolite and ironed with a spray- on starch so they will hold the shape."

"Starched and ironed?" Mildred asked. She laid down the cross. Mildred revered craftsmanship, but she didn't like starching or ironing.

Fran patted the mound of crosses, *there, there.* She would soak them in Woolite, let them dry at room temperature, use a warm iron and a dusting of spray starch to give them body, and then press them with a gentle tenderness the way you seal a special blossom from your wedding bouquet in a favorite book. "What are you thinking about a dress for the wedding?" Fran asked, cocking one blue eye at Mildred in the way her blessed memory of a husband Gritz used to do when he wanted to get someone's attention.

"Not much yet," Mildred replied truthfully. "You said yourself I have a lot going on here," she said, growing defensive.

Buying a wedding dress was a sore subject with Mildred Budge.

Fran grew steely. "Uh-uh. You know you have to wear a dress to my wedding. No pant suits at my wedding. I'm thinking of putting that in the church bulletin."

"You're always thinking about what message you would like to put in the church bulletin," Mildred replied.

"They should let church ladies post more messages. We have a lot to say that we don't get to say."

"You can say it to me anytime you like," Mildred promised. "But you better not try and tell other women what they can and cannot wear to your wedding."

Mildred fetched the old mustard yellow Tupperware bowl and unsnapped the lid. They had been eating oatmeal cookies together for more years than they could count. They each helped themselves to a couple of cookies. They were kind of dry, but, as a general rule, Mildred did not mind dryness in oatmeal cookies. You can dunk a dry oatmeal cookie in milk or coffee if it bothers you. She took a hard bite of a very dry cookie and chewed long and thoughtfully.

"You remember our deal?" Fran demanded.

Mildred chewed and nodded. A tension had gone out of Fran now that she had told Mildred what was worrying her. *The Lunch Bunch! Who did they think they were?* And now she was leaving the Lunch Bunch, too. The realization struck Mildred that she was changing and making changes, and it wasn't scary or happening too fast. You could budge without fretting or grief.

"My maid of honor wears a real dress—the kind that real women wear to real weddings-- and my best friend is my maid of honor, and I'm really getting married. Have I told you that I am terribly, terribly in love?"

"We are best friends, and you have told me that about being in love. I believe you," Mildred said, nodding. Buying time to think, she took another smaller bite of the oatmeal cookie. It was very dry. *How long had those cookies been in that Tupperware bowl?* She couldn't remember when she had bought them. *Had the words 'low-fat' been on the label? Low-fat was a synonym for dry.* Mildred eyed the cookie with disappointment and then took another bite.

"The deal is that I don't make you go shopping with me for my wedding dress, but you will buy a new dress to wear to my wedding. It doesn't matter what color. Just a dress. A pretty dress!"

Mildred nodded and took another cookie.

"Offering to bake the wedding cake does not let you off the hook about wearing a dress to my wedding."

Mildred met Fran's gaze. *How did Fran know*? Mildred had already in the very deepest part of her mind been thinking that maybe it did. Maybe baking the wedding cake meant she could wear pants to the wedding after all. There was a pants suit she had bought five years ago hanging in the guest room closet flush up against the wall, and it could still fit. It could fit. Miracles happened. And if the pants suit still fit, it would do for the wedding. The color was a familiar shade of year-round schoolhouse green, and the cloth was a shiny fabric with large rhinestone buttons in the shape of a daisy. It was her go-to-good-for-any-celebration occasion outfit! That's what the sales lady had promised Mildred when she had bought the pants suit on sale for a dance she didn't want to attend at the Country Club where she was not a member.

Every now and then, a married couple at church threw themselves an anniversary party at the Country Club, and even life-time single women had to attend. If you didn't attend the anniversary dances of your long-time married friends, you were seen as being so bitter at being single for so long that you were unable to rejoice in the long-time happiness of your wedded friends. Attending anniversary parties was absolute. That shiny pantsuit was Mildred's uniform to fight that battle.

"I will order those cupcakes in a heartbeat if you try to get out of buying a wedding dress," Fran warned her. "And that strange pants suit you wear now and then to other people's parties in that color that has no name won't do. They don't even have that shade of green in the Crayon box. Even if I decided that pants were all right for my wedding, that pants suit won't do at all. You aren't going to make me talk to you about that pants suit again, are you?"

Mildred had planned to ask her best friend to just let her be buried in that pants suit. She didn't want to wear a dress to her own funeral either.

"I told you I would buy a dress, and I will buy a dress," Mildred agreed sullenly.

Outside, they heard the engine of Mark's station wagon crank up, and each woman turned toward the sound of his leaving.

"He's finally going," Fran said. "He worked a long time."

"I thought he was already gone," Mildred mused.

Unaware of how his presence had snagged both women's attention, Mark the Gardener chugged out of the neighborhood with the day's collection of heirloom plants secured in individual blue plastic buckets.

Once the sound of his retreating truck was out of earshot, Fran said, "And don't try to tell me you don't have the money to buy a good dress because I know you do have the money. You bought that house over there without blinking an eye, and you are taking in a stranger's baby without worrying about going broke. When the baby's mother gets out of jail, you'll be taking her in, too. All of that's going to cost some money. And you have the money. Your parents left you well fixed, didn't they?"

"I don't know what well fixed means, exactly, but I can certainly buy a good dress if I need a good dress," Mildred sniffed. Every now and then when she had to give an accounting of her financial status to the government, Mildred was annually surprised to be as well off as she was. Money kind of grew in her accounts. She wasn't rich like Liz Luckie, but Mildred was well fixed. She was well fixed because she was thrifty. Some said, cheap. Others said, tight. In the church they called Mildred's handling of money holy stewardship.

"And some shoes. Some pretty shoes. And some hose in a natural shade—not that weird gray color you used to wear years ago when strangers thought you were a nun in plainclothes."

"When did someone think I was a nun?" Mildred asked, surprised.

"Oh, that was a rumor about you for a while. People thought you had been a nun but left the order and still dressed like one, sort of."

"Who?"

Fran shook her head dismissively. "We should have had this conversation a long time ago. Now that I think about it the people who thought you were once a nun are in the Lunch Bunch. Buy the prettiest dress you can afford and put a satin bow in your hair if you have to! Now I've really got to go. You've kept me here most of the day, and I have lots to do. Thanks for the silver dollar for Winston."

"Tell Winston hello."

"Winston," Fran said with a nod. "He's cooking for me tonight. His sister Jeanne is coming for the wedding."

"You'll like her," Mildred said.

Fran moaned and then chuckled softly. "Maybe we should have eloped."

Mildred had just enough sense not to say, 'It's not too late.'

And then as Fran backed out of the driveway, Mildred whispered to her departing friend, "Kicked out of the Lunch Bunch for falling in love? How in the world did either one of us stay in that group for as long as we did?"

The question caused some others to form, as Mildred went to her bookshelf where she kept an array of cookbooks. She took them to the kitchen table and began to study the index: white cake batters.

She identified three white cake recipes with different flavorings that were worth a try, and as she marked them with sheets of yellow Post Its, she asked another question she didn't know had been on her mind: "Where do you go to buy a good dress these days?"

8
WHAT HAPPENED LAST NIGHT?

The next day, lost in early morning reverie sometimes thought of as the beginning of a prayer, Mildred Budge was suddenly summoned by a specter. Her long-time neighbor Sam Deerborn had come in through the porch back door and was now standing in her living room doorway expectantly.

"Mildred, your car door is open," Sam reported, positioning both hands on his hips. "The light is on, and your battery is wearing down. You're getting mighty forgetful, Mildred. That happens when you get old," he said without sympathy.

His hips were bony now. His flesh had been walked off. All the eating Sam did never seemed to be able to rebuild the flesh that was fading, faster in some ways than his reasoning ability.

Unsurprisingly, Sam was dressed in his regular woebegone outfit, grey stretch pants, a greyish, over-washed T-shirt that he wouldn't let Belle throw away (I've finally got it broken in!), and dirty white pull-on athletic shoes that fastened with Velcro because he couldn't tie shoe laces properly anymore, not without help anyway. Every now and then, Belle tried to place a neon orange baseball cap on Sam so she could see him better from a distance. Belle had bought a few of those orange caps for her husband, and Sam would wear one away from the house, but he never came home with any of them.

"Mildred, your car door is wide open," Sam repeated loudly. He often spoke more loudly than he needed to now, and Mildred wondered if Belle was going deaf or if Sam simply couldn't modulate his tone of voice. "If you don't do something about that car door being open, the battery will go kaput. Then, where will you be when you need to go somewhere? That thing is shining..." He had been able to say the needed words a moment ago, but now Sam couldn't think of the word he meant, and that struggle—that interior search for the lost word triggered a familiar move. Sam's arms began to flap against his sides, expressing his anxiety.

Belle called it his Chicken Little stage: 'Sam predicts trouble coming as a form of conversation now. And he sneaks up on you. He scares me half to death a lot of the time. He moves like one of those Ninja warriors.'

But Mildred didn't think it was only that. The flapping of the arms, the defiant hands on his hips, why, that was Sam trying to regain lost ground—to get somewhere that felt familiar. He might even have been trying to fly. Once upon a time, Sam Deerborn had been very ambitious.

"Did you open the car door, Sam? Is that why the car light is on inside?" Mildred replied softly, slowly rising and moving past him to look out the window where indeed she could see the passenger's side door of her red and black Mini-Cooper was open. She saw, too, that the morning was exquisite again, the sunlight landing in miraculous places on leaves and limbs and grass. Instinctively, her hand reached to the window, touched the glass, reached for the essence of the sunlight. She inhaled slowly.

"I thought I locked the car," she mused softly, her breath now clouding the glass.

"Thinking's one thing; doing's another," Sam snapped, moving closer to her. His right shoulder pressed against hers, and she fought the impulse to move away. Belle's Ninja warrior husband could move stealthily, unobserved from one place to another; but once Sam arrived, he seemed to lose track of personal boundaries. Sam often moved in closer than she felt was comfortable, but Mildred Budge was like most church ladies of the South. She restrained herself from small movements away from others that might feel to them like personal rejection.

Southern women had a private way of living, and they were the only ones who knew what it was. For the most part, they didn't discuss it. Instead, the girls traded the experience of getting along with others through discussion of the Bible in Sunday School and celebrated it in prayer. Church ladies often preached whole sermons with a glance, because they were not allowed to speak. They had raised many children with the common power of love available to everyone. They forgave everyone everything all the time. They passed that lesson on to sons and daughters who became preachers.

"Have you had breakfast, Sam?" Mildred asked, as she prepared to edge slightly to her left and pivot toward the kitchen. Her own voice felt like an echo then. She heard herself speaking slowly in a tone of voice and measured cadence that she had once used with rowdy fifth graders who were either too easily intimidated by authority or felt challenged by it—often wanting to take on a person in authority just because. Mildred knew that feeling very well.

As a young school teacher, Miss Budge had initially used stern personal authority to manage her class, but over time she had learned that gentleness and kindness were in their way much more powerful than loudly delivered dictates and bullying morality stories meant to impart a hidden message. Sometimes a nurturing request has more power than a flatly stated rule. *Love me with all of your heart and one another, too. Won't you?*

Sam eyed Mildred suspiciously.

She smiled at him. "Let's go see what you are talking about," she invited.

Sam fell into step behind her, moving quietly, more quietly than a man his age should have been able to move. Arthritis and other aches and pains had disappeared when Sam's diagnosis of dementia had been delivered. No more heart trouble either—no erratic heartbeat. Sam rarely washed his hands, and he never caught a cold. Friends and kinfolk heard many of the details about living with a crazy person identified as having Alzheimer's, but no one celebrated the absence of aches and pains that had been chronic and were no more.

Gripping the open passenger door with her left hand, Mildred leaned forward to peer inside. The glove compartment was open. Maps and records of automotive service appointments were strewn on the dark grey floor mat. She looked at them curiously and then studied Sam. "Who did this to my car?"

He shook his head decisively. "This car is unlucky, Mildred. While back, it was stolen. Now, it's been— "He couldn't think of the word he meant. "Scrambled. You know, like eggs."

"Ransacked?" Mildred offered, playing the same word game that she played with many of her friends who were not diagnosed with dementia but couldn't readily recall names or find the noun they wanted to use. They worried about the implications of their struggle with words. Sam didn't worry at all. He just used hand gestures and quick glances and, often times, held your gaze as if he thought, *if you just tried hard enough—loved me enough like it says you are supposed to do in the Bible—you could read my mind.* It was an irrational hope, and that expectation was in him. That hope of being miraculously and perfectly understood was in most people, if they would admit it. When it didn't happen, you had to blame someone, didn't you?

Mildred held his gaze fearlessly, softening inside, relaxing into an affection for Sam that had deepened as time went by. That love was built on a church lady's discipline of forgiveness: *forgive everyone everything all the time. Thank you, Jesus.*

"You've been plucked like a chicken," Sam declared.

And she couldn't help herself. Mildred knew better, but she said the words anyway. "Robbed?" she probed. "Do you mean robbed, Sam?"

He swallowed hard, working his jaws and his neck muscles. Then, he coughed slightly. "Messed up," he said. "Not that word you said. Your car has been meddled."

And then some inner veil lifted, cognizance returned, and Sam asked brightly, logically, "Did you keep money or a gun in there?"

Sam did that from time to time. His attention and ability to think could surface on occasions like this and follow a train of thought considered logical by others. His wife Belle said repeatedly, 'Sam can fake people off when he wants to do it. He likes to do it, too, because when he seems normal, people look at me as if they think I have made up this dementia thing. He's so good at it that I begin to think the same thing sometimes; but it's not me. Sam is ill, isn't he, Mildred?'

Mildred always nodded slightly, *yes, yes. Your Sam is growing older faster than we want him to, and this is what it looks and sounds like. They call the speed of his aging dementia. It's not you. You are just one of the witnesses to the event, and they call you caregiver. But you are still primarily and always his dear wife Belle.*

"No," Mildred said. "I don't keep a gun in my car--not even mace."

The only money she kept in the car was in the side pocket of the door on the driver's side to hand to people begging for food or gas money at traffic lights. Mildred walked around the car and opened the driver's door. The money from the side pocket in the door was gone. So was a bottle of water. The only item left was a bottle of hand sanitizer that she used after she pumped her own gas. She had thought of carrying disposable vinyl gloves to put on before picking up a gas pump handle covered in germs. But she had decided that hand sanitizer made more sense even though the liquid gel burned her skin and quickly dried out her hands.

"You better call the police," Sam advised sternly.

"It's too early in the morning to call the police," Mildred answered truly. *Wasn't there some Bible verse that said she didn't have to call the police? Didn't the Bible allow you to just let yourself be robbed and go on with the important matters of your life?*

"Ya got to," Sam argued in an echo of his colonel's voice. "Insurance won't help you if there isn't a police record."

"I don't think insurance is going to replace the five dollars that is missing," she said.

"You better call 'em anyway. You never know what they'll make of something like this. You might have some clues here, and they might need those clues. Could be a crime wave coming. Or worse...." Sam turned and stared out at their neighborhood, hands on hips, his gaze roving, looking for trouble.

"It isn't how I planned to spend my morning," Mildred muttered, going back inside her house and wondering about that phone number other than 911 you call instead. She almost knew it. It was only three numbers, too. Good citizens were supposed to respect the police's time and use the non-emergency three-digit number. Her scrambled car this morning wasn't really an emergency. Hoping she was right, Mildred punched in the three numbers she hoped would be right. The morning's event with her car wasn't an emergency. It was just a nuisance.

Mildred watched Sam outside circling her car. Watching him, she calmly answered the questions that the person on the other end of the phone line asked her. They were simple questions. She gave her name. She recited her address. She stopped herself from saying, "I have been plucked like a chicken" and answered clearly, with a nod to Sam who was now standing guard: "My car has been ransacked."

The voice on the other end of the line promised to send along someone who would write a report she might need later and hung up on her before she could finish saying, "Thank you."

Like her good friend Sam, church lady Mildred Budge respected the reality of trouble, and she didn't like to cause it.

9
WHILE YOU WERE SLEEPING

She changed into more presentable clothes while waiting on the police. The patrol car arrived promptly and parked in the driveway behind her car. A woman in a uniform got out. She was short with taut muscles that indicated she worked out in a gym and that she was almost a half-size bigger than the size of shirt and pants she was wearing. She reminded Mildred of someone.

Mildred walked toward her as the officer spoke: "Mrs. Bulge?"

"Miss Budge," Mildred replied, though Mrs. didn't mean what it used to: being married. Now it meant you were of an age to be called Mrs. whether you had ever been married or not. She almost replied, "Madame Budge," as she thought that the French had a classier way of addressing mature women.

The officer paid no attention to the correction, standing beside the car in question. Mildred was accustomed to the pace of friendly conversation and had to remind herself that the woman in the uniform wasn't making a friendly visit.

"I understand your car has been broken into," the officer said in a perfectly normal tone of voice. Without waiting for Mildred to affirm that claim, she asked, "Do you have the registration?"

"It was in the glove compartment." Mildred walked back to her car and looked for the registration where it should have been in the glove compartment and then found it on the floorboard underneath a red McDonald's French fry box. She hadn't been to McDonald's lately and didn't know where the greasy carton came from.

Mildred handed the crumpled registration with a grease spot on it to the policewoman and said, "For the record, I have not been eating French fries in the car."

The other woman was all business—not the chatty, social type of woman that Southern women try to be with one another in the tradition that has established the reputation of Southern hospitality. "Do you have any grandchildren who might have left that trash?"

Mildred shook her head, mumbling the word "miss" again.

"Would you mind if I dusted the vehicle for fingerprints?"

"Like they do on TV?" Mildred asked, suddenly intrigued.

Sam joined her suddenly again—he had wondered off into the back field and returned-- standing too close to Mildred once more and grinning from ear to ear. "Just like they do on TV. I've always wanted to see someone do that." He elbowed Mildred in her left side and nodded *yes* vigorously.

The policewoman eyed Sam quizzically.

Across the field, Belle came out her back door and called across the back field, the way a mother would if her child might be getting in her neighbor's way: "You all right over there, Millie?"

Mildred fought the temptation to say, 'Come and get your boy. I've got the police here.' But she was a disciplined keeper of other people's children and nodded reassuringly. If Belle could have seen Mildred's disciplined expression, she would have recognized the brown-eyed gaze of trustworthiness that for twenty-five years had promised parents of unruly children that there was nothing their child could do that would rattle her or cause so much disturbance in a classroom that a veteran school teacher couldn't handle it. Miss Budge called upon her experience now to manage Sam while talking to the police.

The resolute gaze existed still, and Mildred's movements matched it. Her body had grown more still after her retirement, and she wondered about that: the encroaching still points of her personhood, which others saw mostly as the burning spark of golden light in her brown, prayerful eyes.

"The black dust for fingerprinting makes a terrible mess," Officer Thomas warned. "I don't have to do it. Most of the perpetrators of this kind of crime have sense enough to wear gloves."

Sam's face fell. He looked over at Belle and waved for her to go back inside the house. *Lemme alone.*

"Go ahead. Fingerprint the car if you have the time and want to do it," Mildred consented.

Sam's face lit up, his grin broad. His eyes shone with anticipation that action was happening; and in some way, he had helped to create it.

"I know how to clean up a mess," Mildred vowed.

"She does," Sam affirmed readily. "If there's one thing Mildred Budge is famous for is being able to clean up a mess. Everybody says so."

"Do you need me to keep you company while you do it?" Mildred asked the policewoman.

The two women swapped gazes. And for a second the other woman's gaze melted, shifting from the cool, objective gaze of a law enforcement officer to the warm gaze of someone who upheld the law but for whom the vocation of becoming a policewoman had been born in compassion—a desire to help others. Compassion surfaced in the moment and created a rapport.

And almost immediately the moment was gone.

Just that quick, the policewoman changed right in front of Mildred's eyes, right back from warm to cool and promised, "It won't take long. There's a lot of this sort of thing going around."

"Breaking into cars?"

"Vandalism, mostly," she replied, tersely, turning to go back to the car and retrieve her fingerprint kit. "No rhyme or reason to it. Troublemakers with nothing to do but make a mess. One mess after another."

As the other woman walked away, Mildred suddenly remembered who the officer reminded her of. Officer Thomas looked like her old friend Margie had when she wore her security officer uniform assigned to her as a senior citizen volunteer who helped with the filing at the local police station after her own retirement as a school teacher. Margie had worn her volunteer's uniform with pride and moved with the kind of perseverance that this police woman exhibited. Margie was gone now—*a blessed memory* is what the Bereans called the class members who had gone onto glory. The last thing that Margie had said to Mildred was, "You have got to keep it real, Millie. One of the ways you do that is to know when your turn is over."

"I don't want my turn to be over," Mildred whispered to herself and to Margie in heaven.

His hearing was uncanny. Sam turned and looked right at Mildred Budge and said clearly, "Me neither."

10
WHAT HAPPENED
TO YOUR CAR?

It took only five minutes of the patrol car's being in Mildred's driveway before her phone rang. Mildred could hear it, but she ignored the commanding sound demanding that she pay attention to whatever was on the mind of the caller. Privately, Mildred Budge thought telephones were uncivilized devices: bullies, even, demanding attention.

The ringing stopped after the tenth time, and the caller discovered Miss Budge did not use voicemail. She had it. She just didn't use it. They could call back. If it was really important someone could get a message to her through a friend. Or even come over. *Maybe I'm the bully,* Mildred thought, and the idea pierced her. *Maybe I'm the rude one, demanding attention in my way on my own terms.* The convicting idea was a solemn one, requiring prayerful thought and, it had been her experience, most likely repentance. That prospect of admitting she was wrong and needed to change did not discourage the church lady. Mildred had learned over time that repentance was a growing strength. When a human being can get to a point where she can see she's wrong and admit it, she can budge. Moments of change always lead to greater freedom. It was freedom that scared people. It was pride that kept them from finding it.

Imprinted with the knowledge that repentance was in front of her to consider, Mildred was about to go and splash some more water on her face before settling into some prayer time when Mark stepped through the gate over at the house across the street and called out to her, "Need some help, Darling?"

It was surprising to see a man standing there like that looking right at her.

It was surprising to be called *darling* the way people in the South call each other that word with ease.

It was surprising to be glad to see this man she had just met two days ago and to hear anything he said and be glad he was close and saying anything.

"I'm okay," she called back.

Mark was standing by his station wagon that was backed up to the gate and hidden in the shade of the bushes and shadows of the house. He was moving blue buckets in and out. And, Mildred thought, he looks at home there. Here.

Aware that the policewoman and Sam were listening, Mildred called out, "Do you need me for anything?"

Mark considered the question and shook his head as Fran zoomed up in Winston's green pickup truck and parked it between Mildred and the man who had called her darling.

Fran parked abruptly, the brakes screeching. Jumping out, Fran slammed the door behind her. Her rubber-soled Ked's hit the pavement running.

"What's going on here?" Fran asked, concerned. "I had a call from Belle that the police are here. Sam's been talking about trouble coming, and I was suddenly just afraid."

Automatically, Fran looked across the field at Belle and Sam's house, getting her bearings. She was a small woman with a protective sometimes pugilistic nature that some people wanted to label as that of a prayer warrior. But that wasn't true of Fran Applewhite altogether. Fran was as ready to brawl physically with an intruder as she was to pray for him. There had been moments when Mildred had wondered if the gentle Winston Holmes knew he was marrying a woman who had an instinct to fight to protect those she loved.

"You got a candy bar on you, girl?" Sam asked abruptly, surprising Fran by coming up behind her suddenly.

Fran stifled a yelp, her shoulders rising and falling quickly as she replied, her fist unfurling for she had clenched it in case a fist was necessary. "Not today, Sam."

Sam routinely asked other people for candy bars now. Some people tried to carry one for him. Not Fran. There were many obligations of friendship to which Fran Applewhite readily assented, but she did not believe in packing snacks for grownup men whatever their condition.

Officer Thomas came slowly over to the two ladies, giving them time to finish their conversation so that she could hand a piece of paper to Mildred.

"Hello," Fran said politely. The adrenaline had abated, and she was now ready to play her part as Mildred's best friend and co-hostess to the police who had come calling. "If she needs a character witness, I can say a few good things about her."

Tommie—that's what the gang down at the station called her—let her luminous brown eyes smile for her. The officer nodded that she knew a joke when she heard one and recited a memorized speech that ended with, "If you have any questions, you can call that number on the bottom of the sheet of paper I just gave you."

"What are the odds that you will catch somebody who has invaded my friend's car?" Fran asked, tilting her head sideways. It was an aggressive question—the kind Fran asked when she didn't get a laugh for one of her sideways jokes. Only Officer Thomas' eyes had smiled. That wasn't enough for Fran when she was feeling testy.

"Yeah, what are the chances you are going to catch the sapsucker?" Sam asked, and there was a sudden belligerence to his tone that was sharper than Fran's.

Gone was the happy boy who was excited about the fingerprinting. Here was the irritable man who thought other people weren't doing their jobs very well.

Instantaneously, Sam changed again.

"Gotta go," Sam announced, looking hard at Mildred and then at Fran. "You two girls don't seem like yourselves anymore," he said with a sudden sharp laugh that caught them both off guard. Spinning on his heel, Sam started to march off only to turn and call, his voice fierce, "Trouble's coming. I can smell it. I can see it. I can hear it." He eyed the stranger in the backyard with his blue buckets, and his voice became intense. "Mark my words. Mark my words. Mark my words. Trouble's coming."

The two old friends watched Sam Deerborn walk a half block away before Fran spoke first.

"Poor thing," Fran said, turning toward the path that led to Mildred's front door.

"Let's not call him that," Mildred said. "Not yet."

"I didn't mean anything by it," Fran said, hearing something in Mildred's voice that caused her to stop and assess her own reaction to Sam. Her voice filled with wonder when she spoke again: "I never see Sam going home. I guess he goes home eventually, but I never see him going anywhere except away from home. He walks all the time now as if he's homeless."

"Sam's not homeless. Maybe his sense of home has expanded," Mildred mused thoughtfully. Hers had, since she had retired. It appeared to others that she lived a very confined life; but in many ways, Mildred had never felt freer—more expansive in her opinions, less fearful of being known—of sharing her life. That had happened because of the last Missions Conference. Good had come of it. Mildred did not want to go on a mission trip, but she didn't keep her doors closed quite so tightly anymore.

Since then, her yellow guest room had been converted into a nursery, and though surprised by the idea still, the retired school teacher wasn't afraid of the baby coming to stay with her while his mother finished her prison term. *I'm having a baby come live with me,* she thought one more time. *A baby. Me? At my age?*

"I didn't just come over here because I had a phone call that you were being arrested and led off in handcuffs." Fran said. "Okay. Belle didn't tell me that. She just said the cops were here, but it was just a break-in...."

"Just my car," Mildred interjected. "Sam's the only one who comes into my house and takes what he wants, and that's not stealing. He forages for food, and I do buy an extra loaf of bread for peanut butter sandwiches and a big bunch of bananas that I know Sam will eat."

"What are you doing out here with your hair not combed well and that very tall good-looking man over in your backyard who has drifted to the gate and looked twice this way since I've been standing here? Don't you want to do something to your face?"

Before Mildred could say, *yes,* Steev the preacher turned the corner and pulled up alongside the two of them.

"I thought he was due in the afternoon," Fran remarked.

"Steev was due yesterday afternoon. He's a day late."

"I know I'm late," Steev said, getting out of his car with a grin. "Life happened to me yesterday. Your house still for rent?"

Mark appeared at the gate and pointed one finger at Mildred.

His earlier question was now embedded in that single move of his pointing finger.

"I'm still okay," she called out to Mark who had come to the gate again and peered in her direction.

The plant man eyed the preacher with suspicion, and Fran elbowed Mildred. "That man in your backyard wants to protect you, Mildred. That's big. When a man wants to protect you, that's very big."

"Talk to Fran a minute, Steev, and I'll go get the key to the house."

11
COME. GO. BE YOURSELF

"That's Mark the Gardener in the back," Mildred explained when she returned to Steev with the key. "He's helping me. He'll have that backyard ship shape soon." She had washed her face better, combed her hair better, sketched in some expressive eyebrows and daubed on a little lipstick with only a faint hint of color--mauve. Red would have been too much color for so early in the morning.

"Fran told me," Steev said, his steady gaze filled with good humor. He seemed shorter in his athletic shoes and orange University of Tennessee sweatshirt. "You doing all right? Fran told me that your car was broken into."

"That's what it looked like," Mildred concurred, peering across the street towards Belle's and Sam's house.

Steev followed her gaze, the smile in his kind eyes growing gentler still. "Miss Mildred, we are being watched."

"Sam does that. And Belle's watching Sam. And we're watching them watch us."

Steev turned away. "You get used to being watched when you are a preacher. Are you going to let me go inside?"

"Yes, but this house is too big for one man," Mildred said.

"I won't be single forever, Mildred," he replied. "A preacher has got to get married or change professions. And while we are discussing fundamentals, down the road, what if I became interested in buying this house."

"I'd be interested in selling," she replied. "I never meant to become a full-time landlord."

He nodded, the idea born and acknowledged between them.

"There's a lot of work to be done yet," she added. "You can get used to the house and see if it feels like home."

The previous tenants had left in the dead of night, taking their boy Chase with them. He was an interior child--an unsolvable problem to his parents, and a mystery Mildred was just beginning to solve when the family had slipped away in the night owing three months' rent. She missed Chase every day and, in an inexplicable way, his parents, too.

"Doesn't matter. Your house is not a church manse," Steev said, taking the key from her. "Let me do that."

"You've got to press hard on it. The lock catches on something."

Steev opened the door easily, smiling to himself.

They stepped inside, growing silent. The house was empty and quiet and peaceful. The musty smell—it might have been the residual hanging fog of marijuana smoke-- was mostly gone. Mildred had aired out the house for a week while she put load after load of useless stuff on the street for the Wednesday garbage pickup. You can tell a lot about people from cleaning up after them, and Mildred had learned that the parents of Chase were untidy people who left behind mounds of clutter and rarely changed the sheets. The mattress on the double bed was unusable, and the boy had been sleeping on a saggy futon in a dark room where he had mostly entertained himself on the computer for hours. The kitchen cabinets were empty except for a handful of crumpled coffee filters and an empty box that had once contained Ramen noodles.

Steev walked slowly down the hallway. "I couldn't have a dog at the last manse because I was afraid a church member going through my house when I wasn't home would let him get out. Churches want you to have a wife. They don't want you to have a dog."

Mildred flipped the light switch. "You can have all the dogs you can afford to feed. There's a nice back yard. Mark the

Gardener is finishing some work out there. He'll be finished soon."

Steev nodded, listening but more interested in looking at the house—taking its measure. They walked slowly through the empty house together. She had vacuumed, mopped, and scrubbed the floors, but the walls were scuffed to the point of needing to be repainted.

When she saw Steev notice the dirty walls, Mildred explained, "I don't think it was all the previous tenants' fault. The former owner of the house had let it go pretty badly, and then Chase and his parents moved in and didn't improve anything. They tried to run an organic cereal business from here, but it didn't work out. I was about to get some estimates on painting the house. It's on my to-do list."

"I wouldn't want to wait for the house to be painted. Besides, I know how to use a paint brush. And between us, though our friend has not complained, I think Jake's ready to have his house back. And, though I have no complaints either, I need to be able to read without an opera or a football game playing in the background. Jake likes both enthusiastically."

"I'm pretty sure this place isn't wired for cable TV," Mildred said. She had been dreading saying those words and dreading even more having to call a cable company to install the line. She imagined prospective renters would want to plug in a TV and watch it right away.

"I don't care about that. What's the rent?" Steev asked, moving quickly through the empty rooms.

She told him.

He nodded. "The location couldn't be better. I could jog to church if my car didn't start."

"That's what I always do," Mildred said. "Don't even break a sweat."

He considered her claim and asked her a different question: "You gonna call the cops on me if I throw any wild parties? "

"Only if you don't invite me," she replied, though Mildred did not really like parties. To much talking at dinner and after dinner cost her a night's sleep.

"You will always be invited. So, we are agreed. You don't mind having me across the street." He studied her kindly.

"I like the idea," she confessed truthfully.

He grinned. "Me, too. I don't think we'll make each other cuss. When can I move in?"

The decisiveness of the question pleased her. *Why shouldn't he move in? He was Steev, the preacher with a great smile.*

"Anytime you like. You've got the key in your hand. I had the locks changed so you don't need to worry about anyone having a duplicate."

"You don't have a lease you want me to sign? Do you want a check today?"

Mildred knew all the rules of good business and common sense, but there was a fortune in plants in her back yard that were being harvested, and the scuffed walls inside that needed to be painted she wouldn't have to paint now. Steev didn't care about having the house wired for cable. And after he moved in, she wouldn't have to worry if something was leaking and causing damage. Steev the preacher would be watching out for floods.

"Bring the check over whenever you like. Move in as soon as you like. Come. Go. Be happy," she encouraged, as Sam walked to the curb on the other side of the street and stood stock still, watching the Garvin house intently. His lips were moving, and Mildred knew what he was thinking and muttering: "Trouble's coming. I can feel it."

"I see Sam walking all over the neighborhood," Steev said. "He goes everywhere on foot."

"Sam's gotten kind of restless in his retirement. He rambles around the neighborhood. We all kind of keep an eye on him. It's nothing to worry about."

"I've got a sermon to write," Steev said. "Maybe I'll call it that. 'Nothing to Worry About'. A lot of people worry about getting what's wrong with Sam."

Mildred just shook her head. "What is there to worry about?" she asked, stepping out the front door. She called out to Sam, "Are you hungry?"

Sam stared at her hard and at Steev.

Steev smiled warmly, nodding to Sam.

Mildred spoke to Sam again slowly. "Would you like a snack?"

Mildred's words circled the neighborhood and finally reached Sam.

"We're going this way to a snack, Sam," Mildred encouraged, moving toward her old friend. Sam waited, eyeing her suspiciously.

Stopping in the middle of the street, the church lady turned to the preacher and said, "I've got a fresh cake baked. It's not frosted, but we can eat it. You want to join Sam and me for a snack?" she asked Steev.

"Rain check," Steev said. "I just texted Jake, and he's bringing my stuff now."

"If you need anything..." Mildred said, letting the words dangle.

Sam fell into step with her, his head down, watching his feet. He took fast, mincing steps.

They followed the worn path from the front yard around to the back door where they could kick off their shoes, and when they entered, they found Dixie sitting at the kitchen table, helping herself to Mildred's unfrosted wedding cake.

12
HELLO, DIXIE

"This cake's not your best effort," Dixie said, unselfconsciously stuffing another bite in her mouth. Dixie was dressed in dark green knee-length shorts with suspenders that stretched over a big white shirt. She wore white knee socks and sandals.

Mildred called this ensemble Dixie's leprechaun outfit. And while the woman sitting at her table was a couple of years older than she, the girl who had chosen that outfit was about twelve years old. Dixie had multiple personalities. Some people added the word disorder to that phrase, but Mildred did not. She simply thought that Dixie lived in a crowded house, and like Sam, Dixie often wanted a snack. She was also very comfortable making herself at home anywhere she went.

Sam reached over and broke off a piece of the cake, plopping down hard, stretching out both of his legs and leaning back in the chair as he took the bite.

"I can help you bake a better wedding cake," Dixie announced. "This one don't cut the mustard. You can't take a cake that tastes like this to a wedding. The marriage would be doomed."

"I'm experimenting with cake batters," Mildred explained, turning to see what Sam was up to. He had risen and gone off into the other room. "Let's go see what Sam is up to."

"You can't run away from your destiny," Dixie growled in a low voice that didn't fit a twelve-year-old girl in a leprechaun outfit. Whenever Dixie used that voice, Mildred envisioned her looking like Popeye, the cartoon character. Dixie had many voices inside of her.

Mildred had tried to figure out a name for Dixie's condition—and Dixie was pretty open to discussing it with her, but like dementia of the Alzheimer's variety, multiple personality disorder didn't match exactly what professionals named as its symptoms.

Sam was opening drawers of the side tables in the den.

"What are you looking for, Sam?"

"The keys to my car. I figure that Belle hides them over here so I can't find them. Where are they, Mildred? You have no right to hide the car keys from me."

"I haven't hidden anything from you, Sam. And your car is broken. It doesn't work anymore, and that's why you can't find the keys."

Sam eyed her skeptically. "You girls just make up stories all the time to hide what you're really up to."

"If that's true, there's nothing you can do about it," Mildred replied easily.

"I think it's true," Sam declared.

"We all make up stories to answer questions we can't quite answer any other way," Mildred said, and a part of her sank heavily when she said the words. They felt very true.

"Is that what the Bible is?" Dixie asked sternly. "I've been waiting for you to tell me that about the Bible. It's got a lot of stories in it. How can they all be exactly true?"

"Now, you know that's not what I mean," Mildred said, choosing her words deliberately. She and Dixie had been reading through the Bible together, talking about what some of the stories meant. It had been the hardest teaching job of Mildred's life, for Dixie was the most ferocious questioner of the Bible she had ever met. Still, Mildred Budge was a former fifth grade school teacher and a current Sunday School teacher, and if she didn't try to help Dixie read the Bible, who would?

Sam turned suddenly and hurried back to the kitchen. Dixie and Mildred followed him.

"What are these?" Dixie asked, pointing to two more eight-inch cake layers that were baked the day before.

"Yesterday's cakes," Mildred replied. "What you tasted was this morning's first effort." Mildred was still thinking about what to do with them. *Which frosting should go on those cakes?*

Sam reached over, peeled back the cellophane, and tore off a chunk of one of the pale white layers. He stuffed it in his mouth. Chewing ferociously as if starving to death, Sam swallowed hard and said, "Dry as dust. Your cake might be better if you put some frosting on it. But don't let me tell you what to do. I know from long experience that you don't like a man telling you what to do."

Sam leaned against the counter, taking another bite of the naked wedding cake. Dixie reached over and pinched off a bite. She closed her eyes while she chewed. "You beat the egg whites too long. That's what happened here. And, it needs more butter."

"I know the cake needs more butter," Mildred said irritably. "I will use more butter on the real wedding cake but right now I'm saving on butter, and I'm testing flavors. That's essence of orange."

"It tastes more like essence of lemon. It's bitter, and I'm your friend so I can say that to you," Sam said. "But don't mind me. I liked that first cake you made from a while back. I had some of that first cake. You said it was your first cake. It was better than this sour lemon cake."

"That first cake was a box mix," Mildred replied tightly.

"If you'd go back to that first recipe then you might be able to get some orders in the future for birthday cakes and more wedding cakes, though I don't believe anyone else will be getting married in our church after Fran and Winston. I think just about everybody is married now. Except you, Mildred."

"I'm not married," Dixie replied stoutly.

"I do not want orders for more cakes," Mildred explained coldly. "This is a one-time deal, and baking a wedding cake is meant as a labor of love," Mildred said. "Fran was going to order white cupcakes from Publix."

"I like cupcakes from Publix," Sam said. "They are usually really good." He eyed Mildred as if she were a troublemaker, keeping them all from having cupcakes from Publix.

Dixie agreed readily, nodding enthusiastically. "Cupcakes are easy to pick up, and you can usually eat two before anyone realizes you aren't taking the second one to someone else."

"I can eat a cupcake in three bites," Sam said.

"I can do it in two," Dixie replied. "If no one is watching. But the icing does get all stuck in your front teeth, so you pretty much have to brush your teeth after that."

"Where's my toothbrush, Mildred?" Sam asked abruptly. "I need to brush my teeth."

"Belle has your toothbrush," Mildred said, as Sam walked off down the hallway to her bathroom, where she was pretty sure he was going to use her toothbrush.

"I'm glad he's finally gone," Dixie said. "Have you ever thought about making a peanut butter and jelly layer cake?"

"No, I have not," Mildred said. Thick peanut butter would not spread easily on a soft layer cake. Unless the cake layer was frozen. A chocolate layer cake that had been frozen and was thawing could accept a thin layer of peanut butter without tearing and some jelly. Plum jelly. Mildred began to imagine how that would taste. The idea appealed to her.

"If you used peanut butter and grape jelly then you could decorate the groom's cake with purple grapes not green grapes and that would be a very harmonious combination, if you don't mind my saying so."

"I don't mind you saying it, but I don't plan to make a groom's cake. I only offered to make the wedding cake."

"You better just order some chocolate cupcakes, then, to serve alongside the wedding cake. That way, if people don't like your wedding cake, they can get happy with a good reliable chocolate Publix cupcake."

Sam returned, wiping his mouth on the front inside of his T-shirt and then across the back of his hand. "Mildred, I don't like the toothpaste you are buying. It has too many bubbles in it, and it tastes, it tastes, it tastes....I don't like the taste."

Mildred didn't like the taste of her own toothpaste either, but she had bought that tube on sale and was trying to use it up. She had heard more than one report that there was very little difference between toothpastes. All of them pretty much did the same thing. So she had bought a tube of no-name toothpaste at the Dollar Tree. She wasn't planning on buying another one. But she wasn't going to throw away perfectly good toothpaste either.

"Go away, old man. We've got work to do here," Dixie said.

Mildred was horrified. Whatever personality was on the surface in Dixie today was being very rude.

Sam laughed out loud. "Careful who you call old, old lady. I'm not much older than you," he said quickly. "But I'll get out of your girls' hair so that you can get on with your shenanigans. This is not your best effort, Millibubba. That first one was," Sam declared again, picking up the rest of the layer he was nibbling on. Then, taking another bite of the bitter cake layer, Sam let himself out the back door and headed off to the field back to his house, where his other toothbrush was.

Dixie sat down heavily with a long sigh, shaking her head at the sight of the mauled sour lemon cake. "I thought he'd never leave," Dixie said. "Have you ever thought of making him pay rent? He's here all the time."

Resigned, Mildred sat down heavily at her table, wondering what she could say to that. She didn't have to figure it out.

Dixie suddenly slammed an open palm down on the table and made an announcement. "Before you start talking about this and that, I need to tell you that I don't really have time to hear your problems today. I've got something to say."

"Then say it," Mildred urged. *Say it, and go home. And let me lock my door and throw away that tube of awful toothpaste, and these cake layers have to go, and I need to start all over. Or maybe we do need to order those cupcakes from Publix.* Mildred was beginning to feel like a failure—too often a familiar feeling.

"I've been thinking about this since old Frannie got engaged," Dixie said, shaking her head. "And what I'm thinking—and it seems clear as a bell to me now that I've tasted two of your cakes. Do you think I better volunteer to organize the Bereans for kitchen duty for Fran's wedding reception?"

Mildred pressed her hand against her mouth, but not for long. This idea needed to be nipped in the bud. Nipped in the bud!

"You haven't been with us long enough to know that certain members of the Berean Sunday School class ran a secret operation during WWII, broke codes for the government that helped win the war, a couple of them flew airplanes to deliver supplies to the front lines, and in between jobs, they also bore children who were raised to become astronauts and presidents of universities. I believe they can handle one wedding reception for a classmate on a Saturday afternoon." Even as she said the words, Mildred Budge regretted her tone, her lovelessness, her fatigue, her sour cake that really couldn't be excused simply because it wasn't frosted. She had short-changed the butter. Her cake was sour and dry, and both Sam and Dixie, who had issues of credibility, had told her the truth.

"Whew! That's a relief. I'm glad to hear it. I didn't want the job anyway. But you girls all seem to need so much help. You just keep trying, girl. I believe in you." The voice that said those words was completely unfamiliar to Mildred.

Mildred swallowed hard, her throat dry with lying and tension. "Other than to discuss Fran's wedding cake, did you have something else on your mind?"

Dixie picked at a piece of one of the layer cakes. She nibbled. "This layer is better than the one that Sam ate."

"It's the same cake batter," Mildred replied.

Dixie shrugged. "What I want to know is what is this business about the Fall of man that happened in the book of Genesis?"

"What?" Mildred asked, leaning forward on the table.

"Yeah. The Fall. Everybody talks about it, but no one can explain to me what it really is. I'd like to know. Start talking, teacher," Dixie demanded, nodding fast and furiously. "I'm really curious about this Fall business. And don't you worry, I've got all the time in the world."

13
MILDRED GOES WALKABOUT

After Dixie finally left, taking the rest of the sour cake with her for later, Mildred put a fresh fat chicken in her oven. The recipe was new. It had called for a cup of red wine and some mushrooms and to be cooked on a low heat for hours. It smelled good. All she needed was a French baguette, a fireplace, and a view of the Seine. Mildred Budge had such an inexplicable appetite for roasted chicken! And change.

Everyone was gone. Her car was locked. She had already repented of feeling impatience, of experiencing covetousness, of being unloving, and for outright lying about the Bereans, none of whom had been code-breakers or bomber pilots.

Her house was calm. The phone wasn't ringing. No one was knocking at her back door. Or her front door. She was finished with cake baking for the day, and now all she wanted was a good supper alone with a good book and a long night of reading before she went to bed at nine o'clock.

Her plan was gently unfolding, the tension in her throat and the back of her neck easing, when she looked out the front window and saw Sam walk by again. He was always walking, walking. *Where did Sam go?*

The preacher's observations about Sam walking everywhere resurfaced. She and Fran and Belle simply accepted Sam's endless walking. But did he go somewhere?

In that moment, it felt like it was her duty to find out.

Wiping her hands on a kitchen towel, Mildred changed into her outside shoes and went out the front door after Sam. She hurried to catch up to Sam, but he suddenly took a sharp turn and disappeared through an opening in a hedge.

"I hadn't thought about that," she said to God. "It did not occur to me that he would not stick to a sidewalk."

Mildred stepped up her pace, catching up to where she could once again watch Sam on his walkabout from a distance. Her body felt as it always did at first when she went for a walk—out of sorts, needing to move in order to be able to move. She had an impulse to groan but was actively trying to teach herself not to make sounds when she moved. "When do we start making old people sounds?" She asked herself in a muttering voice that sounded like an old person muttering to herself.

So, Sam's stalker bossed herself around. "Keep up. Go that way. Hang back a second. Now go." She stayed behind Belle's Sam, whispering to God, bossing herself, moving past the homes of people she knew less and less well, surprised that it didn't take long to get to a third street away—then, a fourth street from her neighborhood where she couldn't name anyone who lived inside any of the houses.

'How limited our lives are,' she thought, walking, walking, her legs growing stronger, her breath growing deeper. She could feel a vitality coming back that had been dormant for a while, and she wondered why she hadn't missed it sooner. *There is a problem with stoicism and with being smugly mature. You get used to the aches and pains of persevering and forget there is this—this exultation and vitality from just being alive.*

And just as the church lady was preaching to herself, Sam took another sudden turn into someone's back yard.

Mildred slowed down, bracing herself for what might be ahead, but what she saw was nothing she had expected. For as she approached the back yard with a metal fence upon which kudzu had lazily threaded itself through the metalwork, Mildred saw her old friend drop his grey jersey pants and take off his T-shirt. Standing sockless in his loose-fitting underpants Sam dropped his shirt by the athletic shoes he had already kicked off.

The ground in front of him appeared to be covered in leaves, but it wasn't ground after all. It was a swimming pool that had not been recently vacuumed. There was matted debris floating on the water. With a sudden spurt of speed and on a brisk day that had a bite of cool to it, Sam dove headlong and fearlessly through the leaves into the deep end of the pool wearing only his underwear.

Mildred said wonderingly to God and herself and to Belle, who couldn't hear her, and to Fran, to whom she had recently said, *let's not call him that yet*: "

Sam really has gone crazy. Poor thing."

She watched Sam swim lazily, unselfconsciously, the matted, floating leaves attaching to his bony arms that ploughed through the surface of the water. He made a slow lap, then another lap, and then another lap, and the surface debris pushed back, eddying in small ripples of water he kept causing. Then, Crazy Sam did the most amazing thing. Sam rotated over onto his back and closed his eyes, oblivious to everything but the water and the sun on his face—and suddenly, instantly, Mildred knew what her old friend was feeling. He was soaking in the cold comfort of the messy water, absorbing the surrounding sunlight, while experiencing the sharp bite of the air against his wet skin. Every molecule of his body was taking nourishment from the particles of creation around him.

Instantly, Mildred closed her eyes and could smell the fallen, sodden leaves, the residue of chlorine in the water, tea olive wafting, a faint hint of someone frying pork chops nearby with a window open—the sharp realization of life happening to all of his senses and in ways that had grown insensitive, in Sam's presence, in Sam's swim, now happening to her senses, too. Mildred's eyes opened, partaking of the scene, and she closed them again, becoming one with the water and the leaves and the cold and the warmth while Sam continued to float as one of his old friends simply sat by hidden from him, companionably living life with him and oddly, unreasonably, through him.

Time slowed. So did her heartbeat. Her thoughts stopped racing. Space opened up, and so did her eyes.

Sam tumbled over again in the water, and dogpaddled to the side of the pool and pulled himself up more easily than he should have been able to, positioning himself on the red bricks that outlined the pool. He was bony and more kidlike than old, and Mildred had the most astonishing revelation that Sam wasn't crazy after all. He had just forgotten to stay grown up, and now he was a kid who was playing—stealing a swim in a neighbor's pool on a coolish day.

While Mildred was coming to this conclusion, Sam dressed himself, moving with agility and confidence, and like a shadow that is erased when a cloud moves, he disappeared around a tree and was gone: just like that. A vapor. A blade of grass. A human being whose days are measured at seventy years, give or take, depending on the Lord's will, and Mildred relaxed into the knowledge that the Bible was true and God was real and that too much of her own life had been spent imitating others, following all kinds of grown-up rules. Even though she had felt the water and known the sunlight while Sam floated and thought the leaves and other debris in the pool unappealing, something about the mess of it drew her; and before she made a conscious decision to do it, Mildred was over at the pool, taking off her shoes, wiggling her toes, and placing her feet in the shallow end of the pool. The water was sharply cold. It felt good.

Tension she did not know was in her dissolved. Coming to attention, she saw an acorn sitting on a bed of floating leaves and felt herself mesmerized by its brownness, its shape, the wet mess of it all that was floating about her and near her, and she was not resistant to being part of it. Instead, she opened her eyes and stared full at the sky and moved her arms out wide, and the breath that came and went inside of her pulsed strongly. She took one deep breath after another. Several heartbeats later, the breaths became prayer. Suddenly, she was praying—praying in a new way, praying with a kind of wholeness that she had never experienced before and which because of Sam's example of floating was mysteriously released in her.

A feeling of profound wellbeing rose up in her, and though she had never experienced the phenomenon of glossolalia, she knew something like how she had imagined it from reports, sensed that the kind of spontaneous prayer pouring forth from her in that moment was under her control and could be quenched or permitted. Mildred Budge let the words stream through her. Simultaneously, she split in her consciousness—not a sharp divide. It was a warm separation of different stances of awareness, and one of them was a congenial awareness of herself that was both poised and energized at the same time. She was aware that goodness and mercy were being poured out through her—not into her. Like blood coursing through her veins and air circulating through her body, she was being cleansed and refreshed and given something, something she could only, paradoxically, accept by giving it away. So she did.

The church lady gave away the blessing. She breathed out loud the words of hope and creation flowing into her, and they were attached to names of people, some of the children she had once taught so long ago. But this was not an alphabetized listing of people in a roll book. The praying of names was ordered by a memory bigger than hers—so vast that the word computer was laughable. The prayer contained an ordering of names assigned to not faces but images, quick glimpses of people, and she said the same words for each of them, "Bless you, bless you, bless you," and "upon you more blessings, tender mercies, streams of goodness...." The utterances were phrases and benedictions preachers sometimes used at the end of a worship service to send people on their way with the wind of expressed good will and hope at their backs.

The church lady knew in that moment that she was being allowed to remember a heart of hers that she had repressed and stifled through the years in the name of common sense. In that moment, she was choosing to love out loud with abandon and hope, for the church lady believed the words in the Bible that promised her she could do just that. The Fall does not hold a believer in its quicksand clutch.

By the still waters, Mildred remembered a kind of reckless trusting abandon that she had been taught to outgrow, and she chose it again.

In that moment of remembered desire, the church lady was imparting a love that she had stopped herself from experiencing but which she had always known was there—true and fierce, this great fierce, protective, giving, love; and this love was coursing through her, blessing others, blessing her, and as long as she wanted to say the names of so many children and people she had known and loved, the love kept coming and going forth endlessly on her breath. "Bless you and you and you and you."

She felt full and empty at the same time, loved and loving, and something she had never dreamed was possible: that it was given unto her to offer this love to others and that she could freely pass it on. Freely say their names. Freely know that her love did matter.

The church lady's attention to each member of the Beloved in prayer had a place in something so big that no prayer paradigm could make sense of it. No preacher could explain it in twenty minutes behind a pulpit. She wanted to live inside that mystery of oneness with the bite of cold air and water and the heat from the sun for as long as the sun was on her and the water about her, so she continued praying through the rolls of former students all grown up and in pain and fear, so old now that they had forgotten what it meant to trust, relax, have faith, have hope, and when the church lady accepted anew this old immense hope yet again, something powerful surged up in her. Faith grew.

She could afford to believe—to hope that all was not resignation, all was not endurance, all was not a form of defeat that Christians tucked under the rug called dying to one's self or martyrdom. There was this: an eternal, uplifting hope that could be breathed for others, and she felt her smile widen as she continued to bless and pray and hope for the children she had known and their children and then, her friends, people so far along in the human walk that they too had forgotten that life— the living of it-- all was not resignation, all was not endurance, all was not travail, all was not repentance. There was more to know, to enjoy, to live out. You could find your life's delight in the presence of God.

She waited, waited for the quickening to release what else was to be known. She felt it expand and encompass--grow bigger still—so big that the image of a great canyon was not enough, nor was a horizon. There was only the sense of it and the knowledge that out there at the end of the distant field the Good Shepherd was always waiting for her and everyone to come home with his arms wide open and his inevitable embrace, sure.

Just that quickly the moment that she would call from then on and for the rest of her life, the anointing of the blessing prayers, receded. Mildred Budge stood up, found socks and shoes, staring with wonder at her feet that didn't look like her own, but they were her feet. They were beautiful. Her body felt refreshed with a vitality that she hadn't experienced since a very young woman, and she thought: 'I could run home and not run out of breath, and I could skip and do cartwheels. I could do it all through Christ who strengthens me.'

Standing, she took a couple of steps through the tall grass and saw something she had not seen before. She leaned over and picked up the broken For Sale sign. Turning, a smile of hope and conviction on her face, Mildred said, "I may buy this house, too, and make it a good place where real people can live. It's a precious place. Just precious."

And with that new idea, the retired school teacher, good neighbor of Belle, stalker of Sam, business partner of Fran, landlord of Steev, and friend of Jesus walked toward home.

14
BLESSING PRAYERS
AND OUR SONG

"Bon jour, Fran," Mildred said. She was home. Supper was already cooked. The chicken with mushrooms roasted in red wine was resting in the oven. Life was good. To celebrate Mildred had made another wedding cake after all: double almond extract plus a teaspoon of vanilla extract. A simple buttercream frosting was all it required. And just as Mildred was approving of this newest recipe effort, Fran arrived with news.

Mildred repeated her greeting cheerily, "Bon jour, Bride!"

"What's wrong with you?" Fran snapped, shaking her head. "I am the one who is getting married, but you are the one who has gotten dreamy all of a sudden," Fran declared, somewhat impatiently. "Is it Mark?"

Before Mildred could say *no,* Fran asked, "What is that song you're humming?"

"La Vie En Rose," Mildred replied simply. "I've been humming it since you told me you wanted to go to Paris for your honeymoon and eat a roast chicken. I've got a red wine and mushroom baked chicken resting in the oven. It's just finished cooking. And a completely frosted double almond wedding cake on the counter. I meant to get a French baguette, but I forgot."

"How are you ever going to eat a whole chicken? That song you're humming reminds me that we need some music for the wedding. I don't want to walk down the aisle this time to the Wedding March."

"Too much Déjà vu for you?" Mildred asked, not surprised that Fran didn't ask for a taste of what could become her wedding cake. It was almost as if Fran hadn't heard her. It didn't matter. *Bless you, Fran. Bless Winston, too. And Steev. And Jake. And Mark. And Belle. And Sam. And, oh yes, Janie—I mean Amanda. And Chase. And Chase's parents. And, well, just bless everybody.* The maid of honor was talking to the bride, but the blessing prayers wouldn't stop coursing through her.

"I did walk to that song before with Gritz. I need a different song for Winston, don't you think?"

"You can skip down the aisle to no music at all. It's your wedding," Mildred replied without thinking.

Fran studied Mildred, and nodded approvingly.

"I like it when you talk like this. What has happened to you?"

The walkabout and the praying had done Mildred a world of good. Fran's maid of honor was relaxed and buoyant with expressed hope.

"What about Winston? What music do you think your beau would like played at your wedding?" Mildred asked, ignoring Fran's question.

Fran changed again. She frowned. "You're in one of your moods."

"What mood is that? Happy? Delighted. Glad to see you?"

Fran shook her head in stupefaction. "Shake it off, kid. And for your information, no one says beau anymore. He's my.... Winston is my guy. I'm not even sure if Winston has a favorite song. We don't talk about music. We don't have an Our Song either," Fran confessed, temporarily stymied by what could be seen by others as a romantic failing—a lack of something vital that portended a dim future for the betrothed couple. Fran tested that superstition with a question. "Do we need an Our Song?"

"Yes," Mildred said brightly. "There are some things one must have at a wedding-- something old and something new, like an Our Song."

"But I already have something else that is new," Fran said, postponing the choice of a song. "I bought a wedding dress."

Mildred was on the verge of offering coffee and wedding cake, but was forestalled in that moment by Fran's declaration of news. A selected wedding dress was big news.

"What color is it?" Mildred asked immediately.

"You always ask goofball questions like that. You didn't ask where I found it or what it's like. You asked the color. It's sort of white," Fran said, eyes squinting.

Fran had been squinting or scowling often lately. Mildred almost asked her how long had it been since she had been to the eye doctor, but she saw that Fran was simply having one of her wedding moods. They came and went quickly these days.

"I read an article that an older bride can wear any color she likes. I just thought you might like a dress with a little color to it," Mildred said. "Like champagne or candlelight—some color like that," Mildred explained without taking offense at Fran's commentary about her questions. There was a word for brides who are frequently in a testy mood, but she couldn't think of it.

"I bought a wedding dress that was on sale," Fran said, taking a hard look at Mildred. "Well, it's not really a wedding dress. It's a dress that will do for a wedding," she added, and the words were almost a dare.

"Do you want to show me the dress or slip on the dress in the other room and come out in it so I can get the full effect? You could stand in the doorway, and I could hum "La Vie En Rose" again. Maybe that could be yours and Winston's song. You could walk down the aisle to that song. You might have to sway a little bit. It's kind of a swaying song."

"Don't be crazy right now, Mildred. First Sam, now you. I don't have time for crazy," Fran warned, reaching forcefully into her plastic shopping bag and extracting a dress that was still on a cheap plastic hanger. Some clerks did that for you: left the purchase on a hanger and folded the garment awkwardly around the hanger and stuffed it in a bag.

Mildred still preferred a box with tissue paper, but most stores didn't do that anymore.

Fran withdrew the dress, and holding it by the shoulders, she laid it across her chest. "This little baby covers a multitude of flaws. It's got some ruffles in the right places, and it has a fullish skirt, sort of." Fran tugged at the side of the dress and stretched out its width. "See?"

The dress wasn't exactly white. There was a bluish hue to the fabric, which was not exactly satin but had a sheen to it. The color wasn't true though. It looked more like it had once been white and washed with something blue and blue dye had faded on this dress. And the sheen of the fabric? It was the kind of coating on a fabric that Mildred's mother had told her while growing up to avoid wearing because, "It makes you look cheap."

Mildred did not say that to Fran. Instead, she searched her mind for something encouraging to say about the awful dress in front of her. Buying time to think, Mildred reached over and touched the fabric, wiggling her fingers afterwards. She felt a waxy residue. Mildred fought a desire to wipe her fingers on the side of her leg. The fabric reminded her of the dresses that dancers used to wear on *The Lawrence Welk Show* when they were going to demonstrate the polka. Baton twirlers wore that fabric on football fields. Ice skaters counted on that fabric to flare when they sailed across the ice rink or performed pirouettes, spinning dizzily, trusting their costume would hold together in spite of intense speed.

Mildred began to list the kinds of activities associated with the fabric and sheen of the dress but never once thought of a bride getting married in a dress made of that cheap looking fabric in an odd shade of blue, not white. Why, the whitish blue was the very pallor of someone very cold and close to death. You might die in that dress, but you wouldn't want to be buried in it. Mildred kept all of that to herself while smiling genially and nodding encouragingly.

"I know the dress needs to be dry-cleaned, and while I like how the cloth holds its shape, the cloth has a funny feel to it, doesn't it?" Fran eyed Mildred. And then holding it closer to her face, she sniffed. "Does this dress smell funny to you?"

Mildred marveled that this was the first time Fran apparently was sniffing the dress, for her friend was a veteran sniffer of all kinds of objects before she bought them for their booths at the Emporium. The fact that she had not sniffed it before caused Mildred a mild alarm. *How was Fran changing?*

Mildred leaned over obligingly and sniffed lightly, the way she did when walking past perfume counters in department stores where ladies dressed in black smocks had drawn-on mouths outlined in black held out little pieces of cardboard spritzed with perfume while announcing proudly, "We are introducing a new fragrance. Do you want to try it?"

Mildred always said no.

Obligingly, Mildred sniffed this time. "I do detect something," Mildred admitted holding back a grimace. It was a pretty bad smell. Worse than mothballs but kind of like that. Sort of sour. Kind of harsh. Not natural—chemical. Yes, a chemical smell.

Fran suddenly slumped onto the sofa, holding the dress in her lap. "I thought it smelled funny in the store; but it was so cheap, I hoped I would leave the smell behind. But the awful smell is in the fabric, isn't it?"

Mildred nodded, swallowing hard. She felt a little queasy from the smell. She no longer wanted her chicken roasted in red wine or a slice of her freshly baked double-almond extract wedding cake. And, yes, she had used real butter and a lot of it!

"I could hang the dress on the clothesline and air it out," Fran suggested tentatively. "Sunshine and fresh air can do wonders."

Mildred just shook her head. "Do you want even a hint of that smell at your wedding?"

"Oh, Millie. I just wanted to get it over with," Fran confessed in a sudden gush of truth—the first crack in Fran that admitted that planning a wedding was too much. Too much! "I saw a dress. It was my size and the color was all right. It was forty dollars, and I had a coupon, so it was less than that, and I just wanted to mark buying a dress off my list of things to do." Fran looked up forlornly at Mildred and said in a repeated refrain that if it were being said by an Alzheimer's patient would have far more dire implications, "I am terribly, terribly in love."

The confession was a constant refrain with Fran now in the same way that Sam was always warning others that trouble was coming.

"Oh, Millie," Fran sighed. "I guess I must take it back and try again."

"It's all right. Don't lose heart. You've bought a wrong dress before and taken it back without much hoopla. It doesn't mean anything. Nothing is jinxed. You are not experiencing bad luck. And, I think you will be happier if you return the dress," Mildred said, taking the dress from Fran and putting it back on the hanger. The receipt was pushed into the bottom of the bag, and she saw the real price Fran had paid. That coupon had been worth thirty percent more subtracted from forty dollars.

Mildred gripped the dress tightly, and understood the allure of it: it was hard to pass up a really cheap dress, unless of course, the dress looked as cheap as this one.

"I don't know why I didn't see it before at the store, Mildred. You're not yourself, and I'm not myself these days. When have you ever known me to buy something that stinks?"

"We'll be a better version of ourselves again soon. Wait. You'll see."

"He loves me, doesn't he? I mean, Winston loves me, doesn't he?"

"Oh, yes. Winston loves you from head to toe," Mildred promised.

"I like the neckline of that dress, don't you?"

"Yes. I think that neckline is nice," Mildred agreed. "I can see how you liked the neckline."

"And the color. This whitish blushing color."

"You don't blush," Mildred said. And blush was the wrong word altogether. This dress had a pale almost deathly pallor.

"I blushed when I was younger."

"No, you didn't," Mildred argued. "You never did blush."

"You didn't know me when I was younger. I could have blushed."

"Very rarely and only when you were surprised—not the way a bride might blush."

"Of course, I am not a blushing bride, and what is wrong with you? Since when have you had an opinion about a dress anyway?" Fran said, growing suddenly cross.

Her moods were up and down.

"You don't even own a dress. Don't spend all of your time baking trial wedding cakes and a chicken, and then tell me you don't have a dress. We've talked about this before."

"I am going to buy a dress for the wedding and make the wedding cake, and I'll ask the Bereans to plan you a special song. No one sings a love song like a Berean," Mildred promised, as she made a mental note to ask Anne Henry to get some of the Berean gals to sing at Fran's wedding. *Is that what a maid of honor did?*

"So, you don't really like this dress?" Fran demanded. "It has to go back?"

"I never said that." Mildred was inching her way back to the fence which she was prepared to sit upon until after the wedding, when they could both go back to being their predictable selves.

"I could see what you really felt about the dress in your eyes. You think this dress is too young for me, don't you? But, Millie, when you are terribly, terribly in love, you feel young again." She looked up at Mildred, willing her to understand. The notion passed, and Fran sighed. "I think the smell could dissipate if I hung it out on the clothesline for a couple of days," Fran said, revisiting her options.

"Can you hear what you are saying? I'm not an expert on weddings, but I think you should try to look ravishing in your wedding dress."

"Ravishing! What is wrong with you? Since when you have you used that word?"

Mildred pressed on. "I am going to buy a dress to wear for your wedding, and it's going to be a beautiful dress. I will ask Anne Henry to get some Bereans together and sing a love song at your wedding and that song can be yours and Winston's special-unto-you Our Song," Mildred said, repeating the plan until Fran the Bride could hear her. "Everything is going to be all right."

"I must take back this dress," Fran said flatly.

"Go shopping for real," Mildred urged. "Let it be the only thing you do. Don't treat it like an errand or something to accomplish on your to-do list."

"Does Winston really love me, Mildred? Really love me?"

"Yes," Mildred said firmly.

"The good thing is with all of this discussion of weddings you ought to be able to write some meditations using a wedding idea and Jesus."

"You would think so," Mildred replied, neutrally.

"You haven't mentioned writing any of your pieces lately." Fran eyed her best friend with interest. "What's going on?"

Mildred stopped herself from saying with arms outstretched, 'This is a precious moment. Can't you see it? Every moment of life is precious. Isn't every moment glorious? We are absolutely loved whether we feel that in the moment or not. Life is such a miracle!'

"I'm living life," Mildred replied simply, a foolish smile on her face.

"You have been living life as long as I have known you and that's a long time, and you have always had time to write your pieces. This wedding thing—it's right up your writing alley."

"Don't want to sit still," Mildred said. "I want to cook and walk, come and go and be myself, and you be yourself, and be with Winston. Be joyful."

"Since when have you let not wanting to do something stop you from doing it? I mean, that's what being a Christian is all is about. Making yourself do stuff you don't want to do or not doing the stuff that feels really good."

"No, it's not," Mildred argued with a smile, because Fran wasn't serious.

Every now and again, Fran Applewhite liked to talk like the world talked just to see if Mildred Budge was paying attention.

Taking a different tone, Fran eyed her best friend and asked thoughtfully, "Seriously, why aren't you writing?"

"Maybe I've said everything I want to say."

"Writer's block? Fran pressed. But she meant more than that.

Mildred Budge depended on the living waters to flow through her and become meditations. When she stopped writing then one might initially surmise that the living waters had stopped flowing—or worse.

Fran went for the explanation of worse. "Are you in sin?"

"Not to my knowledge," Mildred confessed readily. She examined the planks in her own eyes most mornings sitting with her Bible open and asking God to show her anything that he didn't like that she was doing because it was hurting her soul or causing others distress.

"You are answering carefully the way people talk to lawyers," Fran observed.

"You sound a little like a lawyer—and a judge."

"You would do the same for me if the positions were reversed. You have done the same for me. It's awfully hard to see yourself. A real friend will help you take a true look at yourself and face what you see. Sometimes it's not pretty. Sin isn't pretty."

"I know," Mildred said, her hands falling to her side without defense.

"Are you lusting after that man who has been digging up your bushes?"

"I admired the way he looked lifting that pick ax. Mark is beautiful, isn't he?"

"Beautiful isn't a lust word," Fran said. "Did you envy his strength, because it might not be lust. It might be covetousness. I have known you to covet someone else's ability. Mark is strong, and he's in better shape than most of the men we know our age."

"Did you lust after him?' Mildred asked.

"You bet I did. But I came to my senses and repented of it. Knowing Winston has stirred up those feelings again, and you have to reign them in. Sometimes our nature feels like one of those horses you have to break before you can put a saddle on it."

"Or a bit in its mouth. I don't think I am coveting Mark's strength. About all I really want now is time alone."

Fran didn't take that statement personally. When Mildred Budge said she wanted to be alone it wasn't because of any one person and certainly not in reference to her best friend. It was that she wanted to be alone in prayer and to think.

"And your house is getting fuller, and time is passing so quickly."

"It is rushing by, isn't it?" Mildred marveled. *And isn't it glorious and precious? Exquisite, even.*

"But you're enjoying parts of it."

"I have lived long enough to recognize that the one big constancy you can count on is that everything changes. It will change again, and every experience of change—every moment is precious."

"So why do you think you're not writing?" Fran asked bluntly.

"Oh, Frannie. Because life is so good. Really, really good. And no one really wants to read a story about that. They like stories about suffering and witnessing and testifying and getting born again and being martyred and, at different times of year, they like to read familiar stories about Faith Promise, the Mission

Conference, Bible Conference, Women's retreats, Easter, Christmas—the reason for the season—Stewardship."

"Ain't it the truth?"

"Yes, it's the truth. And there's more."

"And Jesus is his name."

"And I am seeing him everywhere. His likeness. Everywhere I look—the lost, the found, the young, the old, the joyful, the despairing. I see Jesus' likeness everywhere, and there is such a joy in his creation and such a love for everyone...."

"Even Liz Luckie," Fran injected knowingly. "You are able to love Liz Luckie in ways that most of us can't. And Dixie. You actually enjoy her company!"

"Liz is not such a mystery. Just a lonely woman who flirts instead of making conversation. She reaps what she sows and doesn't know how she got it. I'm not sure Dixie isn't some kind of eccentric genius. I don't really understand her, and that's one of the things I like most about her. We talk about the Bible often, and she frequently has a fierce point of view. I like that fierceness about her. She demands to know the truth in a most unladylike way."

"Have I told you that I love Winston? I love him terribly. I am terribly, terribly in love."

"Yes, you have told me that," Mildred confirmed. She didn't stop herself from saying, "And I believe you."

For Mildred Budge, the church lady, understood why one must cry out when in love. She understood why her friend couldn't stop testifying that she was terribly, terribly in love.

"But not all the ways that I love him. I can't name them because they grow so quickly, I can't keep track of how much I love Winston Holmes."

"That's happening to me. I can't name them either. But that's happening to me, and it's why I'm not writing. I'm losing track of the ways I am growing to love everybody and am changing into someone unfamiliar to me—someone new-- and I'm happy about it. Just to be alive is wonderful enough."

"So, are we going to eat that chicken?" Fran asked. "It smells really good."

"That chicken is for you and Winston until you can go to Paris."

Fran looked at her friend with wonder. "You're giving us a whole baked chicken?"

"All you have to do is put some tin foil over it, carry it home without dropping it, and you've got dinner readymade. Dessert, too. Wedding cake."

"I'm out of Sister Schubert rolls. And I don't have any peas."

"I have both. You can have it all."

"You wouldn't want to take this dress back for me?"

Mildred said readily, "I will if you really want me to."

"You hate department stores."

"I do," Mildred agreed.

"I'll take the chicken, the rolls, the peas, and I'll take that awful dress back myself."

The two old friends went to the kitchen and packed up an early honeymoon supper for the bride and groom. Mildred placed the latest wedding cake inside the insulated bag she used to send along food to homebound people. She would bake another one soon. She wouldn't mind baking a wedding cake every day because every day was a good day.

At the car while Fran placed the sack with the dress on the passenger seat and Mildred situated the chicken in the back on the floorboard, where a plastic mat would catch any drop of broth that might splatter, Fran looked up suddenly, quizzically and asked, "Did you know that Irving Berlin's second wife Ellin married him in a dress that needed to go to the dry cleaners?"

"I did not know that," Mildred replied. She didn't ask how Fran knew. Fran had become fitful at night and often turned the TV back on at three o'clock in the morning when she couldn't sleep.

"I saw a documentary. Ellin and Irving had been courting for about two years, and her daddy didn't want her to marry him.

Irving was a widower and a Jewish man, and Ellin was a rich Catholic girl whose daddy thought she could do better than Irving. They kept trying to get everyone's blessing but couldn't. Irving called Ellin early one Monday morning and asked her to meet him at the courthouse and get married—they had been courting for nineteen months-- and she was trying to get one more day's wear out of an ordinary dress. She was headed to the hairdresser's when Irving called. After he said 'let's get married right now,' that girl didn't even stop to change clothes. Ellin was terribly, terribly in love with Irving Berlin. He gave her the song "Always" for a wedding present. Can you imagine such a gift from the one who loves you?"

Mildred nodded. It seemed like everyone had been terribly, terribly, terribly in love at some time in their lives.

"Thanks for the chicken and the cake," Fran said finally, and closed the car door with a loud bang. Then she rolled down her window and said, "I've got a good dress that needs to go to the cleaners. That's my back-up dress if I can't find a ravishing one."

Mildred nodded and laughed, stepping back so Fran could back out of the driveway without killing her.

Waving good-bye to Fran, the maid of honor looked around. Steev's light was on inside the house, but he was over at the church. Belle was sitting on the back-door stoop watching for Sam, and somewhere in the neighborhood her friend Sam was walking, walking.

All was calm.

All was bright.

People were terribly, terribly in love. And Mildred had been humming blessing prayers without ceasing, her soul expanding.

"This is a precious moment," the church lady said out loud to God and to her neighbors. From then on, that statement would be a kind of benediction for her, a different version of amen for a life that was spent in prayerful consecration to Love, its existence, the hope it brought, and the pain and fulfilment too.

For the rest of her life, though she did not know it then, church lady Mildred Budge would hum a kind of love song in the background of all her breaths taken. If she had ever stopped to name it, the song would be called "This is a precious moment. Oh, yes."

15
A WEDDING DRESS FOR YOU

The next morning Mildred dialed Liz Luckie's phone number from memory, a number she had learned after the baby shower when she had determined that she must be Liz's friend whether she liked her or not.

It was difficult to be someone's friend when you did not like her very much.

Liz answered, her voice guarded. It was a self-protective "Hello" that caused Mildred to repent one more time of her own reservations about trying to like the woman who had been widowed four times.

Mildred forced her own voice to sound cheerier than she felt. "I need a new dress for Fran's wedding, and I have lost track of where to shop here in Montgomery."

"Oh, my dear Mildred," Liz said with greater warmth. "Your words are music to my ears. I cannot tell you how long I have lived with those words unsaid in my home. Husbands simply do not understand what a woman means when she says she needs a new dress."

Because the words had brought Liz such delight, Mildred repeated them, her voice stronger this time. "I really do need a dress. I have needed one for some time, but...." Mildred allowed her voice to fade away.

It was difficult to explain how you could let go of having a dress. It had been at least two years since she had worn one-- longer than that since she had bought one. Mildred Budge had been living in pants. They were comfortable, but you gave up something for pants—something that Mildred had not taken the time to name. The word *it* would suffice.

Liz's voice filled with a rapturous delight, and though Mildred could not see her in that moment, she knew what Liz's blue eyes looked like. They were wide open and glowing with covetous zeal.

"There is a store about a hundred miles from here—a magical place really-- where you can find a perfect dress. It's a day trip." Lowering her voice, Liz whispered into the receiver, "I give you my word. It's worth every mile."

"A whole day to buy a dress," Mildred said, thinking that as a steward of one's time that seemed like too much time to spend on what was, of course, vanity.

Liz decided for her. "I'll just come get you now, and we'll just go on over there. Cancel whatever other plans you have. Take it from me. Buying a wedding dress is more important."

"We'll just go on over there," Mildred repeated automatically, thinking about her schedule. Another chicken was thawing on the counter. She had planned to cook it for herself for supper having lived with the smell of the one roasting the day before but not even tasting it.

And, too, Mark had come by unexpectedly after Fran left to give her an update on which nurseries had replied to his emails and pictures about what he had harvested. He had dropped off the first check. "Just a hundred fifty dollars, for now," he had said. "I subtracted the lad's mowing fee."

"Thank you," she said, honestly. *A hundred and fifty dollars was enough to buy a good dress, wasn't it?*

"It's early yet," Mark said. "But things are looking kind of promising. More than that, actually." He had said those words wearing his Brooks Brothers jacket. He smelled like a green bar of Irish soap again, and he had stood in the foyer hungrily sniffing the air and the scent of yesterday's slow-roasted chicken that had not completely dissipated.

"You've been cooking," he announced awkwardly, holding a small pot of violets which he explained sheepishly were for her windowsill.

When Mildred did not reach for them, he walked across the room in five steps and placed the small pot of violets on the living room windowsill. A small trail of dirt followed him.

"Roast chicken and wedding cake," she replied without further explanation.

"I bet you're a good cook," he remarked, taking in the room. "I suppose it gets kind of lonely eating a meal like that by yourself."

"No," Mildred replied blithely. "I cook almost every day, and I'm never really lonely." *Anything but.*

Her words caused a stricken look. Mark's small talk dried up. His gaze became instantly furtive as he made his way back to the foyer and the front door. "I didn't mean to intrude," he said, his forest-green eyes clouding over.

"You aren't intruding," she promised him brightly. "People come and go here all day long."

Mark kept walking, didn't even wave as he drove away.

How strange.

After Mildred closed the door, she wondered why Mark had changed so suddenly. Men were a mystery. But that mystery had caused her to want to bake another chicken the next day. If Mark dropped by again, she'd make him a to-go plate to take home for his supper. He probably didn't get too many home-cooked meals.

"Comb your hair, and let's go," Liz said, growing excited. "I can be there in thirty."

There was nothing else to do. Mildred needed a wedding dress, and she had no other options. Mildred agreed to Liz's plan and popped the thawing chicken back into the fridge. Cooking it would have to wait until the next day. It only took Liz twenty minutes to arrive at Mildred's house, and she blasted the horn.

Grabbing her purse, Mildred hurried out to Liz, her hair mostly combed, her lipstick a quick swipe, a glance in the hallway mirror with the oft-asked question, 'Is that what you really look like now?'

"We are going to have to get a move on. I forgot that they are on Eastern Time over there," Liz explained, as Mildred climbed into Liz's new Mercedes. Liz always drove a new car. She traded up every two years.

For most of her life Mildred had driven a car for ten years or so. She hated to trade in an old dependable friend, like a faithful car. That didn't mean she didn't enjoy Liz's taste in vehicles. Her car was always a luxury sedan, most often a dark color with a lighter interior. Leather seats, of course.

And her cars were always spanking clean. The kind of clean that meant someone who was paid to clean had vacuumed it out with a nozzle that fit into thin seams and narrow crevices. There was no grease inside on the door hinge.

Inside the car, there was plenty of room for her feet. Mildred automatically clasped the seatbelt, surreptitiously letting it out a couple of inches while glancing at her watch: 9:20 Central Time; 10:20 Eastern. An hour and a half to get there. Two hours to shop. Lunch.

As Mildred considered the plushness of the Mercedes, she began to fear that the cost of a dress where Liz Luckie shopped might well be beyond any dollar figure she had ever envisioned spending on any dress during her lifetime.

Mildred wanted to ask: 'How much does a dress at this shop cost?' But she didn't. It was far too late to ask that question.

And Liz was too happy that they were going. Besides, time was running out on dress shopping for the wedding.

"It's been ages since I tried on a St. John frock," Liz confessed suddenly.

"It's been ages since I said the word frock," Mildred replied, as Liz squealed out of the subdivision and headed to the connection for the interstate.

Liz drove with the kind of confidence that Mildred associated with men. As her chauffeur aggressively cut someone else off at the access ramp and raced onto the interstate, reaching 65 mph faster than Mildred had ever experienced it, Mildred double-checked her seatbelt and re-centered herself to be directly in front of the airbag.

"What a beautiful day to go shopping," Liz exclaimed. "Not a rain cloud in sight. Who knew when we woke up that we would be having such an adventure?"

"I didn't," Mildred replied, and then she settled back against the leather seat, and the strangest peace came over her. A different peace. A surrender to being driven, guided, challenged. The blessing prayers began again, humming inside of her low and sure. Instantly, she began to see a stream of people she had loved throughout her life, and they were all beautiful, lit up and secure but needing more and more light. Mildred's heart prayed for the Light to keep them warm and safe. Whole and holy. Comforted. To heal them of any infirmity. Let aches and pains fade to shadows. Give them beauty for ashes.

Staring out the window, the prayers receding to an unceasing hum that played in the background of her consciousness like music, Mildred confessed to her reflection and to Liz: "I have always hated shopping. I have always pretended when I was with others that I was fine, but I hate shopping."

"Oh, my dear Mildred! Who doesn't? It's a horrible job. Worse than writing one's resume where you have to face all of the inadequacies of your life which don't exist in your mind; but when you go to write them down, you face how your view of yourself doesn't fit with how the world sees you in terms of the factual truth. Shopping means you must face the facts of your deficiencies. The way you want to look and think you do look is not how the clothes fit you. But you will like this store. And you'll love Miss Julia. She's very old school. I don't know why I haven't been back to her store. I used to love it. Why do we stop doing the things we love?"

It was a rhetorical question. Mildred didn't try to answer it.

Liz drove with her eyes fixed on the road and her hands balanced perfectly on the steering wheel. The speed limit was 70 mph, and she had set the cruise control for 75 mph. "Cops don't stop you for going five miles over the limit," Liz said, making a sharp twist of the steering wheel, and passing another car before settling back in the right, supposedly slower, lane.

"The store used to be called Two Sisters. Did you know that store?"

Mildred shook her head. She had never heard of it. Talbot's was the only store she used to really like, but that was because it was smaller and had a really nice ladies' room. They didn't sell wedding dresses—not the kind of better dress that she needed for Fran's wedding, anyway.

"I think one of the sisters died, and the remaining sister changed the store's name. She couldn't call the store One Sister, and she couldn't keep the name Two Sisters. That would be too sad, wouldn't it?" Liz didn't wait for Mildred to agree.

Liz was a woman who lived alone with no one to talk to, and she was now experiencing talker's relief. "Miss Julia specializes only in good dresses for special occasions. It's called "A Dress for You." That's a better name than One Sister and right on the target. It says exactly what you want."

"A Dress for You. It does sound hopeful—as if finding a dress is possible," Mildred murmured as they soared past a billboard advertising Calloway Gardens. She hadn't been there in years.

A long time ago the gardens were very pretty, but Mildred hadn't been back to see if they still were. She had heard that they had added a butterfly room of some sorts.

Liz shot Mildred a strange look. "Of course, having a dress is possible. Anyone can have a dress."

That had not been Mildred's experience. She had shopped for a dress quite a while before giving up a couple of years ago. Department stores were too big, and Talbot's, well, their sizes had changed, her arms had thickened, and it was too depressing to try and find anything there now-- and especially a dress.

Mildred did not explain how the wrong dress could make you feel. Instead, she thought back to the three dresses in her lifetime that she had really liked: the navy blue imitation-leather dress her mother had given her when she was twelve for a Christmas present; a brown and cream tweed dress with brown leather buttons that she had worn to a bridal shower when it was her duty to write down the names of people who had brought gifts and what had been given; and the absolute best dress of her life, a Kelly green dress with a mock turtleneck collar, long ruched sleeves, fit at the waist and a full skirt that folded prettily around you when you were seated and swooshed and twirled when you walked. It had been a size 10, and Mildred had found it at Loveman's Department store so many years ago she couldn't have named the year or her own age. But she had been a young woman with a discernible waistline in her twenties. It had been an ageless dress, stayed young in her memory as Mildred had aged. She had yearned for that green dress and the girl she used to be in it from time to time.

"And here we are," Liz said suddenly, taking a right turn off the interstate.

"You couldn't have driven a hundred miles."

"We have a few more miles or so to go on this road. Miss Julia's place is off the beaten path. This is the turn."

It was the kind of old Southern road that Mildred loved. There was no sign of a strip mall in sight. No sign of any retail stores really. There were two gasoline stations where you could go inside and buy a cup of coffee and a fried peach pie, but Liz cruised right past them.

"I thought Miss Julia's was closer to Atlanta."

"Outskirts and sideways. This is a back-door route. We can miss all that airport traffic. Atlanta traffic makes me cuss."

On route, Liz pointed out various possible trails this way and that which led to other adventures, but she didn't take any turn.

"We don't have time today to follow those trails, although if you have never seen FDR's summer home you would enjoy that small town. Warm Springs is that way," she said with a wave of her hand, and her nails were polished a pretty shade of pearly pink.

'That color would make a good wedding dress,' Mildred thought.

Driving faster than Mildred ever drove, Liz said, "I ate at a restaurant over there once, and although I have never thought of myself as someone who likes fried chicken livers, I ate some there, and they were good. I can't remember the name of the place, but it was up on a hill. I like big old buildings that sit high up on a hill, don't you? If it's on a hill, there's always a nice view."

Mildred's ears perked up. Her appetite quickened. Occasionally, Mildred enjoyed eating fried chicken livers cooked in sherry and spooned over a mound of warm jasmine rice with some peach chutney on the side.

She could have revisited her recipe for chicken livers and cooked them and some peach or even brandied fruit chutney in her mind, but there wasn't time. Liz veered right sharply and eased up to a large house that had once been a grand old home. "Here's our last turn. Paradise, here we come," she said.

Liz drove up a long winding road, while Mildred silently prayed something other than the blessing prayers. Liz talked animatedly, pointing out more sights--gas stations, and a rustic beauty parlor that she was surprised was still in business and had the name: The Wild Hair.

And suddenly there it was. Tara'
s twin sister on a hill. A Dress for You. It was bigger than Mildred expected, and there weren't very many cars parked in front. Liz zoomed right up to the door and parked in a handicap spot. The car jolted to an abrupt stop, and she turned off the engine, her smile widening. "It's so good to be here. Reach in my glove compartment and get me the handicapped card, won't you?"

Mildred slipped her fingers under the lip of the lock and opened the glove compartment. There was a blue handicapped card that had a couple of more months on it before it expired. She handed the card to Liz.

"Husband number 3 needed it," Liz explained, hanging it on the rearview mirror.

It was the kind of move that bothered Mildred. Somehow in handing over of the card—the lie—and the hanging of the lie that attested that one or both of them was handicapped truly bothered Mildred. They could have parked one slot over and not needed it. And then she watched Liz, who exited the car and crossed in front of it while Mildred was still figuring out if she needed to repent of a lie that she had somehow been co-opted into making. Then, whispering "Sorry" to Jesus under her breath for being a part of it all—the Fall was real, and this, like cussing in Atlanta traffic, was proof of it-- Mildred got out of the car and braced herself for what was next.

There were six wide pale gray steps leading to the porch and a ramp on the side. Before Mildred could make a decision to take the stairs or walk up the ramp, the most elegant woman Mildred had ever seen in person appeared in the doorway.

"Welcome, ladies. I am so glad you are here," the woman said, and her eyes changed into a deep purple as Mildred climbed up the broad steps. "You have come on a good day. A bridal party is scheduled for later; but until then, you have the place to yourselves."

Mildred had seen that type of woman on the big screen when she had still gone to movies, but she did not know that a woman with that kind of Grace Kelly class, Rosalind Russell independence, and Rita Hayworth sexuality existed anywhere in real life.

Mildred smiled her own response while sending an emergency message to Jesus: *What have I gotten myself into? This is going to cost more than a hundred and fifty dollars.*

16
WANT SOME TEA
AND BUTTER COOKIES?

Immediately upon entering, Mildred saw that in spite of the specific name of the shop, the elegant foyer was dedicated almost entirely to luxury handbags. Purses were hung on coat racks and displayed on marble table tops. Small glittering change purses—or maybe that's what women put cell phones and a lipstick in! —were inside a curio cabinet, the glass panes freshly cleaned and a small light inside that lit them up. Mildred didn't have a cell phone, and she didn't like going out at night, but she wanted one of those glittery evening bags right away.

"Elizabeth, it's good to see you," Miss Julia said warmly.

Mildred waited for the two Southern women to swap air kisses, but they did not. Instead, they met one another's gaze like businesswomen who are about to trade important information and make a deal.

With the same resolute gaze of a trustworthy business partner still in her eyes, the mistress of the shop turned to Mildred, and in a conspiratorial voice as if she were sharing private information, said, "Shall I tell you briefly about the layout of our store?"

Mildred adjusted her gaze, continuing a slow sweep of the expansive foyer, which she realized, suddenly, was in the shape of a circle rather than a rectangle. She rotated slowly inside the foyer, feeling as if she were alive in the center of the world.

"Immediately to your right is a place to rest. If you get tired, just sit down for a spell and gently recall why you have come.

Then, once you have regained your bearings and remembered your intended purpose, we will all try again. We are not without mercy here, and you are not alone unless you want to be."

A rest station in a clothing store. No need to hide out in a dressing room and ask Jesus to come and get you—*to pray that you are ready to leave this world and move on into your mansion in heaven.* A rest station in a clothing store was the most sensible idea Mildred had encountered in any retail establishment.

Her chin tilted slightly up, her gaze thoughtful and calming, her hostess said reassuringly, "A cup of hot tea is always available should you find yourself feeling weak for any reason. We recommend sugar in your tea to keep up your energy even when you may be feeling over stimulated or dieting. Sugar is not always the enemy others can so harshly assert."

"Sugar," Mildred repeated. She had always felt that way about tea and sugar. In spite of the warnings about sugar, Mildred believed that one needed sugar to live. A spoonful of sugar in a hot cup of tea could help you to take the next step, whatever that step needed to be and whatever the destination.

"In the opposite direction are the finer underthings. Slips. Hose."

"Slips and hose," Mildred said. She could not remember when she had last heard those two words mentioned out loud. She had one good slip left, but she had not worn it in years. She inhaled deeply of the memory of the taupe, lace-trimmed slip that she had almost forgotten was in the bottom drawer of her dresser. *Wasn't it?* She hadn't seen that slip in ages or even looked for it. *Would she grieve if it were gone?*

"Now to the dresses. Whose day is it?" Miss Julia asked brightly, her gaze moving between Liz and Mildred.

Liz pointed to Mildred. "I will shop, of course. But our girl here is the one who needs a dress."

Our girl. Me?

118

Mildred was stricken. She did not like to be the center of a saleswoman's attention. She had expected the clotheshorse Liz to talk dresses, and Mildred had planned to trail along behind checking out what was hanging on the racks when they weren't paying any attention to her. She needed a cup of tea with three sugars immediately.

The woman smiled with assurance. "My dear, come this way," Miss Julia said, turning toward the back room that was marked off with dark green velvet curtains—the kind that Scarlett O'Hara had turned into a big dress.

Miss Julia walked gracefully. Her chestnut hair was twisted up in an old-fashioned glamourous style that Mildred believed was called a chignon; she wasn't sure. In the middle of Miss Julia's hair was a bright shining diamond—just one.

That single glittering pin in the other woman's carefully coiffed hair caused Mildred to lose heart momentarily. Even if she could find a dress, she was not going to be able to put a sparkly pin in her hair like that and walk with that kind of self-assurance. Mildred didn't own any good jewelry to speak of, and she had never been able to figure out why people fooled with costume jewelry. Mildred Budge had no need of a costume. She was herself, and how she looked was how she looked.

Unable to escape and needing a wedding dress, Mildred followed the elegant woman wearing a diamond pin in her hair.

"I am going to let you find your dress in peace, Millie," Liz called after her. "I will look at these handbags and the shoes. They are Italian," she added, and her voice was rife with bliss and anticipation. "I came into a little money lately, and it's been burning a hole in my pocket."

Oh. The ten thousand dollars Liz had won gambling. Mildred thought of a cuss word and tried to erase it from her consciousness.

Like a chapel that is set up sparsely to promote meditation and prayer, the designated dress-for-you room Mildred Budge stepped into was a quiet chamber with a green velvet love seat, and it was there that Miss Julia invited Mildred to make herself comfortable. And it was there that Miss Julia asked her first question. "What is the occasion?"

"Wedding," Mildred said simply, repeating Liz.

"Not yours though?" Miss Julia asked quizzically, eyeing Mildred in a new way.

"No," Mildred said. "Not today, anyway." *Where did those words come from?*

"Grandmother of the bride? Aunt, perhaps?"

Mildred shook her head, no. "Friend of the bride," Mildred explained as if the woman in front of her was an usher who would steer her to the proper side of the sanctuary just in time for the ceremony. "Best friend, actually. Sisters at heart." Then holding her shoulders back, Mildred said clearly: "We have endured together. Endured," she repeated emphatically.

Miss Julia nodded knowingly, her purple eyes blinking slowly, slowly. "Then it doesn't really matter what you wear. Your friendship will always endure, no matter what. That takes some of the pressure off, doesn't it? Just remembering that."

The response was incredibly reassuring. Mildred swallowed hard and nodded, tears forming in her eyes. She blinked. Her friendship with Fran would endure. She believed that to be true, but it was good to hear the words said aloud by someone who was wearing a diamond pin in her hair.

Miss Julia tilted her head contemplatively. "You want to look extra nice in honor of the occasion and your friendship, but you need to look like yourself."

"Like an heirloom plant," Mildred agreed readily.

Miss Julia blinked at the description, shrugged slightly and said, "All right. At peace. At home in the sunlight. Able to wait. To receive. To give back beauty to those passing by," Miss Julia said, growing pensive. She tilted her head slightly to one side and her eyelids fluttered slightly as she spoke. "You want to look like a Southern woman who knows her origins and has a sense of place. Most importantly, you want to communicate to your friend the bride and the well-wishers who have gathered to celebrate that your dear friend is getting married and your heart's desire is for her happiness. You will endure the changes sure to come gracefully without complaint or any forlornness. You want to dress for your best self. Your truest self," Miss Julia repeated for emphasis. "Dare I say joie de vivre?"

"We both dare to believe it. God help me. Joie de vivre is exactly right." For there were many unspoken tensions between Fran and Mildred about the wedding, and the talk of the Lunch Bunch, wedding cake, and the music were just the tip of the wedding ice berg.

"But mainly," Miss Julia said, fixing Mildred Budge with an intense purple gaze. "You do not want to look like Queen Elizabeth when she is having trouble with one of her grown children. God bless that dear, staunch woman for the sacrifices she has made for her country and her family."

Mildred nodded solemnly in agreement. "Queen Elizabeth has drunk many cups of tea with sugar."

Miss Julia explained: "Hasn't she though? But we must look to Queen Elizabeth as a wakeup call, if you will. Her fashions have not progressed with the times or her age. And for ladies our age that matters. It is the current affliction of the more mature lady, such as ourselves, that we are often forced by very limited options to emulate the fashion choices of people who are public figures. Their fame sometimes establishes a dressing trend, unfortunately. As a result, we often end up looking like a poor-relation imitation of Queen Elizabeth in a conservative dress with the wrong hat or a highly sprayed hairdo that is woefully out of date. Lord have mercy! When we look in the mirror we are disappointed because the woman we think ourselves to be does not look like the woman in the mirror."

"She does not," Mildred agreed heartily.

Mildred had seen her reflection age through the years, and was often surprised that the way she looked did not fit the way she felt or had ever envisioned herself to become.

"It is most likely why you resist shopping," Miss Julia concluded.

"You see all that?" Mildred confirmed, incredulous.

"Oh, my dear. The truth is written all over you. And, you are not alone in your tribulation. Shopping is so very hard. So hard. The pressures are real and great. We are expected to perform miracles for ourselves on a moment's notice and often during some of the hardest seasons of our lives, like weddings and funerals. We are expected in those moments to suddenly see ourselves clearly and find some dress or outfit to reflect the truth of who we are not just every day but during a season of great transition, and who can?" Miss Julia asked, incredulous at the question.

"Then, we must somehow pass a test—one that ticks some mythical box in an unwritten societal test of womanhood by being able to find the miracle dress that unites our core identity with a socially approved display of ourselves, and that is almost impossible. But, my dear, it feels impossible because those choices are grossly limited by manufacturers and by the bullies who dictate what fashion is supposed to be or −it's not exactly the right word—glamour, and forgive me for saying this.... sex appeal."

Mildred Budge had not heard the term *sex appeal* in ages, longer than the time when she had heard slips and hose. There were other words people used now that didn't make any sense to her but were supposed to indicate some kind of sexual appeal. She didn't understand those words. Miss Julia had strong ideas on the subject.

"What passes for sex appeal in fashion these days is one of the greatest lies ever perpetrated on society at large and women in particular. Skin-tight clothing does not create sex appeal. It suffocates it. Unless of course you believe that random lust someone is experiencing and focuses on you because you are standing nearby is the same thing as sex appeal, and many people do believe that."

"I don't have an opinion on that subject," Mildred said, primly. "I just hate shopping."

"Forgive me. I do wax on here, I know. But because of the nature of my business and the customers I serve, I have thought long and deeply about the abuse of women in terms of fashion and what is expected of her."

"I knew there were reasons I truly hate shopping. Really good reasons like the ones you are saying," Mildred said, looking around. She wondered suddenly if the woman beside her slept in a four-poster bed with a gauzy tent over her and was covered in a heavy brocade bedspread. She almost asked her.

"Which is one of the reasons that you don't wear jewelry. Good jewelry choices are an accessory to style, and you hate to shop so why would you be expected to wear jewelry?"

"I don't think about jewelry until I see other people wearing it," Mildred confessed starkly. It was quite a relief to say the words out loud.

"I don't blame you. There have been times when I have felt foolish for attaching something to my ears, as if I am a Christmas tree wearing ornaments."

"I did not know that someone could understand that," Mildred said in a voice that was almost a whisper. She had lived most of her life believing that no one else thought the way she did or felt the way she did about shopping and clothes.

"Oh, my dear. I know." Miss Julia pointed to her ears. "See these diamond dots in my ears? When I realized that I was the type of woman who didn't grasp why anyone would attach little pieces of metal with a rock in them to her ears, I also knew and accepted that in my line of work, I needed to wear accessories, so I bought these petite diamond earrings. They are all I wear anywhere. I have a pin for my hair and a string of pearls. But the diamond earrings—they just go with everything. Owning diamond earrings means you never have to think about choosing costume jewelry again."

Mildred made a mental note: *Buy diamond earrings soon. Size, petite.*

"That is how one can solve that problem. There are other problems to solve, and the solutions are as simple as diamond earrings if you are committed to tying up the loose ends of your personal fashion history and putting to rest illusions marketed to us by slave masters of capitalism." Sitting taller, her eyes growing opaque with a kind of resolve that label of steel magnolia didn't cover, Miss Julia added solemnly, "As a Christian woman, I simply refuse to be anyone's slave."

Mildred nodded, as if the woman in front of her were a priest and ready to listen to a confession of her sins. Mildred began to tell her the truth from the bottom of her heart. "The clothes they sell in stores don't look like me, so I end up buying the least offensive garments. And because they don't look like me and their only criteria is inoffensiveness, I pay as little as possible."

"Why would you do otherwise?" Miss Julia readily agreed. "But there is a different way to experience clothing. A garment can feel like you. You can feel pretty. You are pretty. There is more to life than black slacks and a top."

Mildred was wearing a pair of black slacks and the blouse with grey Siamese kittens on it. Miss Julia averted her gaze from the kittens, and Mildred confessed softly, "I own another purple blouse with hippopotamuses on it and a green blouse with red birds."

"Bless your heart," Miss Julia said. The shopkeeper made a little moue of concern and compassion which was so delicate that it encompassed about a hundred expressions of understanding, concern, and good will. Why, that simple facial expression was so powerful and wordless that one might even call it a prayer.

Mildred sealed the memory of it in her deepest recesses to store with signature prayers and resolved to pray that soulful expression in the future when she experienced a sorrow for someone else too deep for words.

Suddenly, Miss Julia clapped her hands, softly signaling that she was ready to leave the subject behind. "Enough about Queen Elizabeth. Let's talk about you. You need the right dress."

"I need the right dress," Mildred agreed, and the strain in her shoulders relaxed. The tight muscle in her neck loosened. This woman did not condemn her for being a failure as a shopper or as a woman.

"We have the right dress for you, so you can rest easy about that. In order to know which dress it is, you must disassociate yourself from previous dresses you have loved—those are the loose ends I mentioned before-- and be ready to experience the dress we have here for you that will fit you and look good on you today as you are."

"Not a suit?" Mildred confirmed. Her right hand went to the center of her chest where she experienced a small flutter in her heart. Her breath caught in her throat, and she swallowed hard.

"People are not so buttoned-down these days, and suits still have that buttoned-down effect, don't they?" And then after a quiet pause, Miss Julia dared to add, "Nothing about you strikes me as buttoned down. You are as free as a bird, deep down. Deeply free, aren't you?"

"Even Fran does not know that about me," Mildred whispered truly. "I have flying dreams all the time."

Miss Julia did not ask who Fran was, but she knew that Mildred had not mentioned Liz, and she didn't question that omission. Somehow women like Miss Julia knew the effect that women like Liz Luckie had on other women, and she did not judge any of them. Miss Julia just knew who they were.

In that way, Mildred Budge and Miss Julia were part of a sisterhood of people who accepted everybody as they were without making much of an issue about it.

"We begin with a choice of color naturally."

"I like red," Mildred announced readily.

"Naturally, red is the color of love and has its moments," Miss Julia replied diplomatically. "But we must remember that red is a powerful, dominant color and that is not exactly the tone you want to set at your best friend's wedding."

"That is so true. I don't want to be seen as powerful and dominant at my best friend's wedding."

"Would you mind if I tried a small and perhaps indelicate experiment by asking you some personal questions?" Miss Julia asked kindly. She smiled, and her soft purple eyes crinkled. She had nice wrinkles that arched up her face instead of etching downwards. Mildred coveted the other lady's gravity-defying wrinkles.

"Go ahead," Mildred invited, fighting the urge to reach into her purse for a scrap of paper in case she needed to write down the words Miss Julia was about to speak.

"I shall say some colors out loud, and you just let your face do your talking for you."

"As simple as that?" Mildred asked, the tension in her shoulders dissipating further. The tightness in her jaw loosened. Her scalp eased. Sadly, her stomach growled.

Miss Julia ignored the growl. But she heard it. Miss Julia leaned her head to one side and nodded.

"Pray proceed," Mildred said, dropping both hands at her side. A deeper relaxation came then and moved across her shoulders, beginning at the nape of her neck and traveling down her back. A warmth eased the strain of being away from her home and out of town and questions about rooms with butterflies and what would she have for lunch faded away though she was hungry.

Miss Julia's voice became a song of sorts, and the words she said in a lilting voice were like elements in a poem written by Keats, where ultimately truth and beauty would be interchangeable.

"Green."

The word landed on Mildred like the touch of a flower's petal. She thought of Kelly green, then mint green, then sage green, then yellow green, and finally the green in Mark's forest green eyes. She smiled.

"Blue."

Mildred saw the water, calm and bright—the horizon calling her gaze out to where the sky met the water. Not a tsunami in sight. There was a lush cloud sitting on the top of the horizon, like a big pearl decorating the blue water. She wanted to stretch out on a sandy beach and wiggle her toes expansively.

"Yellow."

The center of a daisy blossomed in front of her, and Mildred's spirits rose. She loved daisies. They were abundant, and anyone could put a sweet daisy in a white milk vase or even an empty Coke bottle and experience the delightful effect.

"Purple."

Mildred sat up taller then, stretching in her torso. She always felt elongated when royalty was mentioned.

"Yellow."

The daisy reappeared, and then a rose. A yellow rose with tinges of a deeper color that had no name at all. Mildred eyed Miss Julia quizzically. The lady was repeating herself. People did that so often, only she hadn't paid as much attention to it until Sam began to do it. People lamented chronic repetition as a symptom of his disease. They ignored it in themselves and other people.

Miss Julia's voice dropped as she narrowed down the colors.

"Sunset yellow."

Oh. She was repeating herself with a purpose. Mildred smiled, and she began to hear a melody in her memory, a Strauss waltz.

"Sunset gold."

The music stopped. The daisy disappeared. And Mildred Budge lit up from the inside and light from her poured out and into the room until it was bright with her attention and hope.

"And there we have it," Miss Julia announced. "Sunset gold is the right color for an early autumn wedding and your complexion....and for other reasons that are none of my business," Miss Julia said. "Although you do have a very affectionate relationship with green, don't you?"

"I like sunsets and green," Mildred agreed readily.

Sitting back and looking analytically, Miss Julia observed, "You have a woman's shape."

"That's what it is," Mildred agreed.

"Your neck is pretty. Your eyes glow. Your arms are thick."

"That's a kind way to say it."

"We need all the strength we have in our arms," Miss Julia stated flatly. "Never begrudge the size of your arms if you have your health and enough strength to do the laundry. Never," she declared. And then rising, Miss Julia said without hesitation, "I shall go and get your dress. Today, you will have a dress the color of a sunset and which doesn't look like Queen Elizabeth when she is unhappy with one of her grown inconsiderate children. Do you need a cup of bergamot tea?"

"Maybe," Mildred said in a small voice. But she wanted one. With three sugars.

Miss Julia disappeared and left Mildred alone with her thoughts, which did not stay tranquil for long. Fear assailed! What if Miss Julia brought a horrible dress and Mildred would have to try it on and then find some reason why she wasn't going to spend—how much would it cost? Three hundred dollars? Four hundred dollars? How would she get out of buying the dress if it cost more than she wanted to spend? Then, what would she do for a wedding dress?

Before Mildred finished imagining the worst possible scenario and was able to plot a potential escape plan, Miss Julia returned with a soft dress the color of melting buttercups draped over her arms. She laid it like a wedding bouquet tenderly on Mildred's lap.

The color of melting sunshine blended with the hues of changing golden autumn leaves that hadn't fallen yet. Those leaves were a deep dusky rose and deeper shades of yellow.

Mildred took a fold of it between her fingers. It was exquisite. "What do you call this material?"

"It has a trademarked name, I believe, but it's really just a kind of hybrid Egyptian cotton. With a polished cotton finish. It won't wrinkle so badly. It's your size. The right size."

"My size is all right?" Mildred asked, her voice filled with wonder.

"Oh, yes. Your size is perfectly all right," Miss Julia assured her.

The words were very comforting.

"The dressing room is right there when you are ready."

"I shall try it on," Mildred announced, but she didn't stand up right away. Her inertia was not caused by fear or dread but by an extreme case of relaxation, relief, and acceptance.

A door opened in the foyer. Girlish laughter followed. Miss Julia turned, her face aglow with the spirit of hospitality, her smile, genuine.

"That's the bridal party arriving. Don't they sound young?"

"They do," Mildred agreed, smiling.

"Aren't we glad we're the age we are," Miss Julia asked playfully, looking to Mildred for friendly confirmation.

"Just the right age," Mildred agreed readily.

"I must leave you for a bit. I shall ask our sweet Olivia to bring you a special pot of sweet tea. She is in charge of refreshments. We take refreshments very seriously here, and Olivia has the gift of hospitality. Try to drink some of Olivia's tea. Try to eat a starburst cookie. We must try to be ever so kind to ourselves during difficult moments."

Mildred had never turned down a cookie in her life. Cookies, like friends and hot tea with sugar, helped one endure.

Once Miss Julia was gone, Mildred stood up. She took the sunset dress into the dressing room and automatically checked the mirror to see if it was one of those trick glass mirrors that made you think you had lost ten pounds, but she looked like herself.

Completely alone, Fran's best friend and maid of honor stepped out of her black pants and slipped off her cute blouse with the Siamese kittens on it. She avoided looking at herself in the mirror. It was always such a shock to see one's self undressed. Instead, she lifted the dress and lowered it over herself.

The dress flowed. The colors melted. The soft material settled onto her like a warm shawl. The dress fit.

When she confronted herself in the mirror, her complexion was alive. Mildred was in fact cast in such a glow of light that she scanned the ceiling to determine if some spotlight had been turned on to make her feel more lit up than was humanly possible.

But there was no deceiving overhead spotlight shining down to make her appear brighter or more harmoniously bedecked.

"I look like myself wearing the colors of a sunset," she whispered, as a dulcet-toned voice on the other side announced: "Miss Mildred, your pot of hot tea is here."

Mildred opened the curtain and saw a young woman placing a silver tray with a small pot of tea, a delicate cup, and a saucer of shortbread cookies on the table. The shortbread cookies were the right size too: thick, not thin. Very thin shortbread just crumbled and fell into your lap. Mildred preferred a cookie you could bite and chew.

"What do you think of this dress?" Mildred asked, holding back the curtain.

The young girl was wearing a black pencil skirt and a white blouse—flat, black ballet shoes. No name tag.

"Olivia?" Mildred asked.

The young woman nodded and smiled. She had a saucy ponytail that swung when she moved. Her dark hair was shiny with good health.

Her face free of make-up, Olivia smiled approvingly. "I think you look lovely," she said. "But it doesn't really matter what I think. It's how you feel in the dress that matters."

"I feel like I want to twirl." And Mildred spun slowly around, taking a turn that wasn't a spin at all—just a kind of exultant rotation of freedom.

Olivia nodded affirmatively. "If you want to twirl in it, that dress is for you."

Mildred turned and looked at her reflection. Standing there taking a good look at herself, Mildred was not embarrassed to see her reflection or wonder what had happened to her. She looked the way she wanted to look. She looked free as a bird.

The price tag was hanging at her elbow.

Mildred had purposefully not looked at it.

"Shall I have shoes and a slip sent to you?" Olivia asked, her gaze sweet and pure. Hospitably helpful.

"Why not?" Mildred said, coming out to where the mirrors placed around the room gave her images in all directions and from different angles.

The girl slipped soundlessly away.

Mildred poured her own tea and sipped it, wondering if there was a bell pull that she could use to summon the girl again and say definitely *yes* to the slip and the shoes in case she hadn't heard her. Mildred had not even told Olivia her shoe size.

That kind of information did not seem to matter here.

Before the tea could get cool, the girl reappeared with a box of shoes that were not any color Mildred had known before. They were made of a kind of bonded lace and were the color of desert sand. And there was a pair of hose, sized as AMPLE that matched the dress, and a slip made of French silk that also fit. Underneath the slip was a discreetly chosen brassiere that had no bows or lace because bows and lace could get in the way or itch. It was a simple bra by a designer Mildred did not recognize. It was a #3—whatever that meant. And it, too, was the color of sand. The fabric was surprisingly cool to the touch as if the garment had been lightly chilled. No wires.

Mildred would try it on, but she knew enough about her own anatomy to know it would fit.

On the other side of the door, young women were laughing and talking excitedly over one another. The bridal party was having fun. Mildred wondered how many bridesmaids were out there. Who was the bride and who was the maid of honor? They would all be younger than she was. And Fran.

In times past, Mildred would have felt left out by bridal parties, isolated, but in that moment, she was a woman with a dress and a slip and the right shoes and hose and what would be, she believed, a modern miracle: a comfortable bra #3.

She still had not computed the price, but as Mildred took a bite of the perfect starburst butter cookie she said to God in a rare moment of shrugging off stewardship and accepting the lilies of the field promise: "I don't care what it all costs if you don't, and you don't seem to be worried about it."

At the register, Mildred handed over her credit card and watched the amount ring up as Miss Julia excused herself from the laughing girls who were sipping champagne from glass flutes.

From her pocket Miss Julia extracted a small glossy black business card. "This is my private number. If you ever find yourself in some kind of dress emergency, I can have something shipped to you in two days. Fed Ex. The key thing for you to remember is that from now on, you are never alone." Miss Julia reached out and patted Mildred's hand. "Diamond earrings can be a girl's best friend but so can the right tunic top. I offer those too if you find yourself tired of animal motifs, and we do change as time goes by, don't we?"

Liz appeared suddenly, extricating herself from the small crowd of laughing girls. "Bye-bye, bye-bye," she said, her face flushed with delight and the effects of champagne.

"You'll never believe the love story I have just heard. I'd forgotten about that kind of love."

"I hear those stories fairly often," Miss Julia remarked, looking past Liz and Mildred to the girls and to the young clerk who was writing things down on a pad of paper.

"Come back soon, won't you?" Miss Julia said to Liz.

"Yes, we will," Liz promised.

"Are you two going to the Bulloch House for lunch?" Miss Julia asked. "They have the chicken livers today."

Mildred swallowed hard. The cookies were good—and she had eaten every one of them on the plate-- but she was hungry.

"You feel like lunch?" Liz asked.

"I could eat a little something," Mildred said, as they walked down the steps toward the car. Turning she saw Miss Julia standing there, the diamond earrings sparkling, her mauve polished cotton dress a sheath of calm and beauty that looked just like her.

The woman offered a light wave, her attention elsewhere, though she was standing there like a guard on her own front porch. Inside younger girls were choosing dresses, telling the stories of their loves and adventures, and sipping champagne. *Why do we ever stop? Mildred wondered. Life is a great adventure all along every turn.*

"I didn't know a place like that still existed," Mildred said, feeling free as a bird.

And then Liz said the most amazing words. "I'm starving. Let's go eat a good lunch."

Part 2
Something Borrowed, Something Blue

17
MARK AND MILDRED
AND HARRIETT II

It was that shopping trip to *A Dress for You* that had made Fran's maid of honor say *yes* when Mark asked her to have dinner with him Friday night. The echoing delight of all those other laughing bridesmaids talking about love and Miss Julia assuring Mildred Budge that she was all right just as she was and could wear diamond earrings, too, if she wanted them had leveled Mildred's usual defenses.

So, when she got home and the phone was ringing, Mildred was already smiling and living in the moment. It's hard to remember to say *no* to anything when you are happily alive in a precious moment.

"Do you get hungry for dinner?" Mark asked after she said hello.

"Of course," she said. Mildred had enjoyed a satisfying lunch with Liz and, yes, she believed that she would be hungry for dinner Friday night.

Then Mark asked: "Do you get seasick?"

"Why would I get seasick?" she asked.

And Mark had laughed, warmly. "Yes, why would you?" he replied, and though she couldn't see him Mildred knew his forest green eyes were laughing, too, and she smiled. And that's how she really let down her guard.

"Since you do admit to getting hungry for dinner, why don't I pick you up Friday, oh, about five thirtyish, and take you to the river..."

"I've already been baptized," Mildred interjected, and she could not explain why she said that, but Mark thought she was playing with him. He laughed delightedly.

"The river is also good for cruising, and I want to take you on the Harriett II and buy you dinner and show you the sunset and my house on the bluff from the water. I live above the river. You've never seen my house, and I've seen two of yours."

There was nothing to say but, "I'll be ready."

And that's when Mildred realized even before the phone was placed in the cradle, "I don't know what you wear on a steamboat."

Mildred had Miss Julia's card. She had Miss Julia's assurance that she could FedEx emergency dresses. But what she didn't have was confidence in calling and asking Miss Julia to select something that she could wear on a dinner cruise down the Alabama River. It would need to be something lightweight, cool, but not sleeveless because her arms were thick. Also, Mildred needed an outfit that she was not unfamiliar with because she didn't want to go to the ladies' room on a boat that was moving and have to figure out what to do with a dress or some kind of sideways zipper she had just met.

So, after a couple of hours of agonizing—strangely, it did not occur to her to pray-- Mildred remembered her Country Club pantsuit in the color that Fran warned did not have a crayon that was named after it. Feet growing heavy with a familiar dread that she was supposed to pass an ongoing test of knowing what to wear anywhere, Mildred made her way to the nursery/guest room and to the closet where Old Faithful was jammed against the wall in the closet that really needed to be thinned out.

The pantsuit was wrinkled. Mildred could hang it over the shower rod in the bathroom and steam out the wrinkles. Once the wrinkles were eased out, it would do for a boat ride, though the oversized rhinestone buttons in the shape of a sweet flower made it a little more sparkly than one might expect on a river cruise.

The truth was Mildred didn't have anything else to wear. After that conversation with Miss Julia, she simply refused to wear black slacks and her Siamese kitten tunic blouse or the one with the hippopotamuses on it or the red birds. Nope. It was going to be the Country Club pantsuit with rhinestone buttons in spite of others' opinion about it. And because that's all she could plan to wear on her date—a date! *Me? At my age?*-- Mildred didn't tell Fran she had a date, because she couldn't handle Fran telling her that her pantsuit was not right. Facing a night out, Mildred Budge didn't have much self-confidence, and she simply could not afford to lose even a smidge more by having Fran weigh in on her fashion choice.

So that's how two nights later on a Friday night Mildred Budge walked across the gangway to the Harriett II dressed fancier than any other lady on board, but comforted by the idea that her date was as over dressed as she. In that way they complemented one another. She was in her shiny pantsuit, and Mark was wearing a different blazer—a simple navy one—and he had a green cravat-thing tied around his neck, which did set off his smiling eyes.

They settled in at a table for two with a view of the shore, and careful not to stamp on his foot with either of hers under the table, Mildred made herself smile while she wondered if the mosquito spray she had used was going to make her itch.

That's what she was mildly concerned about when their extended period of smiling at one another was suddenly and rather wonderfully interrupted by a young man with an excited, high-pitched voice who approached her table and asked, his right hand reaching for her arm and squeezing it: "The Divine Miz B. Can that be you?"

She looked up into the friendliest of gazes from a young man who must have been in his early 30s. He was pink cheeked, with laughing brown eyes and a buzz cut of his bleached hair that made her think he might be in some branch of the military. *Do they let you bleach your hair in the military?*

"Miz Budge, you probably don't remember me, but you taught me fifth grade science."

Her heart instantly flooded with joy. She not only recognized Paulie immediately, she also could instantly recall the faces of the other youngsters who had sat beside him in her fifth-grade classroom. She recalled his too-thin shirts and his ungainly legs that he had a hard time managing under his desk, for Paulie had grown taller faster than his fifth-grade status and the furniture assigned to his grade level. She tamped down the joy in seeing him, for it had been her experience that while former students could gush in their recollections about her, they did not really want you to remember them all too clearly when they had been so young and so very vulnerable.

Miss Budge answered in her school teacherly level tone, her syllables measured and pronounced exactly, "I do remember you, Paulie. You sat on the second row, four seats back and you had two older brothers. I taught Ben and Jacob first." The retired school teacher did not add that she recalled Paulie wearing his older brothers' hand-me-downs and heartily approved!

"That's right. I was Paulie. I'm Paul now," he stated firmly.

Miss Budge nodded. She respected individuality.

"I grew up," he declared, taking a step back so that she could get a good look at him. He was tall and lanky, about ten years away from filling out the way men do in their forties.

"You said I would grow into my legs, and you were right." Pivoting, Paul pointed toward the back of the boat and another table. A young woman waggled her fingers with one hand and placed the other over her very rounded belly. "That's my wife back there. I was hoping you would be able to teach our children, but you've grown up too."

"Yes, I have," Miss Budge agreed. "Only, the way I've grown up is called retirement," she said.

"Do you know what I remember about you?" Paul asked impetuously. He moved closer to the table and pressed his hand on her forearm again. She let go of the wine glass. Former students often wanted to touch her—fought hugging her. She had been bear-hugged by many grown-up students, and some wanted to lift her feet off the ground and swing her around. That had happened twice.

She shook her head, *I don't know what you're about to tell me I used to ask,* while Mark settled back in his chair, amused and comfortable with her reunion.

"It was the question you always asked after you presented some idea. Some person's idea."

She shook her head, regretfully, and said with an ease that she had learned from being Sam Deerborn's friend during his travail: "I don't remember what I said, but I'm not surprised that I repeated myself."

"You always said, 'Now what do you think?' When I remember you, I remember how you always asked me that question. These days whenever anyone says something or makes a claim, I ask myself that question. 'What do *I* think?' I've avoided many a problem by asking that question." He turned and studied Mark, as if to ask him, *'What do you think about what I just told this lady across from you?'*

Mark read his mind and said, his smile easy. "Your divine Miz B. is the most intelligent woman I have ever met. That's why I am fascinated with her."

"So that's what you think," Mildred said. "I was wondering what you thought." She heard her own voice say those words. She was flirting, and she didn't sound like herself.

"What do you think?" Paul repeated, with a quick movement of his head which she understood was an imitation of her own from way back when.

So that's how I looked to him? The retired school teacher did not mind.

"I think it's awfully good to see you Paul and to see that you look happy. Your wife looks happy, too. It's a lovely evening for a cruise, isn't it?" Mildred sincerely hoped that his wife was not a former student of hers, too, for she did not recognize her.

"We are doing great. Our first one's due in three months."

"Me, too," Mildred said, but she didn't pat her belly. Her thoughts leapt ahead to how quickly time passed and how soon the little baby known as Little Mister was scheduled to move in with her until his mama was released from prison.

He laughed. "You always said funny things like that."

And then he finally looked at Mark and said, "You've got a special lady here. A really special lady. Everybody who's ever known her has loved her to bits."

And that was as close as he would come to saying the words, *I love you,* but Paulie had found a way to tell her that, and her eyes misted over. When Mark tapped her foot with his under the table, she knew it wasn't an accident. And that small touch of recognition comforted her.

Paulie walked jubilantly away back to his wife, to the back of the boat where the stars were lighting up over the horizon and casting magic on the water. The air felt fresh and the light breeze tantalizing.

"You're having a good time in spite of yourself." Mark observed.

"What do you mean?" Mildred asked, taking a sip of water. Her mouth had gone suddenly dry.

"You don't go out at night, and you don't drink wine often. You've been toying with that glass of wine—not exactly drinking it."

"I do drink wine sometimes," Mildred said, taking a deliberate sip. The wine burned her throat, her scalp, too. She fought the urge to scratch her head.

"You didn't like for your former student to see you with a glass of wine," Mark theorized.

"That's true," she agreed, for it was true. One never stops being an example to the younger generation. "I was his teacher."

"But you are not his Miss Teacher Budge anymore. You are my darling Mildred Budge, and you can have a glass of wine or two with me. It is all right. As you explained to Paulie, you have grown up, too."

"You are right, and I am wrong," Mildred agreed companionably. But she didn't take another sip. Her student could see her, and so could her mother in heaven.

"You know that the entrée will be some kind of chicken, don't you?" Mark followed her gaze, talking softly in the gentle sway of the water and in the rhythm of the evening breeze.

"I like chicken," she answered truthfully. She would also like a roll. Bread helped with heartburn. She was already feeling the familiar burn of acid reflux from the nitrates in the wine.

Mark reached across the table and covered one hand in his. "You are easy to be with," he said. "That's most likely why so many people keep coming to your house. You are the most popular woman I know."

She shrugged and did not withdraw her hand, though it was her first instinct. Focusing on the horizon, Mildred made herself sit unmoving while the view changed from one lovely vista to another. She had never seen her hometown from the river before. "I like this view," she said, more to herself than to Mark.

"Look up there. Do you see that house on the bluff with the big glass room jutting out? That's my house up there? Do you see?" Mark said, pointing.

Finally, his hand was gone, and she was free. Mildred looked the way he was pointing, trying not to press one hand to the middle of her bosom. Her chest hurt. *Oh, no.* She prayed it was just heartburn. She hoped she wasn't going to have a heart attack in front of him.

"That's pretty high up," Mildred said, reaching for the water glass. She drained it. The water helped. She began to look for the server for a refill of water. She needed more water. Maybe she could stave off a heart attack if she drank enough water.

Mark was oblivious to her sudden discomfort.

"In the evenings I often sit out on my back deck and watch the river traffic below. The river, too. Sometimes in the summer they play a movie over that way on a big screen for people. I can't see the screen, but I can hear people being happy, and I'm glad they are there and enjoying the night." He sounded wistful—and lonely. "They have fireworks on the 4th, and that's something. I see them all from where I sit and watch."

"It's a big house," she remarked as the Harriet II left the view of his house behind.

"Bigger than I need. I'll have to move one day. But for now, there's plenty of good space on the side for my plants. I like growing things in my own house."

"I like people who like to grow things," she approved readily.

Mark brightened and sat up taller in his chair.

The meal arrived, brought by one server who was trying to take care of too many people. The young man hurriedly lowered large platters, first one in front of Mark and then one in front of Mildred.

Mark grimaced. Ladies served first had not been part of their waiter's training.

When the server left, Mark leaned forward and promised, "If the boat begins to sink, I'll make sure you get on the life boat first," he said, shaking his head.

Mark didn't offer to say grace. Mildred didn't make an issue of it.

But just before she sliced into her piece of breaded baked chicken, she paused, knife and fork raised. Time stopped. She inhaled. And when the church lady exhaled gratitude for life flowed out in her breath. Her gaze rested on Paul and his wife behind Mark, leaning into each other, smiling into one another's eyes, and a blessing prayer began. It hummed inside of her as she pierced the chicken. Melted butter with green herbs poured out, blending with the rice pilaf and seeping over to the grilled green beans.

"Chicken Kiev," Mark observed, pleased. "This is an unexpected treat. I'm surprised. Cordon bleu, yes. That's everywhere these days. But not Chicken Kiev. I was in London many years ago and ordered this dish, and a waiter who served it made a very big deal about making the first cut for my..."

"Your date."

"My wife, actually," Mark explained quickly, slicing into his chicken.

Mildred took a small careful bite, asking in an offhand way, "So you've been married?"

"Twice," he said. "Divorced, twice."

And then he began to eat with focus, smiling to himself and at her.

"I've never been married," she said. It was all she could think of to say.

"You're a strong woman to have resisted."

"It hasn't been so hard," she replied truthfully. "Sometimes just having people around who expect you to get married or be married adds a pressure; but if you ignore it, then that pressure does not exist. Do you feel pressured?"

"Most places I go," Mark admitted easily. "I'm what is called an eligible bachelor."

"Do you miss being married?" she asked, sampling the green beans. It was a strange little stack of long green beans wrapped in a charred piece of bacon. They appeared to have been cooked on a grill instead of baked in an oven or steamed. She thought at first it would be awkward to eat them, but the beans were tender and cut easily. The bacon was crisp and tasty. The bacon-wrapped green beans were better than the chicken.

Mark finished his glass of wine and poured more in each glass.

"One of us is driving," Mildred said. And she instantly regretted it, because his gaze flickered, and she wondered if she sounded like a prude or a nag or, worse, a retired school teacher who is self-conscious about sipping wine in public where former students could see her imbibing.

"Montgomery is a small city with very quiet streets often going only one way. Don't worry. I'll get you home safely. Drink up," Mark encouraged. "Maybe I'll even take you to my house first and show you my accordion."

"Then I'll show you my piano," she replied.

"I saw your piano the other day in the den. It sits in a corner in the dark. It looked lonely." He held her gaze, sending some kind of hidden message. She didn't know what he was thinking.

"I haven't played my piano in a while," she said in between bites. The chicken had some kind of bitter aftertaste. Maybe it was the herbs. More likely it was the oily liquid which was too yellow to be real butter.

He waited for her to explain.

"I got a disappointing piano tuning last year, and I can't stand how the middle octave sounds. The F key in particular is tinny. One of these days I need to find a different tuner to undo what the last man did to it. If he can. Or she."

"I don't know anyone," Mark said, pushing his plate away. He had eaten about half his meal. She was relieved. She gave up on the chicken and finished the beans.

He drew his wine glass to him and sipped comfortably. "This is very relaxing. The night falls differently on the water from this position than it does up there on my deck."

"What's the difference?" Mildred asked, nodding *yes* for more water. She pinched off another bite of roll and chewed it while the server topped off her water glass.

"Yawl need sumpthin' else?" he asked, backing away. He asked the question the way a bag boy often did and once upon a time an old preacher who called Mildred and asked if she had required a pastoral call. In all of those instances, the question and offer of help was laden with the hidden plea: *Say, no, lady, I'm busy and I don't really care.* Mildred always felt terribly sorry for people who made offers they didn't really mean. *What was their life like on a daily basis?*

Growing quiet, Mark waited for him to leave.

"Up there at my house the night falls like a shroud. Here the water and the night meet, and we are in between both. I like being here with you better."

"I like it too," she replied politely. While her chest was feeling better, she felt itchy. Sticky from the dried mosquito spray. The view was pretty, but she was ready to be home. She wanted to take a shower and put on her soft clothes.

"And so, you think you might go to dinner with me again even though dinner is at night?"

"I might," she said. And then remembering her student's signature memory of her, she asked daringly, "What do you think?"

"I think the boat is turning around, and we must finish our wine," he said.

Mildred had drunk enough, but she feigned another sip to keep Mark company. They sailed at a faster pace to the shore, and she recalled that there was another group that would take their place on the eight-thirty cruise. And then she knew that Mark had watched many a supper cruise goes by and that finally he was on the boat, too, having his cruise on the river at last. Mark's turn wasn't over, and Mildred was glad she could help him have his turn and was having a turn on the Alabama River with him.

They docked easily. Unlike other times when she was exiting a bus or a train or even the movie theatre, the crowd did not push to forge ahead. This crowd of dinner cruise sailors was lazy, lingering in their places, moving at the pace she preferred all the time. It pleased her—this group of lazy leave-takers from a slow-moving steamboat.

"Coffee?" Mark suggested. "Unless you are in a hurry," he said, his words slurring from the third glass of wine.

"I'm rarely in a hurry, and I don't usually drink coffee at night," she said. The heartburn had eased. She was feeling all right. Her heart was beating fine.

"Espresso decaf in a Columbia roast. A few sips won't hurt you," he urged, his syllables slipping again.

"That shouldn't keep me from sleeping," she agreed, though she was ready to be home. It was not rejection of him or that she didn't like him just fine. Mildred admired the view from the riverboat, and she hadn't gotten seasick. She simply loved being peaceful at home more where she could go to sleep and wake up early alone in the silence of the morning before anyone else who used a telephone was also awake.

She did not like to stay up so late that it caused her to sleep in the next day, for the very early mornings were the sweetest times to be alone in prayer.

Every church lady who had ever lived knew that to be true.

18
THE VIEW FROM RED BLUFF

The valet brought the car, and they got settled in. Just after Mark pressed the door lock, he leaned toward her, patted her seatbelt protectively, and confessed, "I'd kiss you right now if I didn't know you'd get all skittish on me and ask to go right home."

Staring straight ahead, wondering how he could sense that about her, Mildred replied, her voice low and dusky with repressed self-consciousness, "You don't know that for sure," she replied, her voice tremulous.

As if he hadn't heard her, Mark angled the car toward the street, entered back into the crawling traffic and steered them sharply toward the next right turn that led the short distance up the hill toward the bluff where he lived. "We're not going far," he said. "Just a little over a mile."

Progressing slowly up the bumpy incline, Mark grew quieter, confessing haltingly as they reached his long and winding driveway, "I'm not a very good housekeeper. But my yard looks good. Of course, you won't be able to see it in the dark."

Mildred smiled and took a deep breath. She didn't want any coffee—not even a few sips.

Mark steered up the curving driveway. It was bumpy. He took it slow, feeling his way along as he had hundreds of times before. She felt the house at first rather than saw it. A big shadow in the night, the house loomed. There were a number of big houses like it around Montgomery. Mildred had been in a few of them after they had been renovated by people who had enough money to take on that kind of expense. Big houses like this one needed new plumbing, new electrical wiring, and central heat and air conditioning. Even with all the right remodeling additions, the big houses were hard to heat, practically impossible to cool uniformly throughout the house, and frustratingly hard to keep painted because of the relentless Alabama sunlight.

"There's the company entrance around front which hasn't been used in longer than I can remember or this side entrance right here that takes us through the kitchen. Will you feel cheated of a grand tour if I just take you through the kitchen?"

"I love kitchens," Mildred replied truthfully, as she dallied long enough for Mark to reach the car door but not so long that she hadn't opened the door a smidge by herself.

As she stepped out, a light positioned on the eave of the house lit up the side door and her pathway to it.

"Motion detectors," Mark explained. "At first you like them. And then they just get on your nerves. There are six more positioned around the house. This has been a high crime area in the past. Be careful how you step. The flagstones buckle in a couple of places. Step high, and you won't stub a toe."

Mark opened the side door first so he could switch on the kitchen light. It was a massive kitchen with old fashioned black and white square tiles and a substantial aged wooden butcher's block in the middle where food could be prepared or a casual buffet laid out for supper parties. *You could invite all of your friends to a supper party here. There was plenty of room.* Overhead, copper pots hung waiting to be used. The oven was also big. The refrigerator was a doublewide with stainless steel doors.

"You could cook a turkey and a ham at the same time," Mildred observed, fighting the impulse to open the door and peer inside and double check that idea. *Thanksgiving! Christmas! You could invite everybody who was hungry and alone!*

"The woman who used to own this house was a caterer and had that oven special ordered. This house needs a big family. I'm going to downsize one day and let that needy big family move in."

She stopped herself from asking him why he had bought it. *But really, why had he ever bought a house this big?* She followed Mark into the long and oddly narrow hallway. It was dark, and he didn't switch on a light. He didn't need one. He knew where he was going. Her hand reached out to touch the wall as she followed him down past a couple of closed doors and finally to the living room.

He switched on the lights. "I should leave a light on inside when I go out, and I always forget."

"Me, too," she said. "Who's that?" Mildred asked immediately, pointing to a portrait of an elegant slender woman with impressive posture, a porcelain complexion, and the kind of mystery in her troubled gaze that would be hard to forget. The portrait hung above a massive fireplace.

Moving closer, Mildred saw that the woman was sitting in a high-back velvet chair and wearing a black dress that looked like it was made of velvet too. She wore a double strand of real pearls. Her dark hair was pulled back from her face, and a widow's peak created a heart-shaped effect. She wasn't smiling.

Mildred could not name that expression. *What kind of gaze is that?* Mildred wondered.

Peering closer, Mildred saw that the woman in the painting was hiding a vulnerability. Love had done her wrong—or someone had. She was beautiful and wounded and mysterious.

"Who is she? Bless her heart," Mildred said automatically.

Mark looked up, his hands hanging at his sides, his chin tilted as his voice dropped when he answered the question. "She is the woman who broke my heart," he said. "And before you ask," he began with a shake of his head and a dismissive chuckle. "That lady—if you want to call her that," he said with some bitterness. "Is not one of my ex-wives. She's the one that got away."

And then as if that announcement didn't require more explanation, Mark pointed toward the river. "Do you want to see the greenhouse? It leads to the back deck and that view of the river I told you about."

Mildred turned away from the image, her curiosity not satisfied. What stories could a woman like that tell—a woman with that much pain in her eyes, and so beautiful too? "She's very lovely."

"I thought so," Mark said, averting his gaze. She saw him do that—saw him make himself stop staring at the woman over his fireplace. He had done that many times before. She wondered why he didn't just remove the sight of her if her image caused him so much angst.

Mark led the way past the heavy formal furniture and a grand piano that he had not mentioned. A red and gold tapestry was draped over the piano, and an assortment of framed pictures in various sizes were arranged on top.

"Do you play a piano too?" she asked, trying to change the mood.

He had grown solemn. The heavy furniture and darkness of the room felt oppressive.

"Just the accordion and that was mostly for show. That piano came with the house," he said. "One of these days I'm going to get rid of it. I just haven't figured out how. Who would buy such a monstrosity? They use electronic keyboards now."

"Do they?" Mildred asked, mystified.

Mildred was never really sure who *they* were when someone used that word just that way. Before she could file away the question, she and Mark reached the glassed-in patio—his attached greenhouse. Various sizes of shelves and tables held dozens of plants in different stages of growth.

"It's a small jungle," she approved, rotating to experience the size of it. "It's quite something, isn't it?"

On the other side of the glass was the river and the riverboat and the twinkling lights of the downtown restaurants and hotels.

"Our plants are over there. Some starter plants are sprigged in that egg carton. I miss the old cardboard egg cartons, but times change, and we must make do," Mark said, going over to test the moisture in the dirt with a forefinger. And with one move, he became the man she had first met at the estate sale--- at ease.

Mark Gardiner was not the first person she had ever known who was uncomfortable in his own home, but the phenomena of people who weren't happy in their own houses still surprised Mildred Budge. *Why didn't they change it? Why didn't he?*

"I like your plant room. It's like being inside and outside at the same time."

Mildred rotated, absorbing the sight of the plants, the colors of the flowers, and the air which was rich with oxygen. The room was an oasis, rich with life and color. The rooms behind her felt like the ones in a funeral home where you sit with grieving friends until the service begins.

"Didn't you say yes to decaf espresso?" he asked suddenly, too brightly.

"I said *yes* to something," she replied, smiling benignly. And in an instant, this man who had been married twice leaned over and kissed her lightly on the lips. It happened so fast she didn't have time to be surprised. "If I had done that in the car, we wouldn't be standing here now," he said.

"You don't know that for sure," she replied, edging sideways, moving past him out of the jungle and back toward the living room where the woman in the portrait would be her chaperone. "Did you say something about espresso?"

"Meet me in the living room. The coffee doesn't take long." And it didn't.

Sitting underneath the portrait of the woman who had broken Mark's heart, Mildred heard the whir of a coffeemaker.

He returned quickly carrying two small cups. He placed one beside her on the side table. "I don't like trying to hand hot coffee to ladies. I'm always afraid one of us won't be able to hold it."

Mildred nodded, stifling an exhale. She was suddenly very nervous. It had been a long time since she had been alone with a man she didn't really know very well in a house none of her friends had ever visited either. Although she had told Mark she was rarely in a hurry, suddenly she felt in a hurry to leave.

Once Mark was seated across from her, she smiled, picked up the tiny cup nestled in its tiny saucer, and took a careful sip. "There's alcohol in this," she said, balancing the demitasse cup on her crossed knee.

He was handling his tiny cup just fine. She wondered if he sat here late into the night reading and sipping his coffee just that way.

"It's called a night cap. You'll sleep great," Mark promised her, finishing his drink and placing his cup to the side on another small table.

She took another awful sip of the bitter brew and made her face smile again. It was harder this time. "Do you want to tell me about the woman who broke your heart?" she asked.

"No," he said, sipping his coffee. "I'll tell you about either of my ex-wives whenever you want to be bored to tears. But Lana! No. There's no point in dredging up that story. It has nothing to do with us."

"And those pictures over there?" she asked, pointing to the piano where a series of different photos told a kind of story about his history. It had been a long time since Mildred had been in a house where she didn't already know the stories associated with people in pictures on mantels and pianos.

"That's just the past," he said dismissively.

"Tell me," she invited.

He took a few long seconds to choose his words, and then he began, his voice becoming formal. "I was involved in the entertainment industry for a while. When I was young. A long, long time ago."

Mildred waited for him to say more.

"Back then, men like Burt Lancaster and Kirk Douglas were making it on their looks. People told me that I should try to do something," he said with a shrug. "I'm not as old as Kirk. My crowd was part of the Bob Wagner clan though we were a few years younger. Have you seen him playing DiNozzo's dad in *NCIS*?"

Mildred had seen Robert Wagner in that role, but she couldn't remember enough about him to say yes, so she shook her head slightly. "Maybe," she said.

"You're not much of a TV watcher, are you?"

"I like TV," she said, not bothering to tell him how much she watched—about an hour or two at night after dinner if she wasn't in the middle of a good book.

"They thought—some people think—that Bob killed his wife Natalie on a boat."

"Natalie Wood?" Mildred asked. That story came back to her slightly. There were conflicting accounts. The actress had drowned at night. Drinking had been involved. Maybe another man.

"I tried my luck in Hollywood, but I wasn't lucky, not the way Bob and Bill Shatner were. Do you remember *Star Trek*?" he asked.

"Oh, yes," she said. "I like *Star Trek*. The early shows explored very interesting themes."

"I wasn't lucky like either of those guys. My face didn't have what they wanted, though I had a couple of small walk-on parts. And I earned 'em. I wasn't lucky like Larry Hagman whose mama got him a walk-on in *South Pacific*. Now he was lucky! If you like that pretty boy type."

Mark waited for her to say that she didn't like the pretty boy type, but she wasn't sure of her answer. Maybe she did. Was Tony Curtis a pretty boy type. She liked Tony Curtis.

Mark smiled tolerantly. "Larry was in that show with that genie girl, and later he played that rich man in that series set in Texas. *Dallas*. Yes, *Dallas*."

Mildred stopped herself from asking, how old are you?

"J. R. Ewing. He modeled that character on his biological daddy, a rough old cob. Did you watch *Dallas?*"

Mildred Budge nodded gently. She recalled watching the show but that was all she remembered. The theme song was good.

Mark leaned forward, excited. "It was a television show that everybody watched for a while."

"Who shot J. R? Now that was a season." Mark settled back in his chair and decided to smile. She saw him decide to smile: to turn on the smile, and the truest part of her retreated into a shell where she had lived off and on for most of her life.

"Hagman died. I can't remember what happened to him. A lot of that generation of stars has gone on. I came along about ten years later. Yes, ten years, or so," he calculated, growing melancholy. He took a long sip of his wine, drowning his sorrows. "Those boys had used up all the luck by then."

"When did you decide to try a different line of work?" she asked, delicately.

"It didn't take long. Three years of trying and I decided I'd rather eat regularly," he confessed ruefully. "When I wasn't distracted by dreams of Hollywood, I fell in love. And then I fell in love again. And after you're divorced twice with alimony to pay you have to find a line of work that draws a regular salary. The courts are clear about that."

"Children?" Mildred asked hesitantly. The heartburn resurfaced, bubbling angrily in the middle of her chest.

"Not that I know of," he said. A dazed expression appeared in his eyes.

Mildred Budge did not recognize Mark Gardiner in that moment. He was a stranger to her, and she was in his home alone with him. No one knew she was here. *Was Fran home or with Winston at his house?* She didn't know Winston's phone number. "And when did you become free of Lana?" Mildred asked carefully.

Mark took a deep breath of air and released it. "That was hard. We were comfortable. We even had some help at the house. We had a cook and a gardener back then. The accountant managed the bills. It was easy street for a while when we were together. Those were good days, but Lady L got bored with me. That's what she said. The woman said she was bored. With me. Not like Stanwyck who dumped Bob Wagner for practical reasons. Babs was older than Bob. Lady L showed me the door. I got a little severance pay for a while out of what she called the goodness of her heart, but that dried up. I did some radio commercials and, after that, well, you know the rest."

"No. I don't know the rest," Mildred said. "Why do you have Lady's L's picture over the fireplace?"

"Because I loved her," he admitted. "I loved her, and she got bored with me. Can you imagine that?"

Mildred assumed that was a rhetorical question, but shook her head anyway.

Mark took a short quick breath and continued. "I left," he said simply. "Not exactly with only the clothes on my back, but that's what I really owned. Everything else was in her name," he said. His gaze flickered in memory or anger. She couldn't tell which.

"I did not pursue palimony, which was just beginning to become a word. We didn't do that in my generation. I didn't have what you would call marketable skills, but I remembered how the gardener at our house talked about the plants and the flowers and how my...lady friend... liked for them to have a history. And I thought about what I knew was true. Ladies like romantic stories about trees and plants, and that's how I got into the old plant business. I find some plants. Write some stories. Sell them to nurseries who sell to ladies who like heirloom decorations. Women never get tired of romance. No, sir, they do not," Mark said emphatically. "And that's how you see me sitting here across from you with a house up on a high hill looking down on the world below."

Mildred placed the cup down on a small table. "I'm going to let this cool a bit," she explained, standing. She walked across the room to the dark piano.

He pushed himself up and walked over to a small bar across from the piano and poured himself a glass of something amber. He lifted it towards her, a question in his eyes.

Mildred shook her head. When she got home, she would drink a glass of milk very slowly to ease the heartburn from the wine, the oily chicken, and the espresso.

Mark took his drink back to the chair and watched her piece the story of his life together from the artifacts in the room.

"So which is the truest about you? The greenhouse and saving heirloom plants or the picture of the woman over the fireplace who broke your heart?"

He didn't need long to answer. Stretching out his legs, Mark crossed them at the ankles and studied his feet. His shoes needed attention. The brown leather was scuffed, and the soles were worn almost through.

Raising his head, he met her gaze dramatically. "The woman over the fireplace killed me. That's the truth." And then taking a deep breath while he considered what he was going to say, her date decided to gamble. He said, "I feel like the woman in front of me is bringing me back to life. And that's the truth too."

19
HOME AFTER DARK

"You don't really know me," Mildred replied truthfully. "How can you say something like that?

Mark rose and went back over to the liquor cabinet and refilled his glass. He took a sip before turning to face her again. "It feels true, that's why. That's how I can say it. When you feel something is true, that's lucky—that's everything. Did you know I was afraid to show you this house?"

"Why?" Mildred asked, as Mark settled down again into his chair, which was bigger than he was—too big to shift around in a room easily. Mildred had become very conscious of the need to choose or keep furniture that wasn't too big or heavy for her to handle easily.

"Because your house is so full of life," he said immediately. His legs splayed gently, and his left hand opened and spread across the arm rest. His fingers flexed, gripping and releasing the chair. "I was across the street from you for a couple of days. People come and go at your house all the time. You have so many friends, and when I thought about bringing you here I knew you would see—you must see—that my house feels dead compared to yours. No one comes here much," he reported, and took a long swallow of his golden drink.

Then Mark leaned his head back against the oversized chair and closed his eyes before speaking again. Finally, he asked, "Are you going to play that piano? You've been looking at it as if it were a third person in the room that you wanted to include in our conversation."

If that were true it was because Mildred was uncomfortable hearing the very personal details of this man's life. Mark had told her some very personal truths, so she tried to tell him one of her own.

"I don't like to play the piano for other people. Music is so very personal." That was not the whole truth. She had played particular pieces of music for others in the past only to find her enjoyment of the music lessened by its reception. When how someone else hears music affects your ability to enjoy it later, you become careful about sharing music with just anyone.

"Is it?" Mark asked, eyes opening.

She did not know why he was staring at her so. His fixed attention made her nervous.

She began to speak more quickly. "You are right though. I have always loved pianos. Any piano."

That was not exactly true, for Mildred Budge did not find herself attracted to grand pianos. They were too big for her. And there was this idea that if you were going to sit down in front of a grand piano then you were declaring—boasting even—that you are a better pianist than you are. Yes, Mildred loved pianos. No, she did not love grand pianos. Mildred Budge accompanied her friends in Sunday School on an old spinet when they sang hymns; and during the Christmas season, she played carols on the homey pianos of hosts and hostesses who believed in serving eggnog. Mildred Budge loved eggnog, but she didn't care for alcohol in it. Alcohol ruined good eggnog.

There was an old music book propped open on the ancient grand piano. Chopin.

"Do you like Chopin?" she asked.

"Doesn't everyone?" Mark replied too quickly.

That was the response of a fifth grader who was being asked a question about a book he claimed to have read and was trying to cover up for not having actually read it.

"There's a book of Chopin on the piano," she said. "That's why I asked."

"Oh, that book," he said. He rubbed a place in the corner of his mouth with his forefinger. His lips were dry. "Would you like another drink?"

She shook her head and offered him a small smile.

"Go on! Bang away! Make a little noise in this dead old house. Give it your best shot," he said, waving his hand toward the piano. "I'd like to hear what it sounds like anyway. Gimme some music. Something pretty."

Mildred didn't want to play that grand piano, but she pushed herself up. "Has it been tuned recently?"

He shook his head. "Not since I bought the house. There is no one to play it. I saw no reason to keep it tuned until it was in danger of being played."

The bench was cushioned and more comfortable than hers, which was wooden. All the church classroom pianos had wooden benches, too.

Mildred thumbed through the book of music. It was a simplified collection of arrangements, which provided the melody but not the nuances and textures of the richer notes that made Chopin, well, Chopin.

Her hands found the right positions above the keys; and after letting her right hand begin the melody, her left hand joined in. And having made it through once successfully, she began to play it again. The room felt darker while she played, and it was only midway through the second playing of Chopin's Etude that she became aware subliminally that a snuffling sound was emanating from the chair where Mark was supposedly listening.

The song ended. Her hands came to rest on the keyboard, and then in her lap.

She waited for Mark to say something polite, but he didn't. Swinging her legs around, she was about to speak when she noticed his breathing was slow and steady. She stopped herself from saying his name. The room felt suddenly empty, inhabited only by the furniture and the ghosts from lovers past. Her host was sitting in the shadows. There was a light behind him so she couldn't see his features at first—just the shape of him. His outline. She was struck in that moment that the shape of him was all she really knew. In so many ways, Mark Gardiner was a stranger.

Standing, Mildred took a cautious polite step toward him, not wanting to startle him or intrude on his private thoughts, when she heard a sudden low whistling coming from him, the heavy exhalation of someone who was not grieving or remembering and had not died but, in fact, had simply succumbed to the effects of a heavy meal and abundant alcohol. Mark had fallen asleep.

She stood stock still then. Disciplined in being a good visitor, her first church lady instinct was to return to her chair and wait for him to wake up. But that could be a long time, and when Mark woke—if he awoke before morning—he would be surprised to see her. Oh, how she hated the thought of that moment, when his eyes would fly open and he would find himself vulnerable and exposed.

The alternative was worse.

If she woke him right then, he would be groggy from sleep and alcohol and insist on driving her home. She didn't want to get in the car with a groggy man who had been drinking.

Somewhere in this house there must be a landline telephone. If she could find a landline, she could call Fran. Maybe she was home. Mildred recalled dully that she did not know Winston's phone number.

She looked around the living room. Nothing. The plant room didn't have a phone. Maybe he didn't have a land line. Maybe he only had a cell phone.

Looking at him still upright in the chair, though his head had drifted sideways and was tilted against the chair, Mildred could not see the shape of his cell phone in a pocket. She didn't know how to dial a number on a cell phone even if she could ease it out of his pocket without waking him.

Mildred walked toward the kitchen. *Had she passed a phone there?* The kitchen was lit only by the moon and had a sideways view of the river. Traffic below on the water had mostly ceased; though when she closed her eyes, Mildred thought she could hear sounds of life coming from the downtown restaurant center. There were many restaurants now in the restaurant strip called the Alley, but she had only been through it twice when she had attended a fundraiser event for the Montgomery Christian School. Each year they sponsored an art show, and she always attended.

At the back door, she whispered to God and to Fran and to anyone else who might hear her silent cry for help, "I don't know the address of where I am."

Looking over her shoulder back toward to the dark room where Mark was sleeping, Mildred whispered what she was going to do, sending her voice toward him in a gesture of politeness, "I'm going outside to see if I can find the street number to this house. Then I'll figure out what I should do next. Good night."

20
HEADED HOME

Mildred's hand twisted the large brass knob and tugged, listening for a give-away creaking sound that would waken her host. It creaked, but Mark didn't rouse. Once outside, the motion light came on instantly. It was a relief to be alone outside even though night had fallen and the lights below in downtown Montgomery felt distant—farther away than a mile. She could see well enough to take mincing steps toward the street and remembered Mark's advice to raise her feet high to avoid stumbling by catching a toe on broken concrete. Mildred proceeded carefully.

The light from the house's eave did not reach the street and the curb. The driveway was long and sloping, with uneven concrete. She remembered the penlight on her key chain. Fishing it out of her purse, Mildred thumbed the switch and saw with relief the small circle of light that was just bright enough to show her where to step next. Twelve slowly taken steps later, she discovered that there was no street number on the curb. Looking up and back at the house, Mildred did not see a house number by the front door either, nor on any place on an eave, or on either of the two columns flanking the porch.

Mildred had her street number on the curb repainted annually in reflecting white paint. A young man from the neighborhood earned part of his college tuition going from house to house offering to provide this service. After he graduated college, his younger brother took over the job, and

Mildred Budge, who believed in higher education and being prepared, always had her twenty-dollar bill ready. Knowing where you are and making it easy for others to read your address was worth more than twenty dollars. An ambulance can read the street number in the dark, and people looking for your house in the daytime can find it, too.

Looking left and right, Mildred whispered with awe in her voice that she could have gotten herself in such a predicament, "I don't know where I am." There was not a remembered time in Mildred Budge's life when she had ever said those words.

Her options were limited, but her goal was single-minded. She wanted to go home. She started walking down the sloping hill toward downtown center.

The street was winding and steep, the pavement rough. The penlight helped. She walked slowly, carefully. At the foot of the first hill, she looked left—no traffic coming-- and she could see the lights of the riverfront and more brightly the greater lights of the river's wharf, the lights of the Harriett II, and nearby, the main downtown hotel, Embassy Suites.

If she just kept walking, Mildred would be back among the lit-up people and go to the hotel where she could call for a taxi.

She continued a quarter of a mile down the slope, eventually finding a sidewalk. Most of the businesses were closed. The car dealership on the left was dark. The appliance repair place was long shut down for the night. Still, unable to see clearly, it felt to her like other storefronts were simply not in use in daylight or the night. Downtowns everywhere were struggling to stay current, their turn declared over by strip malls and online shopping.

As Mildred continued to make her way toward the sounds of other people, she became increasingly confident that she would get home—sooner or later. "I'm twenty minutes from Embassy Suites," she promised herself.

But before she finished giving herself a pep talk, Mildred spied another hotel tucked on the left side of the street. The

Renaissance Hotel. She had never been inside. The desk clerk at the Renaissance could just as easily call her a taxi as the desk clerk at the Embassy Suites. Scanning the front entrance, Mildred saw the lobby was well lit and inviting. A ladies' room would be inside. Maybe a water fountain. She was awfully thirsty. A person at the front desk would be on duty. Relief began to flood her. A tension she had been ignoring began to ease. Gripping her purse tightly, Mildred went inside.

The whoosh of cool air was instantly refreshing. She stopped just inside and closed her eyes, a prayer of thanksgiving escaping her in a moan. Her eyes opened, and she surveyed the welcoming lobby. There was a fireplace and a grouping of comfortable chairs. She fought the temptation to walk right over and simply sit down. She was safe. There was a phone available on a table for guests. She read the signs, finding the one that pointed toward a ladies' room around the corner, where she immediately went and freshened up, washing her hands and looking up to see her reflection where she told herself, her head slightly shaking, "This could have ended so much worse."

With her own words ringing in her ears, Mildred dried her hands, using the paper towel to grab the door's handle before tossing it into the trashcan. She followed the signs back to the front desk. No one was behind the desk at first; but within seconds, a young lady came out to greet her, smiling, her youthful eyes sparkling.

Mildred sighed with relief at the sight of the friendly girl. It was one thing to hope for help; it was quite another to meet someone who looked like she was ready to give it.

"I am Mildred Budge."

"And I am Brenda, the night manager. How may I help you?" she inquired.

And before Mildred could answer, Brenda tapped the keyboard in front of her and looked up quizzically. "Do you have a reservation?"

Mildred shook her head, no. In that moment of intense relief, Mildred Budge was wordless.

The change in Mildred's demeanor caused Brenda to grow concerned. "Be easy. Then tell me how I can help you."

The sudden offer of sincere help caused Mildred to grow weak, for until that moment, she had been quite strong—had been her resilient, resourceful one-foot-in front-of-the-other-while-you-run-the-race-set-before-you church lady self. But the young lady was so present, so sweet, so helpful, so lit up with sparkling attention that Mildred reached out and gripped the counter, steadying herself.

Brenda saw the older woman orient herself through her fingertips as she gripped the counter's edge.

"You and I are going to sit down right over there," Brenda immediately directed, coming around the front desk. "We're going to sit right over here, and I'm going to get you a bottle of cold water. Don't you worry. I've got you now. Whatever is wrong is going to be all right now. Just chill."

Mildred did as she was told, moving toward the big blue chair that faced the fireplace. She stared at the unlit fireplace while Brenda went for water. When the young lady returned, she twisted the cap off for Mildred and urged, "You take a couple of big sips of that cold water and then tell me how I can help you."

The young lady dropped to a crouching position beside her and balanced on her heels.

Mildred sipped some water, catching her breath and regaining her focus. Then she explained, "I am so very embarrassed to say these words out loud, but my date drank too much and passed out in his chair. I didn't want to wake him because I didn't want to get in a car with him and find out if he could drive me home, so I escaped—slipped away while he was asleep," she amended hurriedly. "He lives up on that hill over that way," Mildred said, pointing. She couldn't believe she was saying those words, and a part of her instantly wondered if she would ever tell anyone else. She was much too old to have been so foolish.

"Ma'am, if he drank so much that he passed out, he should not be getting behind the wheel of a car. You did exactly the right thing. My mama would be so proud of you."

"I just kept walking until I saw you—this place. I thought someone here might call me a taxi to take me to my house in Cloverdale. It's not so far from here. But I just don't think I can walk all the way home this time of night."

The girl's eyes widened in horror, and she bounced up. Her hand reached out and clutched Mildred's hand. "You will not be walking anywhere else this time of night."

Brenda's eyes darkened in sympathy. 'We're very sorry that this happened to you. Very sorry."

"It's not your fault," Mildred said.

"I know what I'm going to do. We have a driver who meets people at the airport in our hotel van and brings them here. He is still on duty. Mr. Bill is good for another half hour. I think he would be very pleased to drive you home in the hotel van."

As Mildred was beginning to say, "I hate to cause anyone that kind of trouble," Brenda waved aside Mildred's objection and walked back to her desk. Stretching across the counter top, Brenda buzzed for the hotel van driver and spoke into her intercom system.

"Mr. Bill is on his way, and again, we are very sorry this has happened to you. It will be our privilege to make sure you get home safely."

"I'm not a guest here," Mildred explained.

The younger woman was shaking her head. "Oh, ma'am. The minute you walked through that door you became our guest. That's how we see hospitality here. We're here to help. Always. I'm going to get you home safe and sound, and this whole experience will just be a bad memory you can forget."

Withing two minutes, the electronic doors whooshed open, and Mildred could see the van with the Renaissance logo on the side. She heard a door slam and then a man appeared, walking toward her. He was a short man with a grey mustache—somebody's grandfather.

"That's Mr. Bill. He's a good one," Brenda said, her eyes growing serious. "He will take you home," she promised. "You are all right now."

"Too kind. Too kind," Mildred muttered, her eyes filling with tears, for it had been her long experience that she was able to go to sickbeds to visit dying people and funerals to comfort the bereaved and emerge dry eyed; but when anyone was nice to her, as this young woman was being, Mildred Budge was often moved to tears.

The sight of Mildred's tears moved the clerk, and Brenda's eyes instantly filled as well. Reaching beneath the counter Brenda extracted two tissues and handed one to Mildred so she could blot her eyes too. Pointing toward the sliding doors and the sight of the shining white van with the hotel's logo on it, Brenda directed, "Go right through there. You are safe now. Mr. Bill will take you home."

"Too kind. Too kind," Mildred repeated, reaching out and clasping the other woman's hand. "I will never forget your kindness."

They snuffled together briefly, each woman moved by the other woman's vulnerabilities and for all of the ways that women are subject to pain and all kinds of disappointments and danger in the world of men and dating and night time and experiencing so much of it in so many deep ways, alone.

Her legs shaky from the perilous trek in the night, Mildred walked stalwartly to the van. Mr. Bill slid back the side door and waited until Mildred had taken that awkward step up and was seated before closing it. She turned to wave at the clerk, but Brenda was already focused on another person who had come to the desk and so there was no final wave, no blown kiss, no solemn nod of gratitude. There was only the sudden eruption of a flashed blessing prayer: "God grant special mercies to that sweet child of yours, and if I ever need to stay in a hotel anywhere, it will be the Renaissance or any hotel owned by Marriott."

Mildred was breathing that vow and prayer as Mr. Bill steered the van in the dark down mostly empty Montgomery streets toward her house and the street number.

"Ma'am, I'll have you home in a jiff and a prayer."

"In a jiff and a prayer," Mildred repeated as they sailed through the night and under the stars. She began to relax, sinking into the plush cushion of the back seat as her shoulders eased down, and she began to accept that the awful night was almost over.

Parked in front of her house, Mr. Bill pocketed her ten-dollar tip. Standing at her door, she watched him turn the van around and head back toward downtown. There at the threshold of her home, the church lady prayed a blessing prayer for him and all of his children and his extended family and was just about to pray for his neighbors and everyone working at the Renaissance and all their guests in every single room, when she saw a movement in her peripheral vision and the light in her Mini-Cooper flash quickly on, then off.

Someone was sitting in her car.

21
NOBODY'S HERO NOW

The car door swung open briefly and when it did, the overhead light came on again. Mildred saw Sam sitting all by himself in her car. Mildred was torn between wanting to go inside and have a good cry or help her friend.

She walked across the crunchy grass over to her friend. Crouching beside the slightly open car door, Mildred asked gently, trying not to sound impatient or worn out with him: "What are you doing out here this time of night, Sam?"

She looked toward his house, wondering why Belle wasn't standing at the back door calling his name the way mothers summoned children home from playing after dark. *Suppertime! Bedtime!*

"Same thing you're doing," Sam replied evenly, his eyes finding her in the shadows. "I'm breathing God's sweet night air. Looking at God's bright night-time lights." Sam inhaled deeply with a kind of satisfaction Mildred had seen somewhere before— felt it too, though she couldn't remember where or when. "I am living life is what I'm doing."

"Aren't we all?" Mildred replied, more to herself than to him. She eased the car door open more fully. The interior light which had flickered briefly before came on and stayed on.

There was a trickle of blood coming from a gash over Sam's eyebrow. He was oblivious. Sam looked up, his jawline more pronounced in the light. He was gaunt. "You look awful pretty, Mildred. What are you all dressed up for?"

"I had a date, Sam."

"Oh, go on, Mildred. Everyone knows you're too smart for that sort of thing."

"Are you here, Sam? Are you really here?" Mildred asked the question before she could stop herself. Sam was present—his old familiar self instead of the new unfamiliar self. It should be Belle who was hearing and seeing her husband be alive, breathing God's air, and seeing the night lights. He was also eating some kind of left-over sandwich from a clear plastic container that looked like it had some black coffee grounds stuck on the top.

"Have you been going through trash cans?"

"Ask me no questions and I'll tell you...." Sam replied tartly, but he didn't finish the old saying. He announced suddenly, "I don't want to take a test on my life anymore." Sam looked up at her, his eyes filled with a need for mercy—understanding.

She told Sam the truth. It was the only form of mercy she could give.

"Me, neither," Mildred said.

Inside her house the telephone started ringing. Fran wouldn't be calling her this time of night. No one who knew who she was would be calling Mildred Budge this time of night.

"Let it ring," she said. "I hate telephones." Turning her back to the car and Sam, she leaned against the warm metal. She counted ten rings before the caller gave up. Looking up at the stars, and then to Sam as if he were a priest, who could hear her tell the story of her life and not repeat it, she confessed: "I have always hated telephones. They're so intrusive. I don't even like the sound of them when they ring. Still, I have learned a bitter lesson. I need to get a cell phone, Sam. And some diamond earrings, though that doesn't sound like an emergency. It feels like it is. Like I am almost too late to even be thinking about diamond earrings." Mildred inhaled deeply. "You getting tired of looking at the night lights yet?" she asked.

You can be fully alive and want to go to bed.

Sam looked up at her as if she weren't speaking English. "You look awful pretty, Mildred Budge. Whatcha been doing?"

"I've been on a date. I like dating about as much as I like telephones."

Just that quickly, Sam didn't understand what she was saying. It comforted Mildred in a way. He wouldn't be able to repeat what he couldn't understand. In an instant of letting go, Mildred Budge was very tempted to tell Sam the whole untold story of her life and how so much of it wasn't what other people saw or knew or said about her as the truth. It felt to her at times that her life story existed in bits and pieces of encounters and confessions, memories and often frustrated hopes. The biggest failure of her life was that she had so often smothered dreams and hopes because it was expedient to snuff out so many small desires. Wise, even. Prudent. Cautious. Careful. Who can you say something like that to and have them understand what you mean?

Sam's voice reached her, low and intimate in the shadows, coming out of somewhere deep inside himself that he suddenly felt free to express. "I love you, Mildred. Have I ever told you that? I love you."

His words hung in the air like points of starlight. Mildred wasn't afraid of Sam's declaration—not the way she had been startled by words like that spoken in the past by others and been unsure of how to reply. She knew how to answer Sam.

"I know you love me, Sam. I love you, too, Sam. And Belle. I would lay down my life for either one of you any time. And you would for me, if you could."

The church lady was doing exactly that right then. She would have preferred to be inside, but she was outside, leaning on the car, talking softly in the dark. The meal and late-night coffee had not settled well in her stomach. Her feet hurt. Her soul felt disturbed. She wanted to be inside her house with the door locked praying for Brenda and her mama.

Sam retreated at the mention of his wife. The outline of him and the force that was his personhood and energy dissipated. Mildred could feel the retreat of Sam's attention and focus. She wondered if he had always been able to do that, and she simply had not been paying much attention until now.

"I'm not Belle's hero anymore. I'm nobody's hero anymore." Looking up at her in the light of the car and starlight above, Sam confessed, his face free of tension and fear. "I'm nobody's hero, Millie. It is such a relief."

Turning to reposition his legs, Sam wagged his foot back and forth. Back and forth. "Belle doesn't know I'm not really here anymore. I'm everywhere else. But I'm not here—not like she expects. I'm not *him* anymore." He said the word *him* with disdain.

The words made sense—kind of. But then so much of talking with a person who had dementia required a kind of filling in the blanks of what they meant or what you thought they meant. Some experts called that activity learning to speak Alzheimer's. But people filled in those blanks in conversation with just about everybody for most of their lives. When you begin to do it on a regular basis with someone who has dementia, you see that you have been doing the same thing for most of your life with most people. The knee-buckling truth was they had most likely been doing that with you. It was a rare brave friendship where the deepest facts of who you are and what you mean and what you are trying to say when you talk are almost brutally exchanged with no hard feelings or fear that someone will use that present knowledge to hurt you.

Talking in the dark and the shadows, Mildred and Sam did that right then, having laid down their respective lives, he in his way and she in hers.

"Where are you right now, Sam?"

The moment was gone. His words left as quickly as they had just come. He was back inside himself, wordless again. Mildred tried to think of what he might say in this moment of telling the truth. *I live in the thin places between earth and heaven, inside here and now, inside the everlasting always trustworthy love of God who holds me in the palm of his vast unshakable hand.*

She waited in silence under the starlight with Sam.

"Mildred, is that you?" Sam asked suddenly.

"Mostly," she admitted softly. "I've left bits of me behind on the Harriett II, some of me was shed inside a mausoleum of a house on Clay Street. I don't know the street number, Sam. I left lots of me behind on the downtown streets I walked on alone in the dark to get to safety, and I was scared at first and then I wasn't scared; and by the time I got to a place where I could find some help, I wasn't afraid at all—just tired. Then I shed some more of myself at the Renaissance Hotel where I met a young woman named Brenda who was very kind to me, and now out here with you, I'm crumbling into dust beside my car with you while stars burn out above and the angels continue to sing over us. And I love you, too, Sam."

"Where have you been?" Sam asked as if he had heard nothing at all.

Mildred had just truthfully answered that question moments ago. The second time she answered it, the content was different. *Did it matter how you told the story of your life and were you lying if how you answered a basic question changed with the moment, your words chosen to fit the ability of someone who could maybe hear you, and what you were brave enough to admit in that moment?*

"Oh, Sam. I went on a date with a man I'm supposed to want to date. He's very handsome and congenial and knows how to talk to women. Once upon a time he was in the movies, and I don't care about that. Because I'm supposed to want to call that kind of talking a good time, I said *yes* to a dinner date. But I never really wanted to go. I went because we are supposed to go on dates when someone asks us. I was polite. We went on a dinner cruise on the Harriet II, and I had two glasses of wine I didn't really want. He drank four glasses. I was afraid to let him drive me home because he had been drinking too much—or at least I thought so, but maybe I'm naïve. I could be. Maybe people often drink four glasses of wine and drive just fine. But I wasn't sure. When he said 'Let's go to my house right over there for coffee,' I said *yes* because I thought he needed to drink some coffee before he tried to drive farther. But when we got to his house it was like a big movie set furnished with antiques that were too heavy to lift, and nobody had dusted lately. I don't need more furniture to dust."

Sam appeared to be listening. Maybe he was.

"That's not all, Sam. As soon as I saw Mark in his own setting—his house—I saw him differently. I got the uncomfortable idea he was playing the part of himself. We all do, I know that. Over his fireplace was a portrait of a woman in black. He said loving her had killed him, and I pretended I didn't know he had practiced saying that line just that way with just that kind of rueful smile, and I thought I didn't so much mind his saying lines like that, but I didn't want to bear the burden of being his audience for very long. A few minutes was more than enough for me. He wanted to talk, but I didn't want to listen. And then he said that I was the woman who could bring him back to life, and I don't want to be that woman either."

"You can't raise people from the dead," Sam declared, becoming the elder of her church again. "You're Mildred Budge, but you can't do that. No, you can't do that."

"Then he drank some more liquor, Sam, and I played the piano just so I wouldn't have to talk or listen anymore. And, Sam, this is the saddest part of the whole evening."

Mildred waited for him to say 'trouble is coming, I can see it, I can feel it,' but he didn't. The blood over his brow was coagulating, and she wondered once again if he had scratched himself or fallen. And it seemed to her that people were changing, disappearing, coming and going and standing and falling and getting hurt faster than she could pray for them or bandage them up afterwards. *It was too much. Too much. Jesus, just come and get me. I'm ready to go anytime. Anytime you say.*

"He made us small cups of espresso. I didn't like it very much, Sam."

"Mud," he said. "What you said. That's what it's like. Mud."

"I left the cup of mud on the table next to a picture of him dressed like a movie star." She was repeating herself. Mildred knew she was repeating herself. There was no diagnosis of dementia to justify it. There was only the need to make sense of her life that caused her to repeat herself. Others, too. "He was in movies a long time ago, and I think I was supposed to be impressed, but I wasn't. And maybe something is wrong with me for not being impressed. I do like the way he can dig in the yard."

"Aren't we all in some kind of movie?" Sam asked, and she wondered if he was prophesying because in the Bible there is a verse that implies old and young men will prophesy and dream dreams. You wouldn't have to have your wits about you to prophesy.

"There was a book of music open on the piano. It, too, felt like a prop. But to be honest, Sam, I used it just that way. I played the piano so I wouldn't have to talk or listen anymore. I played a Chopin Etude."

"Etude. Etude. Etude. Etude. Etude." Sam repeated the word over and over.

Across the field the lights in his house grew brighter as Belle's worried silhouette paced the floor, moving from window to window, wondering where her husband was. *He's coming. I'll be bringing him to you as soon as I can talk him out of this car,* Mildred promised her friend. Behind her, the front door to her own house was still locked, her clean bed waiting, the phone no longer ringing, and tomorrow would be here sooner than Mildred felt like she could face it in that moment. *In less than eight hours I need to get up, get dressed, and go sell stuff at the Saturday Sidewalk Sale. You can't call in sick when you are one of the booth owners.*

"I played Chopin, and Mark grew drowsy, and I played it a second time because pianos are different, and your hands land on the keys differently after you learn how the instrument reacts, so the first time I was learning the places my hands needed to be, and the second time I was really playing the Etude. I do like Chopin, but that's a sad piece. Mark passed out to Chopin, Sam. Or he went to sleep. Is there a difference? And I got to the end of the music and found myself awkwardly alone in a strange man's house. I had no business being in a strange man's house. When I realized my predicament, I didn't know what to do, Sam. I hate that feeling. I couldn't find a telephone plugged into the wall. I know how to use those, but I didn't know Winston's telephone number and Fran was at Winston's. There was no one to call anymore, Sam." Mildred reported, and there was surprise in her voice, still. "There's a good chance that I will never get over knowing that for a brief time alone in the dark in a strange man's house, there was no one I could call to come and get me."

"You can call me," Sam offered out of the depths of a real friendship that no diagnosis or label could stop. "I love you, Mildred. I love everybody now. Belle misses me. I can't do anything about that," he said forlornly, watching the stars. One burst and suddenly began to fall. "Catch a falling star and put it in your pocket, save it for a rainy day."

"A rainy, rainy day," she replied. Like Sam, she knew the words to the old Perry Como song. "We remember the same music," she said, reaching for his quivering hand. "Did you know that simply humming a song makes your brain light up in ways that it doesn't when you are only speaking? We should all hum more."

Her friend resisted her at first--resisted the tug to get out and stand up.

"You can't sleep out here, Sam. Belle will be too worried."

"Belle misses me," he replied, coming out of the car, leaving a plastic container behind with the portion of a sandwich that would attract ants.

Mildred reached around Sam and grabbed the box with food in it. Without caring where it landed, Mildred tossed the plastic container and its contents over her shoulder onto the ground. She would find it in the daylight and throw it away. Sam had likely retrieved it from someone's trashcan. She couldn't let herself think about that anymore.

"Sam, would you like to go home now?"

"No more tests," he said. "No more tests."

"I forgot," she admitted easily. Sam had helped to teach her to say those words.

He blew a long stream of air out, and his breath was sour.

"Sam, let's go home," she invited. "Walk with me."

"I'll walk with you, Mildred. I love you, Mildred."

"I love you, too, Sam."

And unlike the previous days of her life, Mildred did not say *and Belle*. She just let the words stand on their own anyway they could.

Mildred closed the car door softly behind him. Sam held out his arm in the old-fashioned way that ushers offer visitors to a wedding as they lead you down an aisle to a seat where you can watch a wedding and try not to call out just before the vows were taken: *Trouble's coming, I can see it, I can feel it.*

"Thank you, Sam, for helping me," Mildred said quietly. "It's dark and walking in the dark seems farther than in the daytime. I see Belle."

"Belle misses me. I'm not around much anymore."

"Some of you is sometime," Mildred replied truthfully, companionably as they fell into step.

"Sam. Sam. Sam. Sam. Sam," Belle said, repeating his name from where she was standing on the top step at the back door. "Come on in this house, you rascal, you."

Sam moved up the steps in slow motion, the pace of living in the here and now. Mildred waited for him to turn and say goodnight to her, but Sam did not turn and speak again.

By the time Sam had passed his wife, he had forgotten his neighbor Mildred Budge was there.

"A happy ending after all," Mildred whispered as she turned and walked back to her house, fearlessly but carefully in the shadows of the trees.

22
SUPER SATURDAY
SIDEWALK SALE

"Mildred. Mildred."

The voice came to her from far, far away. Mildred heard the voice, but she couldn't open her eyes.

"Mildred. Mildred," Fran said, standing over her.

Mildred felt hot fingertips pressed purposefully against the pulse of her neck. "Are you dead, Mildred?"

Mildred's eyes flew open. "Am I dead?" she gasped, blinking rapidly.

"Good Lord Jesus, no. When you didn't answer the door, I thought you were hurt. Or maybe dead. I knocked hard! When you didn't answer, I used my key," Fran admitted, as she attempted to steady her breathing. She patted the middle of her chest with her left hand, consoling herself.

"But here you are still in bed," Fran said, her voice shifting immediately to exasperated.

A different person would have mistaken Fran's tone for anger, but it was really fear coupled with relief.

"What are you doing still in bed? It's Super Saturday Sidewalk day."

Struggling to sit up and drowsy from a deep sleep that had finally overtaken her, Mildred shook her head. She still had not told Fran about dinner with Mark. She wasn't awake enough to start then. "I couldn't sleep at first. And then I did. What time is it?"

"Almost six," Fran said, sitting down heavily on the side of the bed. Relief flooded from her. "When I came in, I didn't smell any coffee, and I knew something was wrong. My feet didn't want to move, Mildred. I made them walk down the hallway. I thought....I thought.... Well, you know what I thought."

"You thought I had died in my sleep," Mildred said. "Would you go switch on the coffee?" And she didn't say, and *then go away, please.* Mildred was not ordinarily hard to get along with; but initially at the beginning of every day, she needed an extended silence and three cups of regular coffee. She had read someone's words about the rhythm of morning people: They love fellowship and cherish solitude. Mildred loved her friends, and she cherished her solitude. While her friends did not always understand that, they sensed it and respected it.

Without a word, Fran padded softly back down the hallway to the kitchen and switched on the brew. When she came back, the fierce glint in her blue eyes was back. "Okay. We need to revise our business plan."

Mildred nodded, her feet in slippers and her thick white chenille robe cinched loosely. "You revise it. I'm getting coffee."

Fran followed Mildred back down the hallway to the kitchen, stalking her. "You're not awake. And you won't be for a while. You're not dead, and that means everything is all right. I'm going on to the Emporium without you. The early bird gets the best spot on the sidewalk. You come along when you can."

Mildred nodded silently, her back to Fran, her eyes on the dripping coffee. "I slept hard," she said unnecessarily.

"It happens like that. I never sleep better than on Saturday night before church on Sunday. There's something inside of us that knows when we need to get moving that keeps us in the bed. Except for me of course. I'm up and raring to go. It's the Super Saturday Sidewalk Sale!" Fran exulted. "I know the spot we want, and I'm going to go get it."

Fran was fired up. It was good to see and hard to hear.

Mildred's hand reached for a cup, and shifting the pot quickly, she held her cup poised under the dripping coffee unable to wait for it to finish its brewing cycle to pour. She hadn't rushed pouring a cup of coffee before it was finished dripping in two years—not since she had retired from teaching, when her mornings of employment had contained that forced pressure of moving faster in the world's pace rather than the speed she preferred: slow.

"I'm going on," Fran declared. And then in a great show of mercy, she said, "I'll take care of things just fine. Come when you can. And if the idea of so many people is too much for you today, let yourself be off the hook. Winston and I can manage the whole thing."

"You and Winston can manage," Mildred agreed quietly, taking the first hot sip, her back to Fran. And Fran understood that sometimes too many people was too many people for Mildred Budge. Mildred had never loved Fran more than in that moment.

Fran reached out and patted Mildred's right arm with the hand holding the hot coffee. It sloshed over the sides and dribbled onto her robe. "You're still alive. I knocked really hard!" She headed to the door, calling over her shoulder, "What did you say before? Come. Go. Be...." At the doorway, Fran turned and said, "Be alive and be easy on yourself. Life is long and hard."

And then Fran was gone into the world of happy go-getter morning people driving toward the Emporium where streams of early bird shoppers would want conversation as well as what was for sale. Fran would enthusiastically provide both.

Fran was laughing and teasing with shoppers when Mildred arrived three hours later. Fran's business partner parked her Mini-Cooper on the far side of the lot so that she would not be using a more convenient spot near the sidewalk that would keep a potential buyer from being able to buy and easily transport what they had purchased to the car. She could still smell the residue of Sam's trash-collected meal and cracked a window to air out the car.

Mildred stepped up to Fran just as she was writing out the sales chit. "Thanks a bunch. You know what to do next," she said, still smiling and nodding as she confirmed that the customer understood the routine of payment and collecting the item. "Thanks for coming by!"

It was a simple process. You picked out what you wanted. Got the sales chit. Took it to the cash register. Paid. Got your receipt, and then picked up your item at the table where you had seen it, or if it was big and heavy, you drove around to the loading dock in the back of the building and let the guys help you load it into your car.

"It's been a super duper morning," Fran reported happily, the light in her blue eyes shining brightly. "Winston can't keep the merchandise coming out fast enough. The Bereans dropped their stuff off just like they were asked to, and Winston has been cycling their donated items out here as soon as there is an empty spot on the table. He's putting the bigger stuff in our front booth and moving some of that stuff below to the basement booth. The Faith Promise fund is going to get a walloping donation at the end of the day," Fran the businesswoman predicted happily. "Our stuff's moving faster than anyone else's," she reported with satisfaction. "What do you think of our spot?"

"It's the best spot," Mildred confirmed, looking left and right and trying to figure out why Fran thought this location for their table was the best spot. She didn't have a clue.

"We may be sold out of the Berean's missions' donations by midafternoon. If so, we're going to leave. There's no rule that says we can't leave. We will go home and put up our feet."

Mildred stole a glance at her watch. Just a few hours to go and she could get back to her house and lock herself inside and not answer the telephone. It was the dream of her life in that moment.

"I'm going to need a bathroom break ere long. But before you take over here, will you run inside and check on how our two booths look? Winston's doing the best he can, but he's managing a lot, and home décor and how to arrange a display is not his strong suit."

"I'll go," Mildred said, moving past Fran and the other vendors who were at attention. There was a steady stream of cars and people moving down the sidewalk, looking focused, looking bored, looking nosey, passing time.

Inside the store, the lighting was muted. Only a few shoppers had gone inside. A couple of the men were sitting near the front entrance in rocking chairs next to the coffee table where there was a plate of free vanilla cream sandwich cookies and the stale but hot coffee. Streeter, the manager, was nowhere to be found. He was probably in the back helping to sort items on the loading dock.

Right away Mildred saw Winston. He was in their first-floor booth rearranging the smaller pieces of furniture. The easy chair and small gossip bench had their backs to the front door. Winston was turning them around to face shoppers. The petite solid pine drop-lid desk was now gone, and so was that wooden breakfast tray. They couldn't stock enough of those either. People said both kinds of items made good laptop tables.

Standing in the aisle, Mildred waited for Winston to see her. When he looked up, she mouthed the words, "Thank you."

He had a translucent innocent face, kind eyes, and a gentle, slow-dawning smile that reminded Mildred of Gary Cooper in one of those old movies where he moved slowly and tipped his hat a lot. She never knew what Winston was thinking. Never. In her presence he was a wordless man who loved Fran Applewhite. Today, Winston took three big steps to come close enough to say, "Thanks for the silver dollar and the chicken dinner."

Mildred had forgotten all about that silver dollar and the chicken--was surprised to hear him mention it. "Glad you liked them," she replied. "I'm headed downstairs. Do I need to carry something with me?"

He stared at the long wide stairs that led below and shook his head. "Nobody's going down there today. All the action's up here," Winston said, as he walked back toward the loading dock.

Mildred went downstairs anyway because she had told Fran she would.

Their basement booth looked fine though the floorspace was under stocked. The cowboy cooker Dutch oven was sitting by its lonesome on the corner of the table. It needed a red bow or something. Mildred figured Fran had shifted some stuff upstairs to fill in up there. After today they would really need some more of their own inventory. The Bereans donations were for missions only.

Fran appeared suddenly. "Got a buddy holding down our fort for a minute. It looks good, doesn't it?" she asked. "Where's my boy?"

"He was here, and now he isn't."

"I'm getting married in twenty-four days. Do you remember that?"

"I remember that," Mildred said.

"Lots to do between now and then." And then as Fran realized that Mildred was not being very chatty, she asked, giving Mildred her full attention. "Is something wrong?"

"I'm still asleep, but I will be awake soon."

Fran accepted that and patted her arm. "Meet you out front," she said, heading to the ladies' room. "Be there or be square," she added laughing. Fran was in her element. She loved visiting with shoppers. She loved talking about odds and ends and furniture and colors and could always remember people's names.

Mildred returned to the table on the sidewalk and nodded to the next-door vendor that she was there to take over for Fran.

Some part of the back of her brain wasn't awake yet; and while Mildred was smiling and nodding, she wasn't really present.

And so, she didn't see Mark at first coming from across the parking lot. She did see some kind of movement out of the corner of her eye. But she didn't pay much attention. And it was only when Mark was standing in front of her waiting for her to look up that she finally realized, *Oh. Oh. There he is. An eligible older man. Still something to behold.*

"Hello, there! I thought I'd find you here," Mark said, with an easy-going smile. He looked rested and expectant.

Why wouldn't he? He had some sleep.

Mark paced his smile, letting it ease across his face.

Mildred couldn't resist. She smiled back.

"I never have been able to figure out women," he confessed winsomely, but he didn't mean it. "You disappeared on me last night. Where did you go?"

Did he not remember falling sleep?

"When it was time for me to go home, I did," she explained simply. Her hands began to pet the items in front of her, mindlessly repositioning them this way and that.

"Well, I would have thought you would have told me good-night or good-bye."

"How do you know I didn't?" she asked, remembering distinctly standing in the doorway as she headed to the kitchen and whispering her intentions.

Mark squinted, studying her, the smile still real—still confident. He could sense that there was an undercurrent of some kind—some back story he didn't know—but it didn't matter to him. He dismissed it. "Doesn't matter now. You're here. I'm here. I don't usually go to this, but I knew you girls would be here. I was curious," he said, looking around.

"Do you get a lunch break?" Mark asked, looking past her. "I was hoping to take you somewhere special and..." Leaning forward, he added, his eyes smiling, "Hold your hand."

That last idea startled her. It was as if nothing uncomfortable about the night before had happened. Nothing.

"Do you want to read my fortune?" she asked, that shadowy part of her brain waking up. "I slept in this morning and just got here. I don't think Fran is going to let me go to lunch."

"I didn't think she was your boss," he said, looking around for Fran.

He met the question and the dare in the tone of her voice gracefully. "I could read your fortune. I say it looks very bright," he said. "If you can't do lunch, what about dinner tonight? We could do take out," he said. "How about a quiet supper at your place. I'll tell your fortune, and if you are in the mood, you can tell mine."

"Buenos dias, Marco," Fran said, appearing suddenly. "Como estas usted?"

Mark's bearing changed immediately. "I don't speak Spanish," he replied stiffly. She had broken his rhythm of flirtation.

His gaze grew colder, and his chin went up.

Fran shrugged and stifled a laugh. "I don't either. You buying? Because if you are, I have a couple of Spanish dancer bookends right over there," she said pointing toward the end of the table.

Mildred followed Mark's gaze to the dancer bookends. The first time she had seen a pair like them she thought they were unique and had wanted a set for herself. They made her feel happy when she looked at them. Since then Mildred had seen the dancing couple in many booths, on shelves, on display tables, at estate sales. If she really wanted them, she could have them. But once she had learned she and anyone else could have them, Mildred didn't really care about them anymore. That was true of many things.

"I'm not much of a reader, so I don't need bookends," he said, at first dismissively, and then right before their eyes, Mark changed. A breath in and a breath out, and he grew warmer, his smile friendlier. "Senorita..." he said, leaning toward Fran. He let her feel the warm engagement of his smile.

"Ah, Senora," she corrected him.

"I've always liked Madame," Mildred interjected suddenly.

He fidgeted with the cuff of his blazer. It was the same Brooks Brother blazer he was wearing the first day Mildred had met him.

"Madame sounds like she's had a much more interesting life than Senora," Mildred chimed in. "Senora cooks all the time. Madame dances..."

"And she might go to Paris and eat a roast chicken," Fran added.

The quick exchange between the two old friends confused Mark—made him feel left out.

"Ladies, I've just come to show my support for your enterprise, but obviously I'm interrupting. I would apologize, but I'm not really sorry. I wanted to see you Mildred. You understand that, don't you Fran?" Mark gave Fran a dark look that Mildred had not seen before. It was harsh.

Fran registered the moment, holding his gaze. "Oh, I understand," Fran affirmed quietly. She stepped back to let them finish their conversation, and a small twinkle of victory appeared in his gaze.

Leaning across the counter, he made sure Mildred was looking into his eyes when he said quietly, "Mildred, are we on for later?"

Mildred automatically smiled her polite church lady smile. It was a part of every church lady's equipment and more important than her purse with all of its emergency supplies. Tilting her head slightly to the left, the smile as genuine as human will can make it, Mildred said, "Tomorrow is Sunday. I don't go out on Saturday nights because of church on Sunday," she said.

Fran registered Mildred's answer. Mildred heard herself, too—the echo of her response circling around and coming back to her as it would for a while—a few days until she decided what she really thought about it. In that moment during the experience of the first echo of her *no*, Mildred was going to have to work on saying *no* better than that. Or maybe she didn't always and forever want to say *no*. She would spend her prayer time the next day working through that. With Fran soon to be married and no longer a member of the Lunch Bunch, it was conceivable that Mildred might one day want another lunch invitation from someone. He was a man. He was available. He had good teeth. But she had seen a worrisome glint in his eye— a glint of will and victory, the kind of victory that had not shown up in that first handshake when Mildred had naively believed that a shake of a hand was a reliable way to take a man's measure.

"A rain check then," Mark prompted, expecting Mildred to agree.

Mildred smiled ambiguously turning to help an approaching customer. When the shopper had left, Fran asked her bluntly, "What was that thing with Mark about?"

"What thing?"

"You could cut the tension with a knife," Fran declared.

"You could feel it?" Mildred asked.

"When are you going to tell me what happened? Because something happened."

"Yes, something happened," Mildred admitted as suddenly the customers had all moved past, and no one was in front of them needing small talk or answers.

Fran's face grew worried by the tone of Mildred's voice. "Did that man do something?" she asked.

Mildred turned and said, "I had dinner with him last night, and towards the end, he fell asleep."

"You went out to dinner at night?"

"Chicken," Mildred said.

"Any good?"

"I've eaten that kind of chicken meal many times before. Nothing new."

Fran nodded. "Chicken," she repeated.

"And then Mark took me to his house overlooking the river. I went because he had been drinking wine, and I didn't want to ride in the car with him until he had drunk some coffee. So, we talked a bit. He drank some coffee and something else from his bar, and he fell asleep in his chair."

Fran's face became solemn, her gaze sad, her temperament a fresh version of an enduring patience that was so much a part of her strength. "Men do fall asleep," she said, nodding knowingly. Then, pacing herself, Fran added carefully, "Drinking too much is different. That's something we need to think about."

Waiting a moment, Fran asked another question, "Did you have a good time?"

Mildred shook her head before taking a deep breath and telling her best friend the truth. "I've had a better time at the dentist's office."

23
END OF SUPER SATURDAY
SALE

At the end of a long and successful day at the Emporium, Mildred headed home. She was looking forward to an extended period of silence inside her locked house only to find a yellow Post-it handwritten note stuck on her front door. She saw the flap of paper waving as she was parking and dreaded reading the words. *Oh, no. Oh, no.* A halfhearted rain check was not enough of a *no* for Mark. He wanted something more from her. She wanted to be alone.

"I think I'm being stalked," she told Jesus.

But Mildred Budge was wrong.

The note was from Steev the preacher. "Come across the street to a cookout. Bring more cake or nothing at all!"

Mildred smiled at the homecoming message, for there is always a moment upon crossing the threshold into your own empty house when you want to hear someone call out, "Welcome home."

The door front invitation sounded like that welcome to her. In spite of wanting to be alone, Mildred smiled.

A long breath later, she was inside. Her house felt quiet—undisturbed. Still, she moved through her house like a watchman attuned to signs of trouble, taking an inventory of the sounds that reassured her all was well. The refrigerator was humming. The clock on the mantel was ticking. Nothing was dripping somewhere in the house causing worry.

In her bedroom, Mildred sat down on the side of the bed, wondering if she had time for a shower. She needed a long hot shower. The need for rest and the long day caught up with her. Leaning back on the bed, Mildred put up her tired feet, and before she could question whether she had time for a nap, her eyes closed, and she fell instantly and deeply asleep.

The phone did not ring while Mildred rested.

No one knocked on any of her doors.

No large dense pine cone hit the roof and clattered loudly down.

No squirrel scampered across the roof.

But some sound roused her.

From deep inside that interior awareness, Mildred's subconscious registered that a worrisome sound had occurred. A different sound.

Her breathing slow; her eyes fluttering awake, she opened them slowly and replayed the extant noise in her memory. More curious than alarmed, Mildred lay still and listened. She didn't hear anything else. Instead, she saw only that the late afternoon sun had given way to a purple twilight.

Squinting, Mildred could barely make out the time on the night stand clock. There was no time for a shower if she was going to the backyard cookout across the street.

Mildred was on the verge of making the decision to take an end-of-the-day shower, put on her soft clothes, and stay home inside the restorative quiet of solitude when a second jarring thump occurred just outside her front door again. The abrupt bang jolted her, this time causing a slight adrenaline rush.

The noise didn't sound like someone knocking. It was really one loud abrupt rap. It could be a bird flying into the door. That happened at certain times during the year when the red berries on vines ripened, and the birds pecked at them and got drunk on the juice and impaired their radar systems. At least that had always been Mildred's reasoning to describe the antics of Hitchcockian black birds flying haphazardly in the early fall.

Just as she was talking herself into believing that, Mildred heard another thud—not as loud--and it wasn't a knock. It was like a newspaper being thrown and hitting the door.

Was Sam throwing things at the front door?

Did she have to care?

Did she have to look?

Who would know if Mildred Budge, the lady of the house, leaned back on the bed, ignored whatever was happening outside, closed her eyes, and drifted back into that interior space of solitude closest to prayer? It was her heart's desire to be simply quiet and enter into that stillness.

And then she heard a whimper. She knew that sound. *Didn't she?* It sounded like that old curious cat Jinx which used to roam through the neighborhood scavenging for food. But that roving cat had disappeared a while back, and Mildred had concluded that Jinx had migrated to another neighborhood or been killed by a car or a fox. She had seen more than one fox running through the Garden District.

And then she felt a blow to her middle—a blow of realization that maybe Sam had fallen on her doorstep and was lying there hurt, trying to get her attention by banging his weak fist against her front door.

"Sam?" she spoke his name in a hoarse whisper. Making herself move through her dread that Sam was hurt, Mildred hurried down the shadowy hallway—the same one that Fran had traversed that very morning fearing Mildred had died in her sleep-- and turned toward the foyer and the front door.

Time slowed, and in a kind of surreal slow motion, Mildred made herself keep moving. She had known this kind of time experience before. It felt like she was moving through an invisible web and had to push away strands stretching across her path that were intended to keep her from reaching her destination.

The doorknob was cold, and at first, stiff. Dread weakened her. Mildred had to use her will and the strength in both arms to turn it.

She was surprised by how much darker it was outside than it should have been, and she wondered if she had misread the clock. *Is it later than I think? Am I losing it too?*

She could hear the gang across the street at the cookout, and in that very moment, it seemed so very strange to her that the old Garvin house—the preacher's house now-- was lit up.

In slow motion, her right hand reached out automatically and searched for the switch to the front door light.

She heard the whimper of the child sitting in a ball on her front stoop, his small head bowed, and his face buried against his knees. She recognized the back of his head immediately and was about to drop down beside Chase when a car that was sitting in the shadows by the corner gunned its engine. Tires squealing, the car veered right and zoomed away.

The getaway car's acceleration was loud enough to draw the attention of Steev from across the street, who came quickly through the side gate.

Steev saw Mildred lit up in the doorway and called out to her. "Are you all right?"

When she didn't answer, her silence caused Steev to leave the others. "Coming, Millie!" he called out, and it registered with her that the preacher called her by the name her dearest friends used. *We are friends now*, she thought.

Steev didn't reach her before she knelt down beside the child at her door. Her heart beating loudly in her ears and chest, the retired school teacher whispered the automatic truth, "Chase, you're here. You've come home."

She waited for the little boy to speak, but his head was bent into his knees which were pulled against his chest. His shoulders shuddered, and he wouldn't look at her.

"You're all right now, Chase. You're home," she promised, as Steev was suddenly beside her, his face taut with concern. It was the first time she had ever seen him without his kind eyes shining with joy. Steev's expression looked different in that moment. *We are friends now,* she thought again. *We can see each other's eyes change and experience the deep interiority of personhood they reveal when our guards are down.*

"What have you got here, Miss Mildred?" Steev asked, confirming that she was all right and that the person on the stoop was not big enough to threaten her. Gone now was the sweet use of Millie and back was Miss Mildred, but that didn't change what she knew. And she would always know it wherever they were and whichever public social roles they were playing everywhere they went. From then on, Mildred Budge knew that she and the preacher were now more than two people who went to the same church together. They were friends.

She heard more commotion, and looking up, she saw Jake Diamond loping across the street, his stride sure—his face illuminated in the street light. Mildred had served with Jake on the pulpit committee. He was an even-tempered man, resourceful, strong and sure in his identity. In response to what he thought was an emergency, he ran right toward it with purpose.

"Who is this?" Jake asked, huffing slightly and stopping a yard away from them in an exquisite understanding that boundaries needed to be maintained for the small boy's sake. The child was shrinking in front of them, hiding his face, drawing up his legs in self defense as tightly as he could.

In a crouch beside the child, Mildred Budge looked up and said, "This is Chase. He used to live across the street where Steev lives now. But he's returned. He's home now."

24
WHO DOES SOMETHING LIKE THIS?

The boy's hair was cut in uneven patches, pointing in all directions. Mildred refrained from running her hand over Chase's tender head to smooth the hair, an instinct she always felt towards the heads of children and some adults. But restraint was needed more. The church lady held herself in check, giving the small boy her steadfast presence, which sheltered him from the size and height of the two men looming nearby.

"Do you want to go inside?" Jake asked Mildred and, in his gentle way, Chase.

The boy responded by leaning harder against Mildred, who shifted. She stood up slowly and eased the boy up on his feet beside her. "Chase, it is time to go inside."

Steev stood by quietly, understanding instinctively that too many people and too many words would make it harder to help the child. As Jake moved in closer to Chase, Steev retreated until he was standing on the grass, giving Jake and Mildred room to coordinate a plan shaped by nods, pointing, and hand gestures.

Jake fell silent while Mildred coaxed the boy to move. "You remember my house. We're going to step through here and into the foyer."

As she said the words to lead the boy in, Mildred switched on the inside foyer light.

The shock of the light revealed an even more startling sight. Chase's dingy clothes were worn and too small for him. The T-shirt was a burnt orange color with an ink stain on the pocket.

His jeans had holes in the knees, but they weren't fashionable slits and holes like some people preferred in designer jeans. His holes were simply from neglect and over use. Chase closed his eyes and teetered.

Jake scooped up the trembling boy and unhesitatingly carried him to the old yellow and brown tweed sofa in the den. Mildred followed. Steev came through quietly, keeping close to the wall, watching, listening.

Mildred settled down beside Chase on the sofa, her hand on the middle of his back, counting his breaths. Jake stayed standing, raising one finger as if he had an idea, but he didn't stop to explain it. Instead, Jake turned and went back to the front door. Steev followed him, and outside, the two men conferred quietly, making a plan. Jake reentered. Mildred heard him twist the lock.

Good, she thought. For in that moment she felt vulnerable to intruders. Until that front door lock was turned, she had been on high alert.

Jake returned and stood in silence waiting for a cue from her.

"Is there anything else in his bag?" she asked, her arm reaching around the boy to test him in ways he wouldn't understand. Exposed ribs in her hands indicated malnutrition. A slight pinch to the skin on the back of his hand, and she knew he was dehydrated.

"He has a few clothes that don't look any better than the ones he's wearing. Looks like that's his only pair of shoes," Jake reported.

She looked down at Chase's footgear. His once white sneakers were dirty and worn. She could see his big toe protruding at the top of the scuffed canvas shoe. The boy had outgrown his shoes, but no one had bought him a new pair. Resolve took hold in her. Patience, too. For Mildred's first instinct was to be angry at the negligence of the child's care. But the next moment she was overwhelmed with a sense of how much distress his parents must have been in to lose track of their son. When something like this happens to a boy, something awful is happening to the parents. Mildred made herself focus on the boy.

"Would you get me a warm wash cloth?" she asked Jake, looking up in the dim light of the table lamp.

"In just a minute," Jake said. "We need a record of what we're seeing," he said, taking out his cell phone.

"What are you doing?" she asked, her arm growing stronger around the boy.

"Documentation," Jake replied tersely, moving his cell phone, taking recordkeeping snapshots of the boy and his hair and clothes, the lonely gym bag with his paltry possessions stuffed haphazardly in it. The last picture Jake took of Chase was of his right toe protruding through the top of the worn shoe. "One day you may need proof of how he arrived and the level of care he had been experiencing."

Placing the phone in his back pocket, his eyes met Mildred's and Jake promised, "I'm a witness. Steev, too."

Mildred nodded, as Jake went to get the warm wash cloth.

A light was turned on. It cast a glow down the hallway.

Jake returned, moving wordlessly to her and handing her a thick blue washcloth dipped in warm water and squeezed out. She gently wiped the boy's face where days of grime were caked. When Chase allowed it, she moved the cloth up to his head and wiped lightly across the scalp, looking for something she didn't want to name, but she searched for lice nonetheless. Another reason people cut a child's hair was to get rid of lice. The retired school teacher didn't see any of the small creatures that had once been a part of her vigilant routine monitoring of children's heads.

A part of Mildred relaxed, for she had already envisioned trying to contain the space where the child would be sleeping until she could buy the right shampoo that eradicated lice. But that disinfecting process was not necessary. Chase could sleep anywhere in the house—put his head on any pillow or blanket--

and not leave behind bugs and the problems their presence created.

Jake dropped to a crouch. "Who are his parents?" he asked quietly as the boy let his head rotate around under the cloth, his mouth drooping open as relaxation grew in him.

"Just a couple of children not much older in their way than he is," Mildred explained, soberly. It was the truth. And it was pointless to judge big children for being big children unable to take care of a smaller child. "I'm going to get him some water," Mildred said, beginning to rise.

"I'll get that. Stay put."

Jake wasn't gone long and returned with water and a straw that he could have discovered only by rummaging in her junk drawer in the kitchen.

"Good idea," she approved, holding the glass with the straw near Chase's face. He moved toward it, taking the straw, inhaling the water.

Jake drifted into a waiting watchful silence while Mildred let the boy relax against her. Time passed. Before long, the exhausted boy was sleeping deeply, his face pressed against her shoulder, his head bobbing slightly with his breathing while she tried not to disturb him with any movement of hers.

But Mildred needed to move.

Her body was in a strain. She had been awakened from a late afternoon nap—needed to refresh herself in more ways than one, and now she was confined awkwardly with the sleeping boy and Jake.

"He's been under long enough that I think we could stretch him out and let you stand up," Jake said, his dark eyes glowing with assurance. "You need to stand up," he advised Mildred seriously.

Without waiting for her to agree, Jake lightly gripped the boy's other arm and shifted him to the other side of the sofa, where he repositioned a couch cushion to function as a pillow. Jake pointed toward the orange and yellow crocheted afghan across the back. She nodded. He took it and draped it over the sleeping boy.

"I'll be back in a minute," Mildred said, excusing herself.

"I'm not going anywhere," Jake assured her.

As Mildred walked down her own hallway, she heard a gentle tapping at her front door. She ignored the knock and went through her bedroom to her bathroom, where she closed the door and took a fresh warm washcloth and wiped her own face.

And then Mildred folded the wet cloth, draped it over the side of the sink, forgot to comb her hair, and went back to the living room to see if Jake had answered the door.

25
I WILL NEVER LEAVE YOU
OR FORSAKE YOU

Steev had returned. He was waiting in the den with Jake. Both men were watching the exhausted boy sleep, their eyes dark with concern.

"Jake told me about the boy," Steev said. "We think we saw the parents drive off. But I'm back about Sam. Belle asked me to come," he explained apologetically.

Mildred reached out to grip the back of the recliner, holding on. She couldn't take any more bad news. She really couldn't.

"They didn't hit Sam as they drove off, did they?" Mildred asked, her voice hoarse with imminent heartbreak.

Both men shook their heads before the words came out. "Sam's run off. Or at least, Sam ran off when the car sped away. And the old fella hasn't come back yet."

"Are you telling me only that Sam is missing?"

"Belle says so. She was at my house. Sam was, too. And then the excitement happened. And the old boy took off in a sprint. I didn't know he had that kind of speed in him."

"He's pretty agile when he has a mission," Mildred said, her hand letting go of the chair. She inspected the palm of her hand that had gripped the back of the chair, thinking she'd see something there. But her hand was only red from holding it hard.

"Belle's worried, and I know you've got a lot going on here, but she needed me to ask you to keep an eye out for Sam. Belle says that her old man is as likely to come here as go home," Steev said, eyeing her with a fresh curiosity.

"That's it?" Mildred confirmed.

It was too late at night to explain Sam's walkabouts. But her old friend knew the neighborhood. He wasn't afraid of the dark. If Mildred hadn't been so tired, she might have let herself worry just to keep everyone else company. But Mildred Budge was tired.

"Sam will turn up," she predicted with assurance. "And if he comes here first, I'll call Belle."

"What about the boy?"

She looked at Chase snuffling in a deep sleep on her sofa, covered in the afghan her Aunt Betty had made with one crochet hook and eight balls of yarn. Mildred had another blanket crocheted by her aunt that was in shades of cream and which she had stored in a big vacuum-packed bag. Eastertime, Mildred took out the blanket and laid it across her knees and thumbed through her aunt's favorite Bible passages. At certain times during the year instead of visiting her aunt's grave, Mildred liked to visit inside her aunt's Bible and see her handwritten notes in the margins beside certain verses with the dates. There is no more intimate a diary than someone's Bible with potent, life-changing verses marked by dates in the margins with little phrases or names of people written in the tiny scrawl of the one reading that Bible. Mildred's named was etched in margins all through her aunt's Bible.

"The boy is all right for now, though we are going to need to get some food and more drink in him soon. We'll figure out some kind of plan tomorrow. He needs a bigger pair of shoes and larger clothes," she said. They were small details but important ones: the beginnings of a plan.

Steev understood. "Leave that to me," Steev said. "I'll announce it in church tomorrow, and you'll have all you need by lunchtime. Our folks act when they hear a need," he promised moving toward the front door. "I need to go make sure the fire in the barbecue pit is out. You coming?" he asked Jake.

The other man shook his head. "I'm staying here with Mildred. I don't want Sam showing up in the night while the boy's here. It might scare him. And the parents might panic, change their minds, and come back. Mildred shouldn't be here by herself. Our girl has enough to handle."

Steev nodded as if Mildred didn't have an opinion on the subject.

She didn't. "Come. Go. Be at peace," she said spontaneously, resisting the urge to once again grab the back of the chair and hold on—to try and find her stability in something other than the promise that dwelled inside of her: *I will never leave you or forsake you...*

Steev grinned. "You still preaching?"

Mildred smiled wanly. If she was preaching, she had finished. In that moment, the tired church lady had no other words left.

26
SUNDOWNER SYNDROME AND NIGHT OWLS

After the front door was closed and locked again, Mildred said, "I've got to change my clothes."

Jake nodded easily, settling down in the recliner opposite the den sofa where he could keep an eye on the boy. He knew his way around her house. He had visited a few times since they had served on the pulpit committee together with Sam and Liz.

Going to her chest of drawers Mildred fished around for a navy and orange War Eagle T-shirt big enough that she didn't have to hold in her stomach.

"You don't have to stay," she reassured Jake, when she joined him in the kitchen. He had found a can of chili in her pantry and was heating it up.

"Aren't you hungry?" he asked, ignoring her comment about leaving.

"I haven't thought about it," she said truthfully.

"Sit down. We'll eat. We'll talk. It'll be all right," Jake promised, with confidence.

She sat down in Fran's chair. "You do your own cooking?" she asked.

"Of course," he said, scooping chili into two bowls.

"Spoons?" he asked, placing a bowl in front of her. She pointed toward a drawer.

"Stay put," he coaxed with a smile.

And then he brought the spoons and settled beside her, pulling the chair up to the table. "Thank the Lord," he said easily, and spooned his first bite.

"Thank the Lord," she said, adopting his shorthand grace.

And she took a bite. It was just canned chili, but it was good.

"Did you add something?" she asked, blowing on a steaming spoonful.

"I cook with love," he said with a disarming grin. "I bet you don't eat chili at night."

"Not usually," she admitted, taking another bite. "I don't believe I'll be sleeping much anyway," she said.

"It's a rare night when I sleep all the way through," Jake admitted, meeting her gaze. "I get calls in the night from people at the university about..." He looked away, considering how much to tell her.

"Fires and floods?" she asked.

He nodded and told her the truth.

"I am in charge of what goes bump in the night. Noises. Computers. Printers. Hard mattresses. Soft mattresses. Heat. Cold. Something or someone running naked outside at midnight. Something unrecognizable but maybe a fireball or an airplane falling in the sky. Late night or early morning questions about when the semester started or will start." He cocked his head thoughtfully, ruminating, "More than one nervous student who hasn't completed his term paper has rung me in the night to ask 'Did my professor die? I heard he died.' They want an excuse not to go to class. Hard to go back to sleep after that call."

Mildred nodded, spooning chili. It was going down fine. No heartburn yet.

"When a hurricane is predicted, I just go over to my office at the university and wait by the phone for people to call me to turn off the wind and the rain."

"You have superpowers?" she asked, blotting her lips. She was feeling better—more oriented.

Jake pushed his empty bowl away from him and rested both elbows on the table. "When the power goes off, they call me and ask when I am going to turn it back on."

"You have a master switch?" she asked.

"I tell them we haven't paid the electric bill, but I will take up a collection the next day and deliver the money personally to the power company. They usually say, 'Sounds like a plan' and then I don't hear from that person again."

"When the power goes off it can be inconvenient, but I have learned over time that I don't really care," Mildred confessed readily. "It will come back on eventually. I'm not afraid of the dark, and I know how to be still and alone. I have candles. I pretend it's a rare and beautiful snow day, and I revel in the quiet." She was speaking aimlessly, trading inconsequential facts—the way you talk when the power is off and you are trying not to care or be afraid that it won't come back on sooner rather than later. It's how you get through an emergency: there was a little boy sleeping on her couch, and she did not know where his parents were or what was so wrong that they had brought him here.

"You don't worry about the contents of your freezer thawing out and ruining?" Jake pressed.

"I usually need to clean out the freezer anyway," she said. "I just wait till it's over and clean up whatever mess is left behind. Most trouble turns out to be a mess you have to clean up."

He eyed her. "You looking for a job? We're hiring in the building and grounds department."

"Not today," Mildred replied, as she reached over and sliced off a small bite of unfrosted orange wedding cake. She popped it in her mouth. She liked it, but the cake needed something more. *More butter? Less orange zest? More vanilla? Maybe a thin layer of orange marmalade under a seven-minute frosting?*

"Do you play that piano in the other room often?" he asked, sitting back in the chair. She heard the wood creak beneath him.

He was a substantial man. "I've never seen you play at church. And you don't sing in the choir."

"I take playing the piano in spells. I used to play it more, and I used to be in the choir. I do sometimes play for my classmates in Sunday School."

He waited for her to say more.

She held his gaze and told him the truth. "Too much talking too close to bedtime makes me restless. Once a week every Wednesday night after choir practice, I couldn't go to sleep."

"What is it about other people talking that keeps you awake? They aren't gossiping."

"And it's not the prayer requests either," Mildred said, shoulders rising and falling. "I usually know what those are anyway."

"It's the requests no one asks that keep you awake," Jake theorized, speaking carefully, studying her, watching her face.

She nodded quietly.

"You're not antisocial. You are tender-hearted. You feel the pain of others and can't forget it."

"Who says I'm antisocial?"

"The same people who used to say you are an ex-nun."

"Do they really say that?" she asked, incredulous. "I thought that was just something Fran said from time to time when she wanted to make a point."

"No. I've heard that. And that you have the gift of healing. And that you make excellent banana pudding."

She nodded happily. "From scratch. The custard. Good bananas—not too green or too ripe and Vanilla wafers, not the knock-off brittle kind, but the good kind. And real meringue."

Jake stifled a laugh. "I heard you were baking a lot of cakes," he said, helping himself to a piece of the unfrosted orange cake and popping it into his mouth. "But I didn't know you had a banana pudding ministry."

She laughed. It was a common joke in church that anytime you did a chore that involved the church it was dubbed a ministry.

"I also make an excellent pot roast."

"What's your secret for that?"

"It's so simple. You have to buy a very large roast in order to get the kind of drippings that made a tasty gravy. When you have a roast that big, you have to invite a lot of people to share it with you, and that's what makes my roast so good. It's not the quality of the meat or any recipe. Sharing it with others is the secret."

"Sharing it," he agreed. "Steev made hot dogs on the grill tonight. I'm going to tell him about your roast and the pudding."

"Why don't you just come eat with us the next time I make it?"

Jake nodded. He had been invited to dinner, and he had readily accepted.

"You like to sing too?"

She nodded, taking another bite of cake. She didn't like this recipe as much as the butter almond one. "I like to sing the way everyone likes to sing. It makes you feel better to sing," she said.

"Why'd you stop playing the piano this time?" he asked, and the question wasn't just polite. He was truly curious. She saw it in his eyes. So Mildred told him the truth.

"I hired a new man to come and tune it. He did something awful to it. The middle octave sounds tinny, and the F key has a kind of echo, a hollow echo that is very unpleasant. And I can't bear the sound when I play that key, so I have stopped playing the piano until I figure out what to do about it."

"Who was the tuner?"

"Just somebody trying to make a living. He called himself the Piano Man. That's the name of his business, but he had no relationship to music and no understanding of an instrument. I didn't know that about him until I saw him at work. And afterwards, I did call him to come back and repair the problems he had created. And he tried. But the Piano Man couldn't hear the off notes, and that's when I knew he was growing deaf. So, I didn't hold the bad tuning against him, really. I just don't know how to get the piano fixed, and I can't stand how it sounds when I play it. So, I stopped playing."

"You miss it?"

She offered him a scant nod. To say more would be dangerous. Church ladies understood the terrible side effects of complaining or, just as dangerously, admitting you want something you can't have.

"You miss it much more than that very small nod. You miss it a lot," Jake surmised, his eyes warm with understanding.

She smiled and nodded unequivocally.

"Maybe I could take a look at it for you," Jake offered. "I have a knack for fixing things."

She didn't answer him.

"But you're afraid to let anyone else try to work on your piano because you're afraid it will make it worse."

"One of these days I'll know what to do about it. But I don't know now," she replied cryptically. "I'm thinking about it."

"I wish some of the people at the university could wait to act until they knew what to do. Are you sure you're not looking for a job? I bet people could just tell you their problems; and just listening to them, you could figure out how to solve them. Or you would know to wait until you were clear about the answer."

The sound of a horn outside in the dark caused Mildred to stop speaking.

The boy didn't rouse.

The sharp blast of the horn happened again.

"There's someone outside," Jake said, turning toward the disturbing sound.

"That's my car. And I think Sam is probably having a snack in it. I leave the car unlocked for Sam now."

Jake went to the living room and, spreading the slats of the blinds, he peered out. Mildred came and stood beside him.

"That will be Sam," she said. "He wants to drive, but he can't."

"You stay inside with Chase. I'll go out and walk Sam home," Jake suggested.

"I should do that," Mildred replied. "Sometimes he knows me."

"He's a lucky man," Jake said with a flashed grin, heading toward the door. He flipped on the switch and waited. "You're not afraid of the dark?"

"You'd be surprised how not afraid of the dark I am," Mildred said, moving toward the car and Sam.

When she opened the passenger door, Sam was startled. His skinny legs were stretched out in the driver's seat, his right foot pressing the gas pedal. "I can't make it go."

"The car is sleeping right now, Sam."

"Cars don't sleep," Sam replied reasonably.

"Mine does, and people do. Let me take you home. Belle is waiting."

Sam didn't move. His hands were gripping the steering wheel.

We all do that, she thought. We're all looking for something to hold onto. The refrain began again like a melody playing in the back of her mind: *Take my yoke upon you and learn from me for I am gentle and humble in heart, and you will find rest for your souls.*

Mildred walked around to the other side and opened the driver's door. Sam flinched, shifting his body toward the passenger side.

"It's just me, Sam," Mildred said, leaning in.

"Who are you?"

Jake materialized at her side. She looked past him to the open front door and the light from the foyer illuminating her front stoop.

"Do you want me to go around to the other side?" Jake asked.

She shook her head. "No pushing or pulling. No questions either. He hates questions. You have to go very slowly. Words take a long time to reach him. Touch works better."

She placed a hand on Sam's forearm and rested it there companionably.

"You got a Snickers on you?" Sam asked suddenly.

"Belle has one," she replied, because Mildred knew for a fact that Belle had taken to buying bags of bite-sized Snickers bars that would fit into Sam's pants pockets.

"I knew a girl named Belle once. She was a pretty thing."

"Do you see that house over there?" Mildred said, pointing toward Sam's own house.

"Sure." Sam eyed Jake skeptically. "Who are you? You the preacher?" Sam asked, swinging his legs out of the driver's door. Mildred backed up to give him room. "

I've been wanting to talk to you," Jake declared.

"Good, because I want to talk to you, too," Sam replied.

Jake moved in closer. "Belle wants to talk to you, too."

"I knew a girl named Belle once. She was a pretty thing."

"She still is. Let's go see how she's doing," Jake said, his arm around Sam's shoulders.

"You the preacherman?"

"I am his friend. Yours, too," Jake replied, as Mildred stepped back and waited until they were both out so that she could close the car door.

When Jake and Sam were midway across the back field, she went back inside and locked the front door. Then, she went through the den, checking on Chase, and making her way to the back door so that she could hold the door open for Jake.

It didn't take long.

Belle was waiting. Her back door opened. Sam hesitated. Then most likely someone said something about a Snickers bar and Sam headed up the stairs. Jake pointed toward Mildred's house, and she knew what he was saying. "We're right over there if you need us."

Mildred's soul deepened into a kind of grateful rest when she saw Jake make that motion. It was simple to decide that if you have one person who needs you then the needs of another person are no longer a priority. But Sam and Belle were important even when a castaway boy who also needed her was sleeping hard in her den.

Mildred watched Jake walk across the back field. He looked at home among the trees. With each step Jake took Mildred knew what he was feeling. She had made the same walk the night before. He liked the expanse of ground. He liked the size of the trees and the canopy of limbs that stretched across in various places. He liked the way the moonlight fell through the limbs and lit up the ground. He was moving through time and space inside love and a human will dedicated to holy living.

And then Jake reached her.

He stamped his feet on the back-door mat that got a lot of wear.

"Belle all right?" she asked as he came inside.

He cocked his head to the side and reported, "Sam didn't recognize his Belle just now."

"That's happened before. But he'll cycle out of it after a while."

"Do you ever get tired of looking on the bright side?" Jake asked her, sitting down at the table again in what was now his place.

"I never think of it that way. It's just how I see."

27
SUN UP SYNDROME

After very early morning coffee, Jake declined the offer of scrambled eggs. He snagged a quick piece of toast with pear preserves and stood by the sink while he ate a fast breakfast.

"You can sit down," she prompted.

"Got people to see. Things to do. It's Sunday."

"You going to church?" Mildred asked.

"The missions committee is meeting after the service, and I'm on it. I want to go home and shower and change out of these duds."

"I've been on that committee and every other committee. Now I take naps on Sunday afternoons."

"I've heard about you and committees. I was going to ask you to be on the missions committee for next year. I'm heading that. You don't have to answer, because I know what you'll say."

"What will I say?" she asked, suppressing a smile.

"You'll say no—done that. And then I'll convince you that I need you on the committee; and once you believe that you personally are who is needed, you will agree. But you'll drag your feet until you stop, and then you'll be just what we need."

"What do you need?" she asked, trying not to smile.

"You're a handful on a committee. That's what we need. Somebody who rocks a boat from time to time and doesn't mind getting splashed with the backwash herself."

"What is it about boat rides?" she mumbled.

"See there. You think on it. You are cordially invited to serve on the missions committee with me as chair. You can be co-chair or vice-president or as invisible as your little church lady heart prefers to believe herself to be. But we could have some fun, Millie."

"I like fun," she admitted. "But not after dinner. That's too much talking before bedtime for me."

"I'll keep that in mind when I arrange the meeting times," Jake promised. "What do you do when you can't sleep?" He asked suddenly.

"I watch John Wayne movies," she answered quickly.

"You like Westerns?"

"He made more than Westerns, but yes, I do like Westerns. I like knowing the good guys will win."

He eyed her curiously. "Don't you think they do in real life?"

"I don't take the question that far in real life," she said, and an expression passed through her gaze that caused Jake to lean forward and kiss her lightly on the cheek. And when he pulled back Jake said the most amazing words. "More than anything else in my life, I want you for my friend."

"I am your friend," Mildred said truthfully.

"You like everybody," Jake said. "I really want to be your friend."

"I've already invited you to eat roast with me."

"I want to watch a John Wayne movie with you too."

She shrugged and said, "Why not?"

And that was enough for Jake Diamond. He left. And when he was gone the house felt emptier. And she felt strangely lonely.

Mildred got busy. Hearing Chase begin to rouse in the other room, she scrambled some eggs. Standing in the doorway, she said, "Good morning, Sweetie. Go splash some water on your face. You remember where the bathroom is," she prompted. "Breakfast is on the table."

While he was washing his face, Mildred microwaved some Black Label bacon and placed it on a paper plate in front of the boy's chair. She readied the Cheerios box and an empty bowl—fetched a teaspoon and placed the milk nearby. That boy was going to be hungry, but she didn't know what he would eat. She eyed the bacon hungrily but resisted. Kids like bacon.

Chase entered the room slowly, taking peeks at her through sleepy eyes. She motioned to his chair. He sat down, swinging his legs around. His toes touched the floor. He had grown.

She placed a plate of scrambled eggs in front of him. He grabbed the cereal spoon and shoveled them hungrily into his mouth and chewed. She nudged the small plate with the bacon on it toward him. He looked up at her, questioningly. "It's for you," she assured him.

He picked it up and took a bite. His eyes widened.

"So you like bacon," she affirmed.

She scooped her portion of scrambled eggs onto his plate and put bread in the toaster. As he ate, she added a slice of toast and then another.

Then she poured him a bowl of Cheerios and added milk.

He started eating right away before she could even say, "Banana?"

So, she didn't say *banana*.

Mildred hurriedly peeled a banana and sliced it over his bowl, letting the soft pale discs rain down on the Cheerios while he was already eating. He ate a whole bowl of cereal and a whole banana. Only then did Mildred pour a bowl of cereal for herself. Before taking the first bite, she said, her voice rich with intention and truth, "I'm so glad you're here, Chase. I've missed you."

He didn't seem to hear her. She poured him a second bowl of Cheerios. He ate it more slowly than the first, his eyes fixed on the bowl, his hand gripping the spoon tightly.

It was his tight gripping of the spoon that pierced her heart. The flesh was torn at the knuckle. And the boy's fingernails were as ragged as his haircut.

Mildred was assessing what she needed to do first, when the phone rang. She ignored it. The front door was locked. The back door, too. For there are times when you must lock your door and collect your thoughts in order to devise a plan. Although Mildred Budge was not quick to formulate a plan, once she had made a decision she could act swiftly.

"Chase?" she said, and she was surprised by the sound of her own voice. In the back of her mind while she waited on Chase to speak, another interior voice accused her. *You're in a heap of trouble this time. A small hungry boy eating in your kitchen. A newborn baby coming. Your best friend going away just when you need a friend. And you're older than you've ever been. Who do you think you are? This could be the death of you. Do you know that?*

The church lady pushed down the insidious questions that made her back hurt and her knees ache. *Could she even stand up when she tried?*

Chase was waiting for something. For her. For something. She held up one hand as if to signal, 'wait.'

Accustomed to being ignored, the boy shifted into a time out that looked like waiting, but it was something else. Something worse. She vowed to herself in that moment that she would not be holding up her hand like that in the future. While making this calculated, deliberate decision, Mildred stood up. Of course, she could stand up! She led the way to the living room, hoping he would follow her. He did. Going to the *No Peeking* mystery box, she fished around inside it for what she remembered.

Opening the gallon size Ziploc bag, she poured the pieces of Legos on the floor at Chase's feet and dropped down beside him. Arranging her legs to be as comfortable as possible—and that was harder than others knew—she began to connect one Lego to another, asking in the tone of voice she hadn't used since the last time she was with him—and before that mostly with fifth graders she had taught: "What do you think we can make with these?"

While Chase sat in silence before her, she let her eyes smile. Pretending it didn't matter whether he helped or not, she continued to play with the Legos, trying one end against another, murmuring, "Let's see. Let's see. What have we got here?"

His eyes watched her. His body remained stiff and still. Fifteen minutes later, he shifted his weight. His hand finally reached for a piece on the floor. Chase held it up to her as if to ask permission to touch it. She nodded *yes*, blinking back tears.

She handed him the pieces in her hands and said, "Do you want to try?"

He took the Lego pieces from her and began to fashion a shape not unlike something she had crocheted years ago when her Aunt Betty had taught her how to hold the hook and handle the thread. While learning, so engaged was she by the rhythmic movement of working the needle and the comforting positions of her hands, Mildred Budge had once upon a time crocheted a long, long piece of cloth that had no purpose other than to grow longer while she learned the skill. In that moment, the boy was simply learning how to put one Lego piece with another and discover the satisfying sensation of two pieces connecting and a shape beginning to emerge.

Pushing herself back so that she could lean against the recliner for support, Mildred stretched out her legs and watched the boy teach himself to play with Legos. The voice that had tried to tell her that she was stuck, trapped, and too old died inside of her, and she did what she was really good at doing: she waited for a child to finish playing and look up to her for the answer to the inevitable question: *What's next?*

Time passed. Mildred Budge grew older. The phone rang again and was ignored again. Someone tapped on the back door. She did not answer it either.

In that moment the only person who had her attention was the boy.

The boy was losing fear and self-consciousness. Tension in his face was easing. Fear in his eyes was fading.

After a spell, when it appeared he needed something to drink, she asked him, "Would you like some lunch?"

He stood up immediately as if she had commanded him, and she wondered at that. She had only meant to determine if he was hungry again. Chase waited for her to rise, which was awkward. She turned and got on her knees and, using both hands on the seat of the recliner, she heaved herself up, the insistent chant of an old, old voice starting up again. *You're too old for this. You don't have it any longer. Not the energy. Not the youth. Not the strength. And, old girl, deep down you don't really have the desire to give this much of yourself to anyone else and that includes a neglected child, because you don't love others as much as you love yourself. Not really. So much of who you are is an act that you try to hide inside silence, but I see. Others know too. You're a fraud.*

By the time she was on her feet Mildred had heard many fearful accusing words, and when she turned to face Chase, her eyes clouded. A new kind of prayer formed deep inside of her, way below where the blessing prayers lived. Deep inside of her, a knee-buckling moan of a prayer for this boy and his parents, too, began, and she did not quench it. Mildred let the groaning prayer come anyway, masking the moment the way suffering church ladies do when they are trying to put one foot in front of the other to run the race assigned to them by saying brightly, "Let's have a good lunch."

Before she could figure out what that lunch would be, someone pounded on her front door. Insistently.

Chase came and stood beside her, his eyes growing opaque.

"Who do you suppose that could be?" she asked. But the possible answer hung in the air between them. His parents had come back for him. *What would she do? What do you say?* As if reading her mind, Chase moved behind her.

The pounding happened again, but this time, a man's voice called out, "Mildred, are you in there? It's me. Mark."

Mildred reached down and patted Chase on the shoulder. "This will just take a second," she promised. "And then I'm going to fry us some doughnuts for lunch." She had not planned to make doughnuts. It had been years. But hot homemade doughnuts for a Sunday lunch sounded just right. "You will glaze them. It's a skill they don't teach Boy Scouts, and they should. Doughnuts are our friend."

"Mildred!" He pounded again.

"I am afraid he might break the door down if I don't answer it. Do you want to stand here or over there?"

Chase didn't move. The pounding scared him. The determined church lady had no choice but to put a stop to that noise immediately.

Mark pretended not to understand what her body language meant. He stepped through easily, brushing her aside. "What is going on? I've been calling. I came by earlier, and you didn't answer."

Before she could lift her arm and point to Chase whose eyes were wide with alarm, Mark demanded, "Who's this?"

"Chase," she replied simply.

"What's he doing here?" he asked sharply.

She heartily resented his asking the question. She kept her reply to a minimum. "His parents dropped him off last night. He will be staying with me for a while."

Mark's head began to shake. "You're a good woman, Mildred, but I hope you are not letting someone take advantage of your good nature."

He eyed the boy suspiciously. "But you're okay then. Other than having company, you're okay."

"Oh. He's not company. Chase is family. I was so very glad to see him," Mildred said, as Mark eyed her and looked around the room to see if anyone else was with them.

"I meant the guy who left here earlier. The black guy who kissed you in the doorway before he left. The friend of the preacher. Why did he leave here so early in the morning? What was that guy doing here so early?"

"What were you doing watching my house so early in the morning?"

Mark pulled his shoulders back defensively and enunciated his words carefully. "I wasn't watching your house per se. I was running a few errands and thought I'd check on you—just coasting by really, but it was a bad time, because that black guy was taking his time leaving. He lingered with you, Mildred, and you were speaking very intimately."

"He had a question he wanted to ask me. I listened to him."

Mark did not like that answer. He drew back further. "I thought you were a decent church lady—the kind that...."

"The kind that does what?"

"The kind that would be glad to have a very eligible man show some interest in her."

Mildred smiled easily. "I am glad for anyone to show a friendly interest in me."

That eased his tension some.

"So you can't go out to supper tonight unless you bring him?"

"Chase and I already have plans," Mildred said, moving toward the front door. She held it back for Mark. "But thanks for coming by. And for taking a friendly interest in me."

Mark left grudgingly, his steps slow as he tried to think of what he could say next that would move his plan forward. But he left in silence, walking sullenly to his station wagon parked too close to her car in the driveway.

As soon as the door was locked, Chase joined her again, staring at the closed door.

"I didn't ask him to stay for doughnuts because I didn't want to," she explained truthfully. "That's Mark Gardiner, and he wasn't at his best today," she said.

"Tosser," Chase replied matter of factly, turning toward the kitchen. He wanted his hot doughnuts.

Part 3
The Bride's Room

"No one sings a love song like a Berean."

Mildred Budge

28
TIME TO DELIVER THE CAKES

On the day before Fran's wedding, Mildred Budge woke up at ease, relaxed, her body stretching into an X as arms reached up and legs stretched out. She held the pose and released it, examining the ceiling above for hairline cracks. Her world was holding together. Breathing a sigh of gratitude, she wriggled up, her morning prayer starting inside of her and coming out as she stretched her toes and feet out toward the floor before she put her weight on them.

Today, they were going to take the wedding cake to the church. Part one of the two-part drama called Fran's wedding cake delivery plan was going to get accomplished.

It was still early. Absolute silence reigned in the house—the moment! Mildred let herself revel in the quiet for the moment and then the next. Chase was still asleep. No one outside was running a weed-eater or a blower. She smiled and went to the kitchen and performed her morning ritual of switching on the coffeemaker and then taking an inventory of the room. It was clean and tidy. The tools she needed for the day were organized. The shopping bags and Rubbermaid container were ready to be used. She took her pink and grey mug with the first morning coffee to the sun porch, where she could hear Chase when he roused.

When her boy wandered into the kitchen forty-five minutes later, she was prayed up and already dressed. Mildred poured him a bowl of Cheerios and sat across from him while he ate. His light brown hair had grown out and would soon need to be trimmed. She was thinking of buying a barber's kit and learning how to cut a boy's hair. It didn't seem complicated. He was filling out too—not just from eating. He was filling out with a sense of security. The look of fear was mostly gone.

"This is the day, Chase," Mildred said, with contentment. "This is the day that the Lord hath made, and this is the day we take the cakes to the church for the wedding tomorrow."

"What cake?" he asked, without looking up. "Didn't we eat all the cake?"

"Not all of it," she assured him. "Are you tired of cake?"

He considered the question and shook his head. "I don't know," he replied.

Mildred had a different answer. She did know. She was tired of thinking about cake. But she didn't say those words. She said, "After your breakfast, we're going over to the church quietly, Chase. Just you and I. First, to be on the safe side, we are going to take the chocolate groom's cake over and place it in the church refrigerator."

For after Mildred had offered to make the bride's cake, she did not see a way that she could not bake a groom's cake too. *What would Winston think? His sister Jeanne? And the people who loved chocolate? Wouldn't they feel forgotten?* A proper maid of honor did not let wedding guests feel forgotten. If you are going to make a bride's cake, you must finish the race before you and make a groom's cake too.

Mildred did not say all of that to Chase. Catching her breath, she continued, "Then, we're coming back here, just the two of us, and take the bride's cake over. If no one tries to help us, we can get it done."

Chase nodded, as if he understood the implications. Then, pushing his empty cereal bowl away from him, he stood and walked out to the sun porch window and peered out, looking for Sam. Like a forlorn grammar schooler, Chase waited for his buddy, and sometimes when Sam was looking for something he couldn't name, he ended up digging in the dirt outside with Chase.

More than once Sam had brought a football over to try and teach the boy how to throw and kick, but Chase did not have an interest in throwing or catching any kind of a ball. No matter what Sam had said or tried to demonstrate, when the ball came at him, Chase simply stepped aside and let it hit the ground with a thud. Sam gave up, and then when he forgot he had given up, Sam brought the ball over again. History repeated itself. But no harm was done.

Mildred had baked the chocolate groom's cake the day before and had layers for the bride's cake on the counter waiting to be frosted. She eyed them possessively as she ushered Chase out the front door with the groom's cake carefully wrapped in cellophane and situated on a sturdy cardboard circle that professional cake bakers used. She had found a package of them at Hobby Lobby.

"Have you got the grapes?" she asked Chase, who nodded affirmatively.

They were red seedless grapes, and he was carrying a pound of them in a Ziplock bag. Like Southern women everywhere who are schooled in trying to enlist the interest of a bored male, Mildred heard herself speaking brightly to keep the boy moving. "The Bereans will decorate the refreshment table. All we have to do is deliver the groom's cake and the bride's cake."

Before she could finish saying, "You could place your hand on the front of the cardboard and keep the cake centered on the seat," the boy had climbed into the backseat of the car with the grapes.

"Okay. Okay," she agreed. "That's a good way to do it, too," Mildred approved.

Mildred had the car keys in her pocket and positioned herself behind the steering wheel. It wasn't a far drive to the church. The list of chores to be accomplished and outfits laid out and baths to be had and more prayers to be said unscrolled in front of her. With her right foot on the gas pedal, she hesitated-- almost didn't press it.

There were moments like that now when Mildred was about to head off in the direction of her destination and just stopped. Waited. She went through her check list again. One item after another was named, prayed over, and then nodded over.

Finally, her foot moved. Her car responded. Slowly, Fran's maid of honor wended her way to the church, muttering to Jesus, "I may be too old for all of this."

She repeated her plan out loud, as much to reassure herself as to remind Chase. "All we need to do is get this chocolate cake inside, store it on the bottom shelf of the big refrigerator in the back-storage room next to the pantry—not the sister fridge in the kitchen where everybody puts their stuff-- and come back for the white cake. The bride's cake is not assembled yet. Because it's bigger, we are going to take over the layers, stack and frost the layers on the table from where it will be served, and cover it loosely until tomorrow. We're on the home stretch now. It will all work out, Chase, my boy," Mildred promised, more to herself than to Chase, who had become silent.

When Chase didn't answer her, she looked over her shoulder to see if he had fallen asleep. He had not. He was eating the red grapes she had bought to decorate the groom's cake.

29
LET WEDDING BELLS RING!

Not a problem. Not a problem. Not a problem. The words chanted inside of her.

"The grapes aren't really necessary. They were just for decoration. Eat all the grapes you want," Mildred said, as she realized there weren't enough grapes left to put in front of the groom's cake. All right. So be it. If she needed to stop at the grocery store later for anything, she'd buy another bunch of grapes. "Do you want to just wait in the car? I won't be in there long."

Rather than answer in words, Chase left the rest of the straggling grapes and the small spiky, naked vine on the plastic bag they had been stored in, wiggled through the space between the driver's seat and the open door, and climbed out.

"We're going to carry the cake in that direction. So, when I get close to the church door, if you will open it, that'd be great."

Mildred carefully lifted the groom's cake, holding it steady, hoping the layers secured with thick chocolate cooked frosting had set enough so that they wouldn't slide. Chase walked along beside her, and when they reached the back door, he stopped.

"Do you want to open the door?" she prompted.

Chase thought about it and then slowly, slowly gripped the door knob and twisted. Slowly, slowly the boy opened the creaking door and held it with both hands while Mildred passed through.

Inside, she turned and beckoned him, "You can come on in too. We're headed to the kitchen."

She began to repeat herself. "The other cake is in layers. Individual layers because it is bigger and won't transport as easily as this one does," Mildred said, huffing. The lights were off in the building, and the church lady led the way through the shadows—no free hand to find the light switch.

The chocolate cake was awkward to hold. Her chest felt tight, and she was pretty sure that the cake had hit her once in the left bosom. Though there was a big piece of cellophane wrap around it, she feared the frosting had been smudged. To distract herself from this concern, she kept talking to Chase, "I've got a big bowl of buttercream icing already made up. And it is really good. It's got butter, cream, lots of powdered sugar, and a hint of vanilla but not cherry. I thought about cherry and almond flavorings, Chase, but I decided that sometimes flavorings like that don't set well over time. Sometimes that cherry flavoring leaves an aftertaste. We don't want an aftertaste, do we?"

She looked at him, but Chase was thinking other thoughts. Mildred wondered what they were and if she would ever know him well enough to be able to read his mind.

The kitchen was dark, but Mildred did not switch on the light. She knew the way, and Chase was following her fine. She opened the fridge door and a light came on. That was enough light to see to situate the cake safely inside. "We're almost done here," she assured Chase, shifting the cake onto the lowest shelf.

Holding the cake steady with one hand she extracted the shelf above it, and said, "Chase, could you come take this other shelf?"

He didn't hear her.

Somehow, though it shouldn't have been possible, Mildred was able to wedge the cake into the fridge while wiggling the top shelf out. The groom's cake fit snugly into the big refrigerator. "Okay, we're headed home to get the other cake. And then, Chase it's just fun time until dinner tonight. We're going to have our baths and relax and lay out our clothes for the wedding tomorrow. Everything's going to be fine. Tomorrow is the big day, and this whole wedding adventure will be over."

"Right-o," he agreed. "Everything's tickety-boo."

Mildred eyed Chase curiously and nodded. He didn't speak often, but when he finally succumbed to the tension of offering an opinion it often had words like tickety-boo in it.

Back at the house, they loaded the car, with Mildred reciting and repeating nervously the instructions for what was about to happen next. "We're going to take the bride's cake over in layers and assemble it there. I'm going to frost it in the church kitchen, and we'll position it on the reception table. It doesn't need to be refrigerated, which is good because there isn't any more room in the big fridge. The one in the kitchen is very popular. Lots of people go in to that refrigerator in the kitchen. If we tried to store it in that fridge, we'd just be asking for trouble."

She had a big tall Rubbermaid box to transport the layers of cake, the big bowl of frosting, and the wedding bell topper she had bought from one of the other vendors at the Emporium. Who doesn't like wedding bells?

She handed the silver bells to Chase. "Will you carry the bells?"

Chase nodded, looking past her to Sam's house. *Where was his buddy?*

And just that quick, Sam materialized out of nowhere and called out. "Where are you two kids going?"

Chase waved at Sam with the hand that held the bells, and they made a high tinkling cheerful sound. Sam trotted towards the boy.

"What's going on?" Sam asked. "Trouble's coming. I can feel it," he said, looking around.

"Not today, Sam," Mildred replied. "We're not talking about trouble, and there isn't going to be any trouble today. Trouble is not allowed today."

"What's in that box?" Sam asked, distracted.

"The layers for the wedding cake that the guests will eat tomorrow," Mildred replied tightly. "We're not eating this cake today, Sam. It's for the wedding tomorrow."

"I hope it's better than that last cake you made. That last cake was sour."

How could he remember some things and not others?

Before Mildred could make herself repress that question and the clues about human reasoning evidenced in Sam's conversation, Dixie turned the corner, riding a girl's pink bike. It was too small for her legs. Her knees jutted out awkwardly, but she had a blissful smile on her face, which was slightly tilted up toward the sun.

Dixie pedaled up beside the three of them while the car door was still open and asked brightly, "Where are yawl going?" Dixie was wearing her leprechaun outfit: green Bermuda shorts, green suspenders, white long sleeve shirt, white knee socks, and brown leather sandals.

"Chase and I are about to race Mildred to the church. She's fussing about a cake. I know a shortcut," Sam bragged. "Come on, Buddy. I'll show you a secret way."

"I know one too. Last one there is a rotten egg," Dixie challenged.

Off Dixie went pedaling on the bike, while Sam tugged at Chase's arm to follow him back across the field through what was his personal shortcut to the church.

The last thing Mildred heard Sam say was, "This way, Buddy. It's the best way."

And just that quick, Mildred was left alone by her car with the Rubbermaid box containing her special spatula, a round cardboard cake stand, the five white cake layers, and a huge container of icing. Ahead of her were Dixie, Chase with wedding bells in his hand ringing as he ran, and Sam talking nonstop as the three of them raced off together.

Mildred drove to the church alone. She parked close to the back door that led to the kitchen and looked around for Sam, Dixie, or Chase to help her get the cake inside. They were over in the children's playground rocking up and down on the teeter totter. Sam was on one end, and Dixie and Chase were on the other side. Mildred could hear the tinkling of bells. Fran's wedding bells sat dead center in the middle of the teeter totter.

"Don't mind me," Mildred muttered, picking up the box with the cake layers.

The next trip to the car, Mildred fetched the icing and utensils needed to assemble the cake. Inside, she washed her hands, walked over to the window on the side of the fellowship hall, and saw that they were all three still out in the playground. They had moved on to the swing set.

"If I work fast, I could do this alone," she plotted quickly, eyes darting.

Placing the cardboard circle in the center of the big refreshment table, Mildred moved the first layer onto it, and though the icing had thickened, a few drizzles of Half and Half softened it. Mildred slathered the first layer in icing. She added the next layer and frosted it, and the next layer, repeating the process. She watched the icing bowl to make sure the amount of frosting was enough. It should have been. Mildred had doubled the frosting recipe.

Finally, she smothered the top of the cake with white icing and frosted the sides, using the metal spatula just the way she had taught herself to do after watching more than one cooking show on the food channel. She had paid eleven dollars for the special spatula. And when she finished, the church lady concluded, "A butter knife works just as well as this thing."

When she was finished, Mildred stepped back and surveyed her masterpiece. It was a tall, fat, tasty, gleaming worthy-of-Fran-and-Winston white wedding cake.

She forgot about the wedding bells and covered the cake in big sheets of loosely placed tin foil, switched the light off in the room, and said contentedly. "Job done. Now where's my boy?"

30
TROUBLE'S COMIN'

On Fran's wedding day Mildred Budge woke up as she had the day before—relaxed and expectant. She was stretching awake, making the big X in the bed with her body, reaching up and out with her hands and feet while sorting her thoughts, when the phone rang. It wasn't seven o'clock yet. The phone shouldn't be ringing. No good news came before eight in the morning.

Mildred grabbed it before the second ring so it wouldn't wake Chase.

She knew the voice. It was Anne Henry. "Mildred, we've got trouble."

"Anne?" Mildred said her friend's name while her attention began to roam the list of other friends on the current prayer sheet. *Which one had died in the night? Whose funeral was already being planned?*

"Mildred?" Anne Henry whispered. "Are you there?"

"How bad is it?" Mildred asked quietly. "Who has died?" She asked, her voice a whisper. *Trouble was coming.* Sam was right.

"I hate to be the messenger. You know what happens to messengers who have bad news?"

Mildred pressed her right hand over her heart and closed her eyes, waiting for the answer. "Who died?"

"Your cake died. The girls and I got here a few minutes ago to start arranging the flowers and set up the reception table, and your sweet wedding cake was dropped."

"I used tin foil," Mildred said stupidly, as her heart sank.

"It's done for, Mildred. Just an old-fashioned mess," Anne Henry declared and then she went quiet. Anne Henry was thinking. A lot of church ladies stopped what they were doing to think. Other people wrongly assessed that silence or inactivity as slowness due to age, but they were only thinking, and that's what it looks like.

"Anything salvageable?" Mildred asked, though she knew the answer. There are just some questions you have to ask.

"No. I have already thrown it away. There was nothing else to be done," Anne explained.

"No wedding cake," Mildred said, as she heard Chase rouse in his room. She knew his routine. He would be looking for her soon. He liked Cheerios. So, did Sam.

"I still have my boy to feed and get dressed. And I've got to get me dressed. I promised to meet Fran there at 1:30. I can't bake another cake. I don't have it in me, Anne. And I don't know what to do. We just won't have a wedding cake."

That was all Anne Henry needed to hear. Her voice grew stronger. "Don't you worry about it. The Bereans will handle it. We can handle any emergency, and we can handle this. A piece of cake," she said with a quick giggle.

"Good. Because I am fresh out of cake," Mildred replied. She hung up the phone and swung her legs over the side of the bed. Before her feet touched the floor, she prayed. Breathed in. Breathed out. "I only know the problem. I don't know the answer. Don't need water changed into wine. Just need cake," she prayed. The church lady left it at that.

Chase was sitting at the kitchen table with a bowl of Cheerios, and Sam was beside him eating his bowl of cereal too.

"Good morning, boys," Mildred said, with resolve. She waited for Sam to say "Trouble's coming. I can feel it." But Sam just ate his Cheerios, slurping the milk while some of it dribbled down the front of his woebegone shirt.

"Chase, how'd you sleep?"

The boy studied her, holding a spoon of cereal in the air. "Why do you ask me that every morning? I sleep the same way every night. I sleep in a bed." And then Chase took the next bite.

Sam muttered over his cereal. "Buddy, you might as well get used to the questions ladies ask." And then Sam poured himself a second bowl of cereal. "You're low on milk, Millie," he said.

Mildred stared at the empty coffee pot, clutching the front of her robe with one hand while she wondered what the Bereans were doing about the cake problem. She brushed aside the mystery and the problem. She said with conviction, "Fran's getting married, and it going to be a beautiful day. Let's rejoice and be glad in it."

31
THE BRIDE'S ROOM

Mildred couldn't decide whether to stand or sit in the bride's room. The skirt of her sunset dress was full and pretty. She was afraid when she sat down on a chair or the couch wrinkles would happen on her backside. The maid of honor didn't want to stand next to her best friend the bride in front of all of her friends with a wrinkled backside.

Mildred had been in the room many times before, mostly to take her turn in the prayer chair. Taking her turn in the prayer chair was one of Mildred's favorite times of the year. A solitary duty, the volunteer of the day prayed for the service and for all in the building while the service occurred on the other side of the door. So, most times, the small room was called the prayer parlor. But for weddings, when the bride was waiting to walk down the aisle or simply join her groom in front of the preacher in the fellowship hall with long-time friends standing all around, it was called the bride's room.

While Mildred had spent many an hour in the prayer parlor by herself, she had never been present as a maid of honor with the bride. The heavy wooden door was closed tightly. Unlike Sunday mornings when Mildred reveled in the solitude and absolute quiet, that afternoon prior to the ceremony Mildred felt trapped by the confinement.

"So how do I look?" Fran asked for the third time. Mildred had already admired the silver polish on Fran's nails and the small bit of white netting Fran had used on her head instead of a long draped veil. The netting set at a slant and was kind of jaunty--saucy, like Fran.

"Perfect," Mildred replied simply. Truthfully.

Fran had bought an old-fashioned pale blue tea-length dress that fell in gentle folds to just above her ankles. Fran had become suddenly shy when showing the dress to Mildred, for it was unequivocally girlish, feminine, with small seed pearls at the waist, and a youthful heart-shaped neckline which framed Fran's face.

"Is it too young?" Fran had asked, and before Mildred could finish shaking her head, Fran had answered herself, "Who cares? It was the dress for me. This dress makes me look how I want to look on my wedding day. My turn's not over, and neither is yours. I've still got *it,* and so do you," Fran declared emphatically.

"It is the perfect dress for you," Mildred had agreed.

That morning, the two old friends had dressed independently in her own home, and Mildred, who had entrusted Chase to Belle and Sam, had driven over and picked up Fran to take her to the church and sneak her in the side door to the bride's room.

Once the bride was in the room, the chamber was sacrosanct. The groom was forbidden to enter. Even longtime friends knew to find a seat out in the fellowship hall, where Fran had requested her wedding happen at 3 PM on a Saturday afternoon so that her wedding flowers could be moved to the sanctuary for morning worship. "Waste not. Want not," she had explained to Steev, who thanked her for planning her wedding so that the flowers could be used on Sunday morning, too. It saved the church the expense of providing them for the Sunday service.

And the flowers would have a third purpose. On Monday, Bonnie and the other Berean gals would divide them up and take them to shut-ins who couldn't come to church. The delivery of Monday morning flowers told the truth: friends were always dearly missed on Sunday.

Fran had expressly asked that Bonnie send the first of the wedding flowers to the long-time friends on her list who couldn't come to her wedding. And then Fran had asked Bonnie a question. "Don't you think our friends would like one of these crocheted cross bookmarks for their Bibles?"

"Oh, yes. Oh, yes," Bonnie had agreed, taking the delicate crosses as if they were a bag of jewels to be given to their good friends.

Bonnie had taken one soft white delicate crocheted cross out of the bag. Smoothing it out gently and with eyes gleaming in appreciation, Bonnie examined the workmanship. "Exquisite handiwork," she had said. "The bookmark crosses will go out with the flowers to your special friends who can't attend the wedding."

Both Fran and Mildred had their long-time friends on their hearts that morning, when this rumination was interrupted by a rapping on the door.

"Bereans only," Fran called out. Her voice sounded sharper than she intended. The bride was nervous.

Mildred wondered why no one had brought Fran and her a pot of steaming, sugary tea with some shortbread cookies when Anne Henry opened the door and stuck her head in.

Anne Henry whispered, "Girls, it's just me."

"Do we have cake?" Mildred asked, hurrying to the door.

"Oh, sure," Anne Henry said, stepping through. She was slightly disheveled, her face free of make-up except for lipstick, and her signature shade of creamy autumn rose was mostly worn off. Anne was working in the kitchen and the fellowship hall. She wore a thick yellow apron that tied behind her neck and at the waist. There was a new message on it that one of the younger women had insisted upon. *Church Girls Stand on the Rock!* Anne wore the message gracefully, her hands fidgeting briefly behind her to check the knot of the apron.

"Boy, do we have cake," she said with a quick smile. It was a polite smile, a real smile, but it hid something: that wasn't the message Anne Henry had come to give. "You both look just great."

"We don't look better than you do," Fran said. "And thank you for helping. I mean it. Thank you."

Anne waved away the gratitude. A church lady to her core, Anne replied mischievously, "This apron just screams fashion."

Fran and Mildred nodded in sync. They knew Anne Henry had something to tell them, and they were waiting. They didn't have to wait for long.

"I just wanted to give you two girls a heads up." Anne chose her next words very carefully. "Liz Luckie is wearing a black dress. A very smart black dress."

Silence ensued as the ladies considered their tactful and most loving responses. No Berean worth the name ever said anything mean-spirited about another church lady; and in the prayer parlor or the bride's room, she did not even allow herself to think words of condemnation.

Mildred broke the silence, relieving Fran of the burden of trying to think of something generous to say. "Liz is a widow. Thinking of her own losses, perhaps she has decided to wear mourning colors."

"Liz also looks really good in black," Anne Henry remarked. Her right hand brushed against the side of the apron, trying to wipe off something sticky. "Other women don't wear white on a wedding day in order to avoid competing for attention with the bride, but no one has ever actually said don't wear black."

"I think I have heard of black and white weddings," Fran said, ruminatively.

"Whatever the reason, I just wanted to let you know, heads are turning."

Anne stole a quick glance at herself in the mirror and patted her hair. But it was only a stalling technique, giving Fran and Mildred time to consider their response.

"Do we have to care today?" Fran said, finally.

Both women shook their heads adamantly.

"It's just strange is all. Liz has had a lot of attention. Why does she need more?" Anne Henry asked, but it was a rhetorical question. She would quickly join Fran's camp of 'Do I have to care what she is wearing and why?'

"Let Liz have her moment, if she needs a moment like that," Mildred agreed. "Thanks for the alert, Anne. The sight of Liz in widow's weeds might have startled us if we hadn't been prepared."

Anne should have backed out right then, but there was more to say.

"That's not all," Anne said, and her gaze was rueful. She was no longer looking at Fran. She was looking at Mildred.

"We have another small matter that requires sensitivity. The call that went out for needed wedding cakes reached sweet Dixie, and she has brought what she is naming very proudly as a Hunky Dory Groom's Cake."

"But I made a groom's cake," Mildred interjected quickly. "I made it for Winston. A beautiful chocolate cake. I forgot to check the fridge, which is where I put it. The grapes are gone."

"We found that chocolate cake, Millie, and it was fine. Nobody dropped it. Nobody would have dared. But the problem, Mildred, is that Dixie is very proud of her Hunky Dory Groom's Cake."

Mildred understood the question before Anne Henry could ask it. "You want to leave my groom's cake where it is in the fridge and let Dixie's Hunky Dory Groom's Cake have the spotlight on the refreshment table."

"It will, whether you bring your cake out or not. It's that kind of cake."

Fran had heard the story of the fallen bride's cake and was sensitive to Mildred's position. "You made your chocolate cake for Winston?" Fran asked, stepping closer to Mildred. She didn't want her best friend's feelings hurt. "Is Dixie's cake chocolate?"

"Oh, it's chocolate all right," Anne said, stifling a grin. "Dixie bought four dozen chocolate cake doughnuts with rainbow sprinkles and has arranged them in a kind of tier.

"A doughnut cake with sprinkles," Mildred concluded.

"It's actually kind of impressive. Unusual. But festive. Dixie said her cake is low maintenance. No one needs to slice and hand out her cake. People can just take a rainbow-sprinkle doughnut. A couple of the children and Sam already have. It still looks fine, though—more like a tower than a tier. But, it's the Hunky Dory Groom's Cake."

Fran and Mildred grinned. Fran shrugged first.

"Leave my cake in the fridge. We'll send it somewhere later."

"Do you want me to take care of that?" Anne Henry asked immediately. "We are not short of people who like to take away cake from a wedding."

Mildred waved her hands. "My best friend's getting married. Let anybody who wants some cake take that chocolate cake."

Anne waved, backing out of the room, and just before she closed the door, she whispered with a quick grin, "Winston is a perfect dream, Fran. Go get him."

32
STEEV HAS A PROPOSAL

Seconds after the door closed and while both Fran and Mildred could hear Anne's footsteps as she hurried back to the fellowship hall, a second rapping occurred.

"Bereans only!" Fran called out again. She had just discovered that the polish on her ring finger was chipped. She was considering a quick repair when the knocking occurred a second time.

"Ladies, it's Steev. And I would love to be included in your Berean class, but you discriminate against me because I am a man."

"Sweet talking won't work today, Steev. No men allowed!" Mildred called out good naturedly.

A church lady of the South did not get to say those words very often. So often, the opposite was true. There were meetings and responsibilities where only men were allowed to be heard. That didn't really matter to people who lived freely; but on special days when a big change was about to happen, a church lady might call out those words even to the preacher.

"It's bad luck to see the preacher before the wedding," Fran added automatically.

"We don't believe in luck," Mildred said.

The back and forth jibes did not stop the door from moving slowly open. They saw Steev's fingers wrapped around the door, but he didn't push it open—not all the way. Steev stood respectfully with the door cracked, and his head bowed while he waited for the ladies to relent. He knew they would. They knew they would. But they wanted to be coaxed.

"Even though I'm technically not a Berean, I am also not the groom," Steev reminded them. "And I don't believe in luck either."

Mildred walked over and opened the door, blocking his view of Fran with her body. She whispered, "Winston hasn't run off, has he?"

Steev smiled. "You know better than that. Could I talk to Fran for a minute?"

Mildred stepped back. Steev wouldn't be disturbing them if he didn't have a good reason.

Steev stepped inside and closed the door behind him. Fran didn't have her shoes on, and Mildred felt her discomfort. Bare feet! And then she smiled. He was Steev, and it was all right to be caught barefoot.

"Miss Fran, you look just like yourself."

A calm entered Fran's gaze as she patted Steev's forearm. That pat was the real welcome. Everything else was just Southern chit-chat. "You haven't let my boy run away, have you?"

"Winston's not going anywhere without you, Our Fran." Sometimes Steev used the word "our" instead of "Miss" or "Mrs."

Mildred found it very endearing. The names on the prayer list issued each week didn't have that word, but when Mildred prayed for the sick, she said, "Our Lydia," "Our Sam," and "Our Dixie."

If Steev had been wearing a hat, he would have been holding it like a respectful supplicant in his hands. Instead, his eyes wore the humility and need that one didn't see often in a preacher's face. Oh, humility and need existed inside preachers, but they learned to look stronger than they were for the sake of the congregation that depended upon them so heavily. It was one of their greatest sacrifices of pastoral care—to hide their own vulnerabilities in order to help others feel safer and reassured. In that moment, Steev looked humble, young, and determined.

Both Mildred and Fran were moved by his presence.

"I know this is your day, and I know only a little bit about how brides are about weddings, but I have this impulse—a leading but I hate to call it that—that there are other couples gathering in the church who need to be reminded of the vows they made to one another way back when. Sometimes during a ceremony, witnesses standing with you think of those vows while they are hearing the wedding couple exchange theirs. But they are stuck—frozen in place by good manners and protocol. They can't say anything. It isn't their turn to talk, and they need another turn to talk. They need to say 'I'm sorry. I have forgotten I love you.' They can't say any of the words they might need to say and want to say during the vows. And then, there's something that happens at the end of a marriage ceremony. When the couple has said 'I do' and is proclaimed 'Married' those people in the audience—the silent witnesses lose their conviction—lose the moment and their resolve to say what they would have said if they could have been given just a small chance to tell the truth while they were knowing it and were soft enough in their souls to speak love out loud. That's what a vow of love can be. Just a small way of telling the truth that you love someone."

Fran nodded while Mildred listened. Fran was in love with Winston, and she understood. Mildred loved everyone she knew, and she listened, too.

Steev continued, "Often—more than once Our Fran-- I see on the faces of witnesses to weddings regret, disappointment, and a growing bitterness."

"You see all that?" Mildred asked. Until that instant she thought that only church ladies saw the history of people's love lives in the faces of the walking wounded at weddings and funerals and grocery stores.

"I have known a very deep love," Fran injected. "And I know it again. I know what you're saying, Steev."

For the first time Mildred had a start that she really couldn't understand married people—not even Fran, because she did not know where Steev was going with this conversation and Fran, the bride who was leaving behind widowhood because she had fallen in love, grasped his coming proposal instantly.

"I wanted to ask you..." Steev said, with a plea for forgiveness in his young and hopeful eyes.

"You wanted to ask me if you could invite any other couples in hearing distance to join us and renew their vows while Winston and I exchange ours," Fran stated bluntly.

Her hands dropped to her side, the chipped nail polish forgotten. Fran's knuckles were tinged with red, and the skin of her palms was thick from working with them.

Fran Applewhite was a church lady of the South dressed up as a bride, and she knew how much work being in love could be. Her hands proved it.

Steev's face was sober—more sober than it might have been at a funeral.

Fran smiled to encourage Steev. She wasn't offended, Mildred saw. She was just diplomatic and thoughtful.

"Have you asked Winston about this?"

"Winston told me to ask you."

"Ask the whole world to join us. As long as Winston Holmes is standing beside me, I don't care who is beside us saying the same words."

Steev the preacher kissed Fran, first on one cheek and then on the other. And then he took her right hand that already had the small chip on the nail polish on the ring finger. "You are the most beautiful bride I have ever seen in my whole life. One day I hope to find a woman who knows how to love the way you do." And in a sudden surge of supernatural grace, he added deferentially and with affection, "You, too, Our Mildred Budge."

Then Steev turned to Mildred. "Pray for me, Mildred, that I can make the invitation so that broken marriages can get healed instantly today. Instantly." And the same feverish gaze that showed up from time to time when he was preaching zealously came alive in his lit-up eyes.

Mildred had seen it from time to time in the eyes of men and women who were suddenly and inexplicably lit up. Steev was lit up. In the church, people knew what that was. Outside the church, they called that light something else. Mildred Budge was a church lady through and through, and she called it holy.

With purpose and conviction, Steev closed the door softly behind him.

"Do you mind?" Mildred asked, after the door was securely closed.

"I don't mind a thing in this world," Fran said. "I have everything there is to be had, and I am completely satisfied. Other people having what I have or being reminded that they do can't take anything away from me. There's a lot to be said for saying something out loud. It's kind of holds you accountable. Until you say it out loud, it's really just an idea in your head."

Fran was talking to herself and Mildred. And she wasn't thinking about Mildred not having words to say out loud that would hold her accountable in the name of Love. The two old friends didn't keep count or take offense.

"You don't have anybody to walk you down the aisle."

"I'm giving myself away."

"Me, too," Mildred replied automatically. "I've got Chase and Janie coming and Little Mister is on his way."

"That dress looks like you." And in a sudden moment of inspired affection, Fran said, "Wearing the sunset like that, Millie, you look free as a bird!"

And that was the last sentence Fran said to her best friend Mildred Budge before she walked down the aisle and took her place beside Winston Holmes.

33
ALWAYS

Mildred looked around the room of people standing as Fran entered. Such good friends everywhere! Her heart smiled before her face did. And there was Chase standing between Sam and Belle. Belle's face was tight. Sam's gaze was roaming, unfixed, first the room, then the ceiling. *The sky is falling. Trouble's coming.* And then Sam saw Mildred, and it seemed like he didn't recognize her—his attention fluid-- but she nodded in a friendly fashion anyway.

Belle reached out and gripped Sam's shoulder, but he ignored it. And then Chase saw Mildred and started walking. With people milling, people standing, people sitting in the chairs positioned around the fellowship room, Chase walked in a straight line across the floor and stood next to his Mildred. Chase got as close as he could up against her side and took a deep breath. He was home.

Mildred put an arm around his shoulders and held him, lightly. Jake was a witness, and he smiled and nodded in her direction. *How ya doing?* She nodded back: *Doing fine. It's almost over. Praise the Lord.* He pointed toward her dress and made an okay sign. Then, he mouthed the one word, "Pretty." Mildred smiled, resisting the urge to grab both sides of the generous skirt and stretch it out and prove *'this dress can twirl, and so can I'.*

When the idea surfaced in Mildred's consciousness, she stifled a laugh. *We are all such silly people.* And thinking that, Mildred saw Dixie standing by herself in the back corner, looking like she didn't belong. But she did belong.

And then Mildred saw Liz dressed in black. The dress was something Coco Chanel would have loved, and though inspired by the reputation of a little black dress, Mildred knew that Liz had bought it at an out of the way dress store a hundred miles away. Liz's hair was pulled back and knotted at the nape of her neck, and she wore a double strand of pearls. Pain was etched across her face, and Mildred saw that it was taking everything she had to be present at the wedding where someone else was the bride. Liz had dressed for mourning; she was in a chronic state of grief.

'Liz is doing the best she can,' Mildred thought. And in the midst of a joyous day of celebration for Fran, Mildred grieved for Liz Luckie.

Today is your turn to wear black, and it is Fran's turn to wear light blue, and tomorrow you can wear a different outfit, but tomorrow you'll have another turn and the day after that, another turn. That's life. One turn leads to another turn. Grief and joy standing side by side, and then Chase took her hand and held it lightly. And Mildred felt light as a feather and free as a bird and a hundred other clichés that she wouldn't ordinarily use to describe herself. In that moment she was free from trying to find the exact words to describe this precious moment and was happy as a lark to stand there as a cliché: always a bride's maid never a bride-- and happy as a clam about it.

Mildred stood back as she often did at weddings, baby showers, anniversary parties, and receptions of any kind, and watched.

Mildred was quietly with her friend but in so many other places, too. None of them were called Memory Lane. It was time travel. It was human experience layered in her consciousness and magnified by a moment where love was preeminent and truth the vital life force. Mildred was beside the pool watching Sam float in the cool of the water and the warmth of the sunshine at the same time at peace with the messiness around him that was not ordered by his brain. He was not at war with it.

Creation was still happening. Sam was still taking his turn. Among faithful friends, Belle relaxed. Fran was marrying Winston. And now Chase was eating a carrot stick that he had fished out of his pocket, and the retired school teacher who had once decreed no snacks during this and that time now thought that eating a carrot stick at a wedding was all right—not unseemly at all for a boy who had known hunger and loneliness to be in a crowd of people and eat a carrot stick.

Then, Mildred, far and present, cool and warm, at peace in the order of a holy will and surrounded by so many people standing up for the bride, saw Fran enter the room alone and walk surefooted in a straight line to join Winston with no music playing to establish the timing of her steps. She just walked toward the man she wanted to marry. Everyone in the room grew quiet. Everyone in the room smiled. And then there was that moment when Fran was right beside Winston, and he took her hand—no prompting from the preacher, and no one but his sister Jeanne standing in as best man. So far, Mildred had not really been able to talk with Jeanne, but she had a warm curiosity about her.

And that's when Mildred suddenly realized that she was not in the right place. In that moment, the maid of honor was supposed to be on the other side of Fran. But she wasn't.

Mildred knew she was supposed to move, but she couldn't leave Chase. Steev caught her eye, giving her time to walk over and stand next to her best friend. Mildred shrugged and gestured to the boy. Steev grinned. He understood. You can be a best friend and a maid of honor and choose to stand next to a boy who has crossed the room to find you and is standing as close as he can by you because that's his turn, and you are helping him live it.

It was a casual grouping of friends, some sitting, some standing in the friendly fellowship hall. Steev's bearing and sweeping gaze called them to attention. The room grew quiet and almost still. Words of greeting were said. Hands were clasped. Smiles exchanged. Glances, too. Loved ones grew older, took another breath, inhabited multiple realities.

Everyone in the room was changing in front of everyone else. Everyone's turn was starting over in that moment. No one's turn was up. Everyone belonged. Everyone pulsed with a hope much better than good luck could explain.

Steev stopped being Steev who rode a motorcycle and spelled his name so funny that you could hardly believe he knew what dignity was; but when Steev stood there in front of the altar, he spoke with a sobering presence that he mainly assumed when he was making an altar call. And to the other married couples what he said after greeting Fran and Winston was a kind of altar call.

Steev said, eyes brimming with affection and good will: "Are you standing next to someone you love? Have you loved 'em a long, long time but haven't said so lately? Now's the time. Today's the day. Join us. The bride and groom welcome you to come forward and join them in the exchanging of their vows of devotion by reaffirming yours."

That was all Steev the preacher said at first.

And then Steev waited, his eyes warm with invitation, to come and see, join me, join us, enjoy the wedding. *Come. Go. Be in love today while it is today.*

Most people didn't understand at first. They were there for friendship's sake, so they could talk about it later-- for the cake, because surely there would be cake. It was a wedding!

"Take her hand. Take his hand. Has it been a long time since you said the words, we are going to say to day? Have you forgotten what the words mean? Forgotten tenderness? Awareness? The fragrance of love?"

From heaven, the angels began to hum, and a half dozen Bereans who had volunteered to help with the wedding collected themselves in front of the old brown spinet piano and serenaded all of the lovers in the room with the song that Irving Berlin had written for his bride Ellin: "I'll be loving you always...."

Tears flowed some. Hands patted shoulders, fluffed thinning hair. *Do I dare walk down the aisle and confess that I love this old man? This old woman? That I love him more than a lifetime can express?*

Thoughts tumbled. Music played. Winston held Fran's hand while Fran sang the words softly to him, but her voice rose, blending with the sister Bereans. The bride would always be a Berean, too.

And Steev waited while the church ladies sang the second verse more slowly than the first.

When the song ended, Fran and Winston were surrounded by friends who were in love too. Some had forgotten. Some had Alzheimer's. But everyone had each other.

Closest to them were Sam and Belle. There had been a moment when Belle wondered about dragging Sam toward the front. But before she finished thinking about it and before she gave up on the idea, Sam came to himself. Just like that, Sam resurfaced from down under where he lived. Sam heard the love song, heard the preacher's invitation, remembered Belle, and took Belle's hand. He led the way, crowding in close to Winston, who moved over, pulling Fran closer to him. There was room for everyone at the front of the room where only the preacher stood without a pulpit or an alter or a prayer bench. Steev stood solely with the truth—no props—only the words of truth he wanted to say.

What a sight.

All the couples in the room—even the ones who didn't walk to the front-- kind of leaned against each other humming "Always" with the church ladies and the angels.

Couples who had forgotten to think about love and believed they had outlived romance were wooed by Steev's words to remember, their love rekindled by his words, by the flickering candlelight, by the beauty of large bouquets of flowers.

A chorus of lovers, they replied when solemnly asked, "Do you take this woman? Do you take this man?"

And people said *yes, honey, yes, honey, I still do and in so many ways, more than ever,* and the maid of honor nodded encouragingly the way she once upon a time had nodded and murmured words of encouragement to fifth graders who tried so hard to be grown up and often failed. In the nodding and the hoping and the smiling, Mildred's spirit retreated even more—a position of being unseen that was grossly undervalued in society and not a condition of the psyche a psychologist should try to fix.

Church ladies pray in this position. It is a more potent position than kneeling. Blessing prayers flowed unceasingly from more than Mildred Budge.

In stillness and retreat, Mildred Budge was hidden among the candlelight and behind the smiles. While hands were held and intimate words of love spoken all around her, Mildred saw Mark the Gardener fix his gaze upon Liz Luckie, who was standing off by herself, the expression of aloneness captured on her widowed face. That same expression was in the eyes of the woman in the portrait hanging over his fireplace. Mark was magnetized by what he saw in Liz. He stared at her until she felt his gaze, and turning, Liz saw Mark, too.

Mildred saw Mark change, and if she had been holding a camera, she would have taken his picture.

A spark of desire ignited, and holding Liz's gaze, the spark grew stronger. Mark, too, crossed the room like a moth to the flame.

"There he goes," Mildred whispered to Jesus.

And she counted every step Mark took away from her to Liz, and in her spirit, she fanned his movements, *go on, go on.* Mark could not reach Liz soon enough. They needed each other, irresistibly.

Mildred sighed deeply, and her breath blew out the candle nearby, and she was glad, for then more shadows enveloped her, and she was even more invisible. While the chorus of *I do's* were still being whispered and sealed with kisses all around, Liz Luckie woke up out of her pain and smiled at the man who had come to her, smiling, peering intently. *You remind me of someone.* He wasn't a dead man walking anymore. He was coming to life right in front of her, and Mildred Budge could only be glad. This time Liz's love might help a man to live. They wouldn't put a picture of her on a billboard for that, but Mildred would know. And Fran would know. And the Bereans would know. And in the knowing, once Liz Luckie was accounted for and no longer a danger to other long-time married women and their husbands, this different kind of church lady would find a different turn for herself.

The afternoon Fran married Winston, it felt like anything was possible

34
HEAVEN, I'M IN HEAVEN

Fran kissed a dozen friends before she made her way back to Mildred, who was standing at the piano beside Chase. He was sitting in front of it, his small hands on the keys, moving across the surface of the white keys slowly but making no sound.

The boy's fingers were young, the flesh unblemished. They moved with a kind of nimble speed that would improve if he took music lessons and practiced.

"Mildred. Mildred." Fran spoke her best friend's name softly, twice.

Mildred knew Fran was there, but her eyes were closed longer than a blink. They were closed while she listened to her boy not play the piano and to the sounds around her: to the jubilant noise of the Bereans in the kitchen who had gone from singing "Always" to cleaning up and soon to filling a big Tupperware box with wedding reception left-overs for the preacher to take to his house to eat on for the next few days.

Church ladies loved to feed the preacher. Church ladies loved to pack up left overs for someone who did not have a mama or a wife at the house to do for him. There would be pimiento and chicken salad sandwiches, deviled eggs, cheese straws, meatballs on toothpicks, cheese sticks wrapped in thin slices of prosciutto, and containers of snackable portions of grapes, strawberries, and drippy sweet pineapple. In separate Ziploc baggies would be the predictable carrot sticks and broccoli florets. Mildred knew what was in the preacher's take-away box, because she had been packing to-go boxes like that for anyone who was unable to make it to an occasion and was homebound and needed not just some special food but some company and some attention. *I thought of you today, and here's proof right here in this box.*

Fran reached out and touched her best friend's shoulder. "Mildred, I've gotten married," Fran said in a voice that was new to them both. But then her voice should have changed. She was a married woman again now.

"I heard you say 'I do'," Mildred said, her face luminous with satisfaction. The day had gone well. Her best friend was happy. Chase was where he needed to be. The Bereans had given Winston and Fran a love song for their wedding, and in the years to come, they would talk about the occasion, agreeing with wonder and truth: "No one sings a love song like a Berean."

"Always," Fran replied, enigmatically as her attention turned and searched the room until she found Winston who was, in his way, searching for her. "Did you see all our friends tell the world and God himself that they loved each other and intended to love each other? It was like we were all singing together during the vows," Fran said.

"I heard them all. I heard you. I heard Winston. I hear the music of people murmuring now and their heartbeats and their tumbling thoughts. I hear it all."

"You should write one of your devotionals about that kind of music, Mildred."

"There are all kinds of music, and no one's turn is ever over," Mildred prophesied. "Maybe I'll write a piece about that."

"Not everyone hears all the music, Mildred. That's one of your flaws. You think other people can hear what other people don't hear."

"How do you know that for sure?" Mildred asked, lightly.

"Because I hear your thoughts when you tell them to me," Fran explained. "And I know my own. And what I think isn't how you think, so it stands to reason we don't all think the same way."

Mildred pointed to Chase still tilted over the piano keyboard, curiously studying it without making a sound. "What do you think about Chase?"

"I think God gave us someone special to love," Fran replied swiftly. "God is generous that way. That's what growing older is about—at least, for me. Becoming less and less afraid to love more and more people. I do," Fran said, with satisfaction. *It would be her chant for a while.*

"I do, too," Mildred replied while watching Chase. *Look at him right at the beginning of meeting the mystery of music.*

But Mildred didn't tell her best friend what she was exactly thinking. She just turned and smiled an old smile that her best friend knew very well. It was the smile of 'Go be in love with Winston. I'll be here when you come back.'

It was the smile of faithful friendship.

Of hoping for the best.

Of resolving to do all that she could to help others have many happy endings along the way of their long, long never-ending turns.

"Millie. Did you see....?" Fran's voice faltered. Her eyes clouded momentarily with concern.

"Yes." Mildred nodded. "I saw Mark see Liz," she added after a moment and another. She was looking around the room. She saw Steev joshing with Winston, and she saw Jake standing next to Belle, and Sam was eating another doughnut. He was standing beside what had been Dixie's Hunky Dory Groom's Cake, and while handing out cups of punch, Dixie had directed people, "Eat a rainbow cake doughnut! Take one home for later." Her platter was almost empty, and Dixie was ebullient with success.

There were all kinds of cakes and plenty of them, for the Bereans had come through as they always did. News had gone out over the prayer chain, and the message was: We need cakes for Fran and Winston's wedding by 3 pm.

And the Bereans had not failed. There had never even been a hint that they would fail. Bereans live on love and words of love, and they never fail when someone needs an expression of it. The words came unbidden, playing like music in the background of the present precious moment. Love is patient and kind; love does not envy or boast; it is not arrogant or rude. It does not insist on its own way; it is not irritable or resentful; it does not rejoice at wrongdoing, but rejoices with the truth. Love bears all things, believes all things, hopes all things, endures all things. Love will bake a wedding cake fast whenever one is needed.

Fran stepped closer to Mildred. "That Mark. Men can be fickle," she opined apologetically for them all. Studying Winston, she added, her eyes luminous, "Not all men. I found one who isn't."

There wasn't time to explain that Mark had not been fickle at all. The former actor and now part-time gardener had stayed true to the woman whose likeness was hanging over his fireplace until he had seen another woman who had reminded him more of the woman he loved than the one he had first met sitting in a chair at the estate sale. The woman in the picture over the fireplace was the one who had killed him. The woman named Liz who had a reputation for choosing husbands who died was the one now bringing him back to life from his sad, long-time romantic adventure of being tragically in love. Mark was about to change. Liz was about to change. This new turn was just beginning for both of them. If this man came back to life with Liz, why history was being changed right in front of them all. Mark's newest turn was just beginning, and so was Liz's.

"Can we go home?" Chase asked suddenly looking up from the silent piano.

Both women looked at the boy. Fran's bright blue gaze softened.

"Are you ready to be in your own home, Chase?" Fran asked.

Chase and Mildred nodded. People love doughnuts, no one's turn is ever over, and people always want to go home.

"Winston and I are going home too." Fran nodded to Winston. He nodded too. They were headed home together.

Mildred saw Anne Henry come out with a big Tupperware container of sandwiches, raw veggies, and cheese straws. Anne Henry strode across the room to Steev the way her father once had walked with such purpose—and it was so important to know that a daughter may inherit the purposeful stride of her father and in the movement forever keep him close in her heart and in the memories of others—memories that were not maudlin or self-pitying but fresh and vibrant and truth-telling. *Oh, how we loved Anne's father. Oh, how we did love him. And there he is, still, in the eternal way, walking purposefully in Anne—still among us in spirit.*

Anne Henry told Steev what to do with the box of food the Bereans had prepared for him, and Mildred saw the young preacher mouth the words, "Yes, ma'am. Thank you, ma'am." If he hadn't needed both hands to hold the big box of food, he would have saluted. Anne Henry brought out the instinct to salute in certain men. No one talked about that much, but it was as true as the purposeful stride she had inherited from her father. One day others will know someone who elicits respectful salutes, and they will think of Anne and her salutes and her stride and her packing up of care packages.

"Have you ever seen so many cakes in your life?" Fran asked with satisfaction. "I had more cake than anyone else who has ever gotten married here. I shouldn't be proud of that, but I am. There was Italian Cream, German Chocolate, Red Velvet, plain yellow with chocolate, chocolate with chocolate, lemon cake with drizzle frosting, and I think I saw a carrot cake. I wasn't sure. I didn't get to eat any of them. But they looked good. We have great friends."

"I think Dixie's doughnut cake was the most popular."

"Aren't we glad about that?"

"We are."

Steev came over carrying his container of sandwiches and cake. "Girls, the gang is coming to my house to eat more sandwiches and wedding cake and doughnuts under the stars."

"You and the gang are doing that, my dear. I'm going on my honeymoon," Fran said, her gaze telling Mildred *see you later.* "Thanks for wearing a dress to my wedding, Millie."

Mildred couldn't wait to take it off. She loved her sunset dress and wanted it hanging in her closet now. There was too much cloth.

"Mildred?" Fran said, as if there was something more to say.

"Come. Go. Be joyful all the days of your life with Winston."

But Mildred wasn't sure her best friend had heard her. Winston had turned and his gaze had found Fran across the crowded room, and Fran couldn't hear anything else from anyone else. Fran walked toward Winston, and she did not look back.

"I'm headed home," Steev said to everyone and to Mildred. Turning, he asked, "You coming? Those of us who didn't get a chance to eat are going to eat now. Miss Anne has fixed me up."

"My boy is tired," Mildred said, watching Chase who was talking with Jake.

"If you change your mind, you know where I live." The preacher turned toward the back door, and pivoted, grinning broadly as he said: "Come. Go. Be Mildred Budge."

35
LET'S GO HOME

They could have walked home. The church wasn't far from Mildred's house in Cloverdale. Alone, although more tired than the boy with her, the church lady might have done just that. But the boy was with her. Before they could get to the side door that led to the parking lot and their car, Anne Henry brought another container of refreshments for Mildred and Chase.

"You didn't get any cake, Millie," Anne Henry said. "I put together a sampler of cakes for you, and I was able to snag two doughnuts. Chocolate with rainbow sprinkles. I don't know about you, but that doughnut cake idea may be repeated often in the future. A Hunky Dory Doughnut Cake is pretty, easy to serve, and who doesn't like a cake doughnut?"

Mildred grinned. "I like doughnuts better than cupcakes."

"And, I wanted you to know that we found some wedding bells out on the teeter totter. They must have come off your cake, but we don't know how they got there."

Mildred could have explained. She knew how the bells had made it to the playground, but all that really mattered was that they had been found.

"The bells were gritty. I washed them. Then, I put the bells in with Fran's and Winston's to-go box. I can see them sparkling in her china cabinet right now."

Anne Henry didn't say the words so that Mildred Budge would thank her. She said them because she knew Mildred would wonder about that—*were the bells clean?* Of course, they were clean. A Berean cleaned.

"I've never seen so many cakes," Mildred said, pleased.

"Wasn't that fun?" Anne was gleeful, relishing the good time they had all just enjoyed. "The girls and I all agreed to go ahead and clean up tonight so that no one has to come back on Monday and face it."

"Cake," Chase said, taking the box away from Mildred.

"Go on," Anne said. "Everybody knows you would stay and sweep and mop if you didn't have other things to do. As maid of honor, you've done enough. Go home. The Bereans will handle this."

"Another time," Mildred promised.

Anne nodded, seeing for the first time Liz with Mark, both standing close together talking, talking. They weren't aware of anyone else in the room. Anne eyed Mildred, concerned. The news of Mark's initial courtship of Mildred Budge had quietly infiltrated the ranks of her Sunday school chums. And now Anne Henry was wondering if she needed to blame Liz Luckie for this travesty against one of their own—man stealer!

Mildred waved away the questions Anne wanted to ask—and with that single wave, Anne would forgo all questions. The same woman who inspired salutes respected the boundaries of personal privacy. She strode purposefully back to the kitchen, a Berean in heels.

Mildred walked stalwartly out the side door with Chase beside her, and they were home again before too many stars had burned out.

The front porch light was burning. She locked her car and was just about to open the front door when Jake's Forester pulled up across the street and parked over at Steev's. Quickly, Jake was out of his vehicle and calling to her: "Millie, are you coming over?"

"Not tonight," she called back, surprised that her voice would carry. "Chase and I have had a long day."

Jake jogged lightly across the street as if he hadn't heard her. But he had heard her.

"Let me carry that inside for you, Mildred," he said, taking the cake box.

Mildred pushed open the front door and motioned Chase to pass through carrying the box of cakes. "To the kitchen," she said, turning to Jake who closed the door.

"Your friend Mark..." Jake said, stopping himself.

"Yes?" Mildred asked, turning. Already Mark was a distant memory. She almost couldn't think of his last name.

Jake nodded. "If you were coming to Steev's, what I wanted to say was to warn you that your friend Mark is coming with Liz Luckie. They somehow got themselves invited."

Jake watched her face carefully. He couldn't see much. Mildred was a skilled church lady. "I'm so very glad they've been invited. I don't want anyone to ever be excluded."

"Mildred," Jake said.

Chase reappeared in the doorway, waiting for what they would do next. "Popcorn?" he asked. He was already wearing pajamas that fit and socks on his feet. He was home.

Chase waited for Jake to acknowledge him, and he did: his eyes warming at the sight of the boy. "Our Mildred, did you see your boy in front of the piano?

"I saw," she said. "We're going to have some popcorn. You want to stay?"

"I love popcorn," Jake replied.

"Chase and I sometimes watch a John Wayne movie," Mildred admitted. "Are you staying?" she asked. "We've got a lot of sandwiches and cake too."

Jake nodded slowly, a smile dawning on his face as he realized he was welcome. She wasn't just being polite. The church lady wasn't just practicing the discipline of hospitality.

Across the street other friends gathered at one of Steev's backyard potlucks. Stars shone. A half dozen couples came and went, laughing and calling out in the street. Belle and Sam went home early. Later, she would hear that Mark and Liz were the last to leave. Steev told Mildred the news about Mark and Liz, cautiously, clearly, truthfully. Preachers who have read the Bible talk like that.

But all of that happened later.

"You go get comfortable. I'll get Chase to teach me how to make the popcorn," Jake said.

By the time she returned, Chase and Jake were sitting on the couch with a large bowl of popcorn and the TV tuned to the Western channel. Both looked up at her and smiled.

"We've been talking, Millie," Jake said, as she sat down on the other side of the boy. "We're going to have to get that piano tuned so you can teach the boy how to play it." Holding her gaze, Jake told her, smiling, "I'm going to help you with that piano."

She nodded her assent as across the street the sounds of another bridal party carried to them; but they were inside their own, getting quiet, getting comfortable, getting settled. We come. We go. Trouble's always coming, but everything is all right in the bride's room.

'This is a precious moment,' she told the Lord, as the blessing prayers began again coursing through her. *Oh, yes.*

BONUS EXCERPT: LOVEJOY

I was past my prime but not yet old when I met my match, Mr. Lovejoy. The distinguished widower had been part of the background of my community, an old Southern church where tradition is as romantic as the scent of magnolia and the fragrance of the gospel is as abundant as the scent of that flower that ladies in social clubs use for tabletop centerpieces.

Through a natural reluctance to join myself to a ladies' social club that defined me by my gender or marital status, I kept myself apart in the Southern society where God had placed me. I lived on the perimeter where spectators observe and often have opinions. In Sunday school I sat near the wall. In church I sat near the back, where I was occasionally shaken out of my church-time reverie when I heard a man belt out "Amen" whenever the preacher made a point that might have gone without attention otherwise.

Heads turned at the sound of one of us agreeing out loud with the preacher. Eyes widened to discern the rebel among us-- the man of the Amen. He wasn't hard to spot. The man who vigorously agreed with the preacher was Franklin Lovejoy, a widower of two years.

A handsome man, Mr. Lovejoy sat by himself five pews up from me, and often I watched with amusement the number of ladies who attempted to establish a stronghold beside this older available man. They came and went. I don't know what he said or didn't say that did not encourage the ladies to return. Some did come back, for a while. There were even some Sunday mornings when a single woman nestled in on Lovejoy's left side and another lady snuggled in on his right.

Sunday mornings became like a soap opera to me. I watched, taking note of the women who came and went while the preacher positioned himself behind the pulpit, oblivious to the sexual tensions brewing in the pews.

Most early morning church goers arrive a quarter to the hour in order to get our preferred pews. For that early rising, we not only win our respective cherished pews but are treated to ten minutes of slow-down-and-get-silent-before God music. After the bell chimes announcing the hour, the preacher stands—often shyly. I never like the preacher more than when he first approaches the pulpit with both diffidence and courage, self-protection and openness. A deep silence comes over him just as he is supposed to say a few words about this and that. Then, in the midst of words about love and mercy and beauty and truth that point us toward the God of Wonders, wonder of wonders, Franklin Delmar Lovejoy, a great encourager of deacons, elders, and younger men who try to preach, would release at exactly the moment when the preacher needed a pat on the back, his signature one-word cheer of encouragement, "Amen."

Instantly that single word created a bridge that connected the preacher to all of us. We were one--created to be one in a breath all together. I marveled at the happening, and kept my eye on Mr. Lovejoy, who made it happen.

He was the only one to do it. (There isn't much talking back to the preacher in our church.) I liked the sound of Lovejoy's voice, too. Often when people are described in terms of their attractiveness or appeal the effect of their voice on you is not mentioned, and it should be. The timber of a voice can be very comforting (or surprising); but in Lovejoy's case, his voice was seductive—head-turning. Irresistible. Preachers who wanted to be great preachers coveted Lovejoy's resonant truth-carrying voice and its stirring effect of commanding attention.

The Bride's Room

Sometimes I whispered the word "Amen" after Mr. Lovejoy just to hear myself speak in church because mostly women don't speak in church, not in the South, anyway; and if you do, it is to cheer or encourage a man in his walk of faith. And so, I was not skilled in speaking and even kept my ideas to myself, believing, rightly I think—amen? —that I simply don't know enough about anything to have a worthwhile opinion.

However, upon whispering "Amen" after Mr. Lovejoy during the church service, I began to learn the sound of my own voice and the power of agreeing and, sometimes, the extraordinary freedom of disagreeing.

No one was more surprised than I after being on a committee called Tender Mercies that I would one day find myself speaking up loudly and with many more words than the man who said, "Amen." But it was Franklin Delmar Lovejoy who had somehow initiated my freedom of speech.

One amen can cause a ripple effect in others. An amen has the power of contagion.

Mr. Lovejoy had tapped into some kind of unnamed restlessness in me, and his amen had triggered my speaking up in the Tender Mercies meetings. Only my words were not about agreement; they were a loud and serious questioning of perpetuating helplessness in others by helping others too much in the name of Tender Mercies. It is a surprising situation to speak out against giving too much help in the name of mercy in a church where mercy is the sister word for grace. Yet, I without a plan to be one, became that voice of dissent.

My position in the church community changed as a result. It didn't happen the first time I suggested a background check on a stranger who had come in off the street asking for help with his electric bill. I wanted to know if chronically seeking help from neighborhood churches was how he made his living. Later, when one missionary candidate requested plane fare to reach his mission field, I muttered the unpardonable: "That's the place Pat Sajak on "Wheel of Fortune" often sends people as a prize trip when they spell an easy word correctly on the TV game show. I wonder why so many missionaries end up in destinations that are places given away as jackpot prizes on America's game shows."

That's the statement that finally landed me in the dog house outside the perimeter of what is considered good behavior at church. I felt the earth shift under me and heads duck as they calculated how many more months, I was scheduled to serve on the Tender Mercies committee before they could finally show me the door. I eyed the door myself, thought about making up a physical condition that I could offer to excuse myself from future committee work; but, in a fit of menopausal madness I spoke to God while looking at myself in the mirror, "What's sinful about having an unpopular opinion?" So, I stayed—mainly to find out what, if anything, would be done about the problem—me.

I walked the widening fault line created by my questions, growing increasingly apart and alone as others who knew of my meddlesome troublemaking began to turn gently to the side when I passed by. You don't have to be formally rebuked at church, put in time out by the elders, or receive a formal letter of warning that you are in danger of excommunication to know you are on the outs with church leadership. The more powerful event at church is to be very quietly and effectively shunned. Most people leave a church of their own accord as an effect of shunning, sheepishly disappearing into the future with nary a backward glance. But I lived in the neighborhood, and I didn't want to find another church far enough away so that my reputation would not precede me or close enough that people who knew me here would know me there and know about me. So, I stayed in my pew, whispering "Amen" after Mr. Lovejoy, and keeping my eye on the calendar to count down the days of my impending expiration on the Tender Mercies committee. People do forget, over time. After a while they would forget my trespasses, and in the forgetting, forgive?

That hopeful plan did not stop me from continuing to speak and question spending decisions in committee meetings, however. No matter how many times I gave myself a talking to about being quiet and more agreeable, in the very next meeting someone would paint a scenario that required mercy, an expensive hand out to someone in a sports ministry or to a cowboy on the rodeo circuit who wanted to tell people about the Lawd in between bronco bustin'. That night, I said, "Tell that good ole cowboy if he's not a good enough bronco buster to win the rodeo prize money and support himself with his chosen vocation, maybe he should open a lawn service. Like the Apostle Paul, you can make tents and earn a living cutting yards while you tell homeowners about the Lawd."

I've been witnessed to by a number of lawn mower men, coffee-serving waitresses, and hair-cutting artistes. You can do all kinds of work, testify to the good news that salvation is through faith alone in Jesus, and not take money from the church to say those words wherever you go.

It was a long meeting with lots of sighin'. I ended up sitting by myself at the end of the long conference table, and I understood why. The implications of saying no to people needing tender mercies were not hard to understand. If we stopped giving out the money then the Tender Mercies committee and the person in charge of the committee was out of a job. Then there would be no stories to tell to elicit more contributions from the congregation to give to people who needed money, and down the road after a while, eventually, surely, the gospel.

That was a sticking point, you see. I kept saying, "Tell 'em about Jesus, and then tell them to get a job. After that, teach that working man to tithe and let the Lord show him how to become a good steward of himself, including the gift of labor. Work is a gift. In so many ways, a hand-out is not the gift we think it is."

In the year of the 500th anniversary of the Reformation out of the blue and on a low humidity morning when my freshly trimmed hair with newly added streaks of blonde and a saucy little flip of a curl on the left side of my bangs that "Gives your face a lift, Miss Cindy, so please don't try to iron it out," said my hair dresser, Mr. Lovejoy of the Amen asked me to lunch.

But first, he extricated himself from the presence of a woman I greatly admire who was well groomed, wore taupe tummy control panty hose without gasping for air, could walk in black patent leather high heels without teetering, had thick brown lustrous Grand Ole Opry hair that was immune to humidity, could make small talk better than Paula Deen, and her laugh was a light tinkling sound that made you think of Christmas bells. Mr. Lovejoy excused himself from the lady with the tinkling Christmas bells laugh and asked me—the church leper-- to Sunday lunch.

Thinking that it was about time someone delivered the criticism from above formally that my opinions were proving problematic, I lit up girlishly, automatically, and said, sweetly, with a honeyed smile on my face, "Oh, thank you so much" to his invitation to Sunday lunch in order to get this problem of being rebuked by the leadership behind me. Go ahead, Mr. Lovejoy. Tell me how wrong I am and that I have been excused from further service on the committee, and I will turn the other cheek and disappear like the vapor I am. And in that moment of planning my reply to what he would surely say during lunch, I wondered if much of what I had been saying on the committee was perversely spoken to get myself kicked off the committee so that I didn't have to formally quit.

I hate quitters and deep down I didn't want to be one.

(The novel LOVEJOY is available through most online book retailers.)

BOOKS BY DAPHNE SIMPKINS

The Short Adventures of Mildred Budge (short stories and a novella)
Miss Budge in Love
The Mission of Mildred Budge
Miss Budge Goes to Fountain City
The Adventures of Mildred Budge (novels)
Mildred Budge in Cloverdale Book 1
Mildred Budge in Embankment Book 2
The Bride's Room Book 3
Essays and Memoirs
The Long Good Night
A Cookbook for Katie
What Al Left Behind
Blessed
What Makes a Man a Hero?
Other Stand-alone Titles
11 DIY Holiday Small Talks for Activity Directors and Groups
Christmas in Fountain City a standalone Christmas novel
Nat King Cole: An Unforgettable Life of Music, a children's biography of Nat King Cole

ABOUT DAPHNE SIMPKINS

Daphne Simpkins is a Southern church woman who
wonders what other church ladies really think. She tries to
satisfy that curiosity by writing the adventures of Mildred
Budge. Connect with her on Amazon, BookBub, Twitter,
Linkedin.com, and Facebook.

Her books are available through most online bookstores.

Daphne Simpkins

Made in the USA
Las Vegas, NV
03 July 2022

51058087R00164